TALK OF THE TOWN

Rich, famous, and gorgeous at the age of forty, Tracy Callaway O'Neal turned heads whenever she walked down Yorkport's sleepy streets. She filled her mansion with guests whose names were essential to the society columns—novelists, politicians, artists, actors—and the local people watched them come and go with wonder and envy.

Yorkport natives marveled at Tracy O'Neal's new home, the most spectacular and daring house ever built in the quiet town on the coast of Maine.

When Tracy O'Neal announced a housewarming party to be held on the Fourth of July, all of Yorkport was agog about her guest list—it included not only her famous friends, but some local people as well.

What those who were invited didn't guess—what Tracy herself never imagined—was that there would be some shocking fireworks on the Fourth—fireworks that would ring in the ears of Yorkport for many years to come!

(Cover Photograph Posed By Professional Model)

Also by Peter McCurtin:

ROCKWELL
MINNESOTA STRIP
SOLDIER OF FORTUNE *SERIES*
SUNDANCE *SERIES*
LOANSHARK
SADDLER *SERIES*
MURDER IN THE PENTHOUSE

SUMMER FRIENDS

Peter McCurtin

LEISURE BOOKS   NEW YORK CITY

A LEISURE BOOK

Published by

Dorchester Publishing Co., Inc.
New York City

CHAPTER ONE

The huge silver Rolls Royce (in the $100,000 class) left the state road and purred its way in to the small shopping center, and to an interested and history-minded observer it might have suggested an elegant Spanish galleon of the 15th century gliding into port on a glassy sea. However, it was unlikely that any of those who turned to gape at it, perhaps to hate it, had any such idea. For this was southern Maine on a bright, breezy morning in early July; and most of the people who stared at the car, or resolutely ignored it, were tourists, tradesmen, small children, and store clerks. The little people.

"That's some cah," a local man said in the

accents of Maine.

"You bet," his companion agreed. "Will you get that niggah driver. I would say that jig has a good time with that lady."

The first man said, "Better move the pick-up, Eben—you're blockin' traffic."

The truck, which had been taking up two parking spaces, backed out and moved away to the road, allowing the Rolls to drive in with hardly a sound. The mall was not enclosed as some rural and suburban malls are; open to the elements, it was nothing more than a long row of stores and businesses. A big hardware store sold everything from firearms to cast-iron stoves; another store sold books; another building supplies. At the far end was a very small barber shop, the kind that still offer SHAVES.

The black chauffeur, a handsome young man in a black suit, got out and ran around to open the door.

The most famous woman in the world got out.

This was Tracy Callaway O'Neal, widow of the late President Daniel P. Callaway, assassinated in Paris by an Iranian fanatic during a tour of the European capitals; and though they were said to be a "dream couple," just a few years later Tracy Callaway had married an elderly Texas billionaire named Earl O'Neal. He died, too.

Tracy O'Neal was just forty, beautiful, deeply tanned and with the lanky figure of a tennis player. Huge sunglasses were pushed up carelessly on her dark blond hair, which was cut short and brushed back.

Most staring at her knew who she was; others recognized her immediately, for her face had appeared on countless magazine covers throughout the world. The Soviets pictured her as the final example of American capitalist decadence, but she sold magazines in Moscow just like everywhere else. Reporters and hand-held television cameras pursued her in swarms and only here in reticent Maine could she find a measure of peace. A member of a hundred fashionable committees, she was a sponsor of all the arts. A homosexual novelist, himself fairly famous, once called her "The most successful adventuress on earth."

People loved or hated her in a manner quite removed from their own lives. But whatever their opinion of her, they all knew who she was.

Democratic for all her fabulous wealth, she murmured "Good morning" to an old farmer with a bag of cement on his shoulder.

"You bet," he stammered and all but dropped his burden.

While he waited, the driver handed her a shopping bag, with the name of Bloomingdale's department store printed on its side, and she carried it into a large super-market. Those inside hadn't seen her yet, and when the door whooshed shut behind her, the girls at the check-out counters became almost frightened, although there was nothing menacing in her queenly entrance. One girl giggled, another dropped change. Tracy O'Neal smiled at them.

The young blond man who rushed to greet her was Bruce Whipple, assistant manager of the market. On weekends Bruce worked as a lifeguard on Yorkport's famous beach, five miles away. Muscular, handsome in a doltish sort of way, he made out with many of the pretty girls who had jobs as chambermaids and waitresses in the hotels, which were open only in the summer. In winter, they went to colleges in many parts of the country. Indeed, Bruce Whipple was a college man himself: the University of Maine.

Tracy had known the Whipple boy for several summers and she always considered him a credit to his working-class parents.

"Well hello there, Bruce," Tracy said in her celebrated husky voice. She smiled at him, still holding the Bloomingdale's bag.

Bruce blushed and some of the check-out girls giggled.

"Nice to see you again, Miz O'Neal," Bruce said. "Goin' to be with us the whole summer?"

Tracy nodded and said, "Just got in. You

8

know I always feel like I'm coming home when the car crosses the bridge at Portsmouth and I know I'm back in Maine."

"Nice to have you back," Bruce said. Then remembering his manners, for the bag was still in her hand, he politely took it from her. She followed him to one of the counters and began to remove empty Coke cans from the bag. All the cans had RETURNABLE: 5¢ stamped on their lids. This was the law in Maine.

Now quite serious, Bruce counted the cans and put them in a cardboard box. "That'll be sixty cents, Miz O'Neal," Bruce declared.

Taking the coins—two quarters and a dime—from the cash register, he handed them to Tracy.

"Thank you very much," Tracy said. "We have to take care of the ecology, don't we?"

"You bet," Bruce said. "I wish everybody would be as considerate as you are. I mean, the country would be in better shape. Ecology-wise. People throw bottles and cans along the highways something awful."

Tracy smiled, refusing to pass harsh judgment. "I'm sure they aren't thinking when they litter the roads."

Bruce offered humble disagreement, knowing that Tracy O'Neal wasn't stuck-up. "Well, they should know better."

Tracy grew serious for a moment. "That will

come, Bruce. Now I have a list of things that will tide me over until I get myself organized."

"Oh sure, and I'm standing here gabbin'. I'll make the rounds with you."

"Thank you, Bruce," Tracy said.

Bruce got a shopping cart and the first item on the list was a dozen Cokes. Tracy followed demurely while the young assistant manager took things down from shelves. He advised her on good buys and she thanked him. A mild sales war was going on with a larger supermarket down the highway and some of the canned goods had been marked down.

As he put six cans of whole mushrooms into the cart, Bruce said, "How's the new house comin' along? That's all they've been talkin' about around here since last year. They say it's goin' to be a beauty. There was a big story in the *Yorkport Star* two weeks ago."

"Oh, they shouldn't have bothered. It's just a great big old house." Tracy frowned becomingly, but they both knew that it was the most spectacular and "daring" house ever built in the Yorkport area, which had many big summer places. Designed by a famous New York architect, the new house had been written up in many magazines.

Tracy frowned again and said, "It's just been completed, the house itself, but there's so much additional work to be done. I'm practically camping out, for goodness sake. My dear friend Lafe Tatum, who decorated the house, is coming up today to make a few changes I decided on. I'm sure you can understand what a lot of work it's been for me."

"Wow! That must be some house."

"Well, I think it's very nice. I took a little hand in the designing of it, did you know that?"

"Why shouldn't you?" Bruce said loyally. "It's your house."

"Thank you, Bruce."

"You going to have a housewarming, Miz O'Neal?"

"How did you guess?"

"Be a shame not to," Bruce answered, inspecting a bunch of bananas with great care.

"Of course you're right, Bruce. I'm going to have a very nice party just four days from now."

Bruce, deciding the bananas were top quality, put them in with the other groceries. "I think a Fourth of July party is a neat idea, Miz O'Neal."

"How nice of you to say so."

"I mean it, Miz O'Neal. A lot of summer people—not that we consider you a summer person, you're more like an honorary native—wait till Labor Day to give the big party of the season. I think Labor Day parties are kind of sad because people are leaving."

Tracy said she thought that was sweet and

waited while Bruce crossed off the last item on the list. She took the list and checked the prices he had marked beside each item.

Walking with the most famous woman in the world, Bruce was in his glory. Some boy his own age grinned and said hello, but all he got in return was a haughty nod.

At the counters, Bruce waved one of the girls aside and checked out Tracy himself. He knew such personal service would be appreciated; it was only polite. He tore the long tape from the cash register, knowing that Tracy Callaway O'Neal checked everything. It wasn't that she was stingy or anything like that. Jealous people liked to think so, but he always reminded them that rich people have their money because they're careful with it. It made sense.

"I'll take everything out for you," Bruce said.

"That's very nice of you."

"No trouble at all."

Bruce knew that when he came back inside the girls and some of the customers would kid him like crazy. Last year they did it all the time, telling him that he had some kind of inside track with the billionaire lady and could well wind up married to her. Well, why not? Gregg Dodge married a cop named Moran, some Irish Catholic state trooper from down around Hartford. And what about Patty Hearst? A cop named Shaw.

12

Bruce was trying to remember the names of all the other lucky guys who married rich women, but by then they were at the car and Tracy was saying something to him. He jerked his thoughts back to the present and saw that she was offering him a fifty-cent piece.

The black chauffeur was out of the car and had the trunk open to receive the grocery bag.

"Oh gosh, no! You don't have to do that," Bruce protested. "I'm always glad to help. What I *am* sorry about is being out of Perrier water. More should be coming in today and I'll bring it right over."

"I could send Ralph for it."

Bruce could be stubborn. "Not a chance, Miz O'Neal. I go to business school—maybe I told you—and they tell us the personal touch is what counts."

"That's very wise," Tracy said, smiling.

Still smiling at him, her lovely green eyes widened in delight at her own cleverness.

"You must come to my party, Bruce. I know you have your young friends—your young ladies—but promise you'll come. You must promise."

"Oh, sure," Bruce said.

The chauffeur banged the trunk of the Rolls a little harder than he had to, and stood waiting.

Now Tracy was in the car. The chauffeur was about to close the door when she waved him to

13

stop. She gave Bruce another smile. She said, "You know, you're the first local person I've invited to my party."

The car drove away, leaving Bruce Whipple numb.

CHAPTER TWO

Sarah Bannard and Dee (Dorothy) McWilliams were having one of their fights. Some of them could be violent; so far this one was just getting close to it. But anything could happen with Sarah and Dee. The police kept away from them except when they did something outrageous in the village, where people could see them. Of course they were never actually arrested because Sarah had so much money. When they got really wild, like having a clawing match in the bank, the chief of police and his two officers would hustle them home in the patrol car.

People always said you could get away with anything in Yorkport. If you had money.

Their hilltop house, though on the small side, was one of the loveliest in the town. One wall of the living room was all french windows; the furnishings of the house were what they used to call "a symphony of good taste."

Now on this sunlit afternoon a sprinkler turned on a small lawn made greener by chemicals. Water from the whirling sprinkler struck the french windows, giving everything a pleasantly fresh look.

It was one o'clock and Sarah was having her third bullshot of the day. Bullshots had a lot of nourishment in them, she liked to say, although this was not intended to explain her heavy drinking, because in her own words, she didn't give a flying fuck what anyone thought of her.

Sarah, with a long leg hooked over the side of a chair, smiled at Dee, who had her back turned and hadn't said anything vicious for several minutes. At the moment she was opening a box of new books shipped to them by a Boston bookseller.

As everyone in town knew, Sarah was the one with the money: about two million dollars inherited from her father, an Atlanta distiller. Handsome rather than beautiful, she always wore the same uniform—chinos, Western-style shirt with snaps instead of buttons, a Marine Corps belt with a brass buckle—except when she was going to the Yorkport Theater, or to a party. Now in her mid-thirties, she had attended or fooled around in many colleges and schools: Sarah Lawrence, Bard College, The Art Students League.

Still smiling at Dee, she rustled the local newspaper, the *Yorkport Star,* a weekly, and in a husky Southern voice she tried to get the jealous Dee going again.

Dee, for the moment, refused to be baited; Sarah knew she would. It was fun to tease Dee, the butch half of the family. Her husband.

Sarah and Dee had met during a season at the Margo Jones Theater in Texas. An actress who didn't make it, Dee held on to Sarah like a leech; without her she would have to work. Since Texas they had lived in many places— Puerto Vallarta, Catalina Island, Taos, Tangier, Rome—and had been expelled from a lot of them.

Sarah rustled the newspaper again, saying, "I don't give a fuck what you think. I'd like to meet her. Look at those legs. Jesus!"

There was a full-page photo of Tracy O'Neal on the front page.

Dee turned in sudden fury. "Why do you keep looking at that wimpy-voiced cunt? Everybody in the world knows she fucked and sucked her way into money. She'd fuck a donkey for an extra five dollars."

"Lucky donkey," Sarah murmured.

A small town Californian, Dee hated all the

17

Boston Irish Callaways, who were a power in the Democratic Party. When President Daniel Callaway was assassinated, she insisted on throwing a party in their villa at Antibes, where they were at the time. At the height of the party, quite drunk, Dee screamed, "What we need is a few more Iranians with rifles. Then we could get rid of the rest of these motherfuckers."

"You better not keep that up," she warned Sarah, who was still staring at Tracy Callaway's photograph. "I'll tear your fucking snatch off if you do."

"You're just jealous. Why can't gay women be liberated like the rest of the pussy?"

"I'll fucking murder you, you cheap whore!"

"Oh, come on now," Sarah said. "How can you say I'm cheap? Why, haven't I given you everything? Have I failed you in some way? Tell me, sweets. Please do."

"I know you fucked that sailor in Mexico. Down in that grass house by the beach. Did you blow him too?"

"My psychiatrist says I'm probably bi-sexual," Sarah said with pretended thoughtfulness. "Dr. Quackenbush says everyone is without being aware of it."

"Fuck you," Dee said.

"Oh, but you have," Sarah said.

Of course there was no Dr. Quackenbush, but Sarah did like a big cock now and then.

18

Why not try everything there was to try? What was the point of having money if you couldn't experiment? Actually, though Dee didn't know it, she *had* tried it with a donkey. The burro became frightened though; had kicked her, had run away braying. But he had dropped about ten inches of dick before he got nervous.

So it was true about donkeys.

A light summer shower moved across the lawn, making rainbow colors as it mixed with the sprinkler. Then it went away and the sky was clear and blue once more.

"Lovely day, isn't it?" Sarah said pleasantly. Everyone liked her husky Georgia voice, and she knew it. Her voice—just her voice—got men and women horny, she liked to say. Sarah was a woman of many opinions, all eccentric.

With gentle malice Sarah knew that Dee was nervous because of her interest in Tracy O'Neal. Well, that was natural: they had money, and poor old Dee had none. Not a cent. Not a sou. Sarah couldn't think of any other coins of infinitesimal value. Then she did: a centavo. If she kicked Dee out on her ass, now grown slightly fat, would that soap opera in New York take her back? Who could say? Perhaps the fucker wasn't playing any more.

Looking at Dee, Sarah realized that all life was sadism. And it was fun. The bullshots were good and she felt good. To make herself feel even better, she popped a Methedrine tablet.

19

Dexamyl was all right in a pinch; Methedrine was the real thing. With Meth and 100 proof Finlandia vodka in your veins, life took on a rosy glow. You could practically scramble up the outside of the Empire State Building. Better still the Twin Towers. Oh, the two things combined could get you into trouble. But fuck it! Wasn't it fun the time she got a balloon seller to fill up a whole bunch of condoms with gas and she released them in Notre Dame during High Mass? Sarah finished the third bullshot and smiled at the memory. The fucking French deported her for that. It was time to get another drink.

Dee, still inspecting the books, stared at the glass when she brought it back from the kitchen.

Smiling, Sarah said, "You look like Carry Nation."

"You promised you'd taper off a little. Take it easy."

"I've seen you raving drunk plenty of times."

"Not as much as I used to," Dee said. "Not until after six at least."

"I don't own a watch," Sarah said sweetly.

She sat down on the newspaper and sucked loudly on the enormous drink, knowing how much that annoyed Dee. Dee liked to think she came from a good family. Like hell she did! Her father was a druggist in Alhambra.

In a moment she said, "Listen to this kid.

Would you believe it! I'm sitting on Tracy O'Neal's face."

"I'll shoot you!" Dee was screaming, but she hadn't attacked yet.

Sarah screamed too. "Oh, tongue me, Tracy! I'll give you ass and you give me tongue! I can't stand it, me darlin'."

Dee, wild-eyed, threw a biography of Kandinsky full force, missed Sarah, and shattered a window.

Sarah turned and looked out through the broken window. "That sprinkler's going to ruin it," she said in that sing-song voice small children use when they threaten to tell mommy.

Dee stood her ground. "Who gives a shit, you cunt?"

"I do, darlin'," Sarah said in her Tallulah Bankhead voice. "That's my fucking book. Go out and get it—*now!* Get the book or go upstairs and pack your little cardboard suitcase from the five and dime. I mean it, sister. I really do."

Tears came into Dee's hard brown eyes and she stood in the center of the beautiful room with slumped shoulders. "You can't mean it! We've been together seven years. After all that you'd just tell me to go? You're so rotten to me, Sarah. You limit my checking account to a hundred dollars, then you tell other gay women about it. You promised to give me a legal share in this house and you didn't. God damn you! How can you be so mean?"

"Get the book. It costs seventeen-fifty. Now *go!*"

Dee trudged out and got the book and went to the kitchen to get paper towels. "It's not ruined," she said miserably. "Would you really throw me out?"

"I'd think about it," Sarah said. "Oh, Jesus Christ! Don't start crying again. I was just joking."

"I hope you were. You know how much I love you."

"There! There! I love you too, sweetheart."

Crying, Dee ran to Sarah and put her head between her legs, but Sarah pushed her away.

"Not before six, angel," Sarah said. "I'm trying to taper off. Now don't be offended, poopsy. I don't feel like it right now."

Dee got up. "But say you love me and mean it."

"On a stack of Bibles," Sarah said, raising the glass in her right hand.

Dee went back to the box of books. "I feel better now. I do love you, Sarah. You forgot to order the Kandinsky—you like him so much— but I didn't forget. I phoned the order in."

Sarah drank the rest of the bullshot. Then with an open-faced smile that was quite false, she said, "You're a good man, Charlie Brown."

Dee began to put the books in the white-painted shelves that lined the room to half its

22

height. The top shelves were so high that she had to use a wooden step-stool to reach them. "I was thinking . . ." she called out to Sarah who was in the kitchen making another drink.

Sarah came in spilling some of the bullshot. On her way to her chair she patted Dee on the ass and Dee was delighted.

"What were you thinking, love?" Sarah asked, drinking heartily. "Tell Mommy what's in that pretty little head of yours. Come on now. Fess up, Shirley."

Dee got down from the stool and sat on the carpet in front of Sarah. Her eyes were red from crying.

"What you need is about a pint of Visine," Sarah said.

"No listen, this is serious."

"Nothing's that serious, dollink."

"This is, really. If I tell you something will you listen and not make jokes and call me silly names?"

"I sure will, pardner. Sorry, that just slipped out. Say it straight, like they say in Texas. No more cryin', hear?"

There was a wistful smile on Dee's face as she began, and she gulped a little. "You know how desperately I love you. All right. Just let me talk. The last few months I've been think-ing that we ought to settle down."

"We're on the old homestead right now. For the summer, anyway."

23

"That's what I mean. But where will we go when the summer is over? We don't even know. All we have is a lot of travel folders and absolutely no plans. No real ones. I don't mean to criticize, you know that. I've been just as wild as you are. But now you're thirty-five, I'm thirty-seven. That's not so young."

"Speak for yourself, John Alden. Me, I'm just a kid."

"Please don't joke. I don't mean it's *old*-old. What I'm trying to say is every summer we come back to Maine something bad happens. Why don't we close up the house and go away! Find some place and try to get ourselves together. Oh, I don't mean we can't have a good time, go to parties and everything. But *quiet* good times. In this damn town they'll be talking behind out backs when we're sixty."

"That would be awful," Sarah exclaimed in mock consternation. "But get to the point, will-ya? This new place of yours, where is it?"

"I'd love to live in England. London or some lovely old town not far from it. Or maybe Charleston?"

"You do jump around. How about Australia?"

Dee made a face. "I don't think I'd like Australia."

Sarah mimicked Dee's grimace. "Neither would I."

"All I want to do is go away from here."

"Because I've been looking at Tracy O'Neal's picture!"

"Well, yes and no. But you said yourself she's a conniving bitch."

Sarah smiled confidently. "She won't connive me. Look. I wish you'd stop all this stuff. We'll have a good summer and find a new place in the fall. My God! We just came here all the way from North Africa. Came all that way and you want to pack up and go. That's just silly. Won't do it."

"Promise you won't get involved with her. I've been told she swings both ways."

"Who told you that?"

"Buffy Winship in West Palm Beach."

Sarah smiled knowingly. "Well, she ought to know if anybody does.

"Promise me, Sarah. Right now."

With five bullshots in her, Sarah was at least half drunk. She reached for Dee's hand and squeezed it. "I promise. I promise."

"I'm so happy," Dee said fervently.

Lying back in the chair, Sarah said, "Get me the book on Kandinsky, will you? I'd like to look at it." Sarah did like Kandinsky: he painted the way she thought.

"Of course." Dee got up quickly and went to get the book.

And then for the next twenty minutes all was quiet in the beautiful house: Sarah paging through the biography, Dee looking through travel folders. But when Dee looked up again, Sarah had a mad grin on her face.

"What is it?" Dee asked in some alarm.

The grin grew madder. "I'm just wondering what Tracy's party's going to be like."

As she said it the shower of folders came at her. Dee came after her then with clawing fingers, and she was screaming. Then, locked in combat, they fell to the floor.

So fierce was the battle that they didn't even hear the truck roar past the house.

CHAPTER THREE

Burly Leonard Gately was Sarah and Dee's closest neighbor, and he spat out the window of the customized, chrome-laden Ford pick-up as he passed their house.

"God damned lezzies," he mumbled to himself. And he wasn't just like other people who have an aversion to homosexuals. Gately hated them with all his heart. He'd like to kill them, or at least make them wear yellow stars on their arms like when the Fuhrer was in power, God rest his brave, brilliant soul. The big man smiled grimly. Now that the New Right was in the saddle maybe they could get on with the job. He wasn't sure he trusted Reagan. That fucking *actor!* But that actor was a beginning, and if he proved to be a false prophet, shit, they'd get rid of him too.

Leonard Gately, for very sound reasons, was known as the wildest, craziest man in Yorkport, perhaps all of Maine. In the back window of the glittering truck a Marlin lever-action rifle hung on a rack in plain sight. Once upon a time the chief of police kidded him about how this wasn't Mississippi and why did he have to carry a thing like that in his truck?

Roaring down the hill toward the village, Gately remembered how he had read the law to old baggy-pants Brown. There was no Maine law against it and what business was it of his and why didn't he go bother that new faggot bar in the village? The swish place where the creeps danced together and bad stuff went on in the men's room. There sure as shit was a law against *that*, and if the chief didn't know what it was, well then, sir, he'd look it up for him.

"Drive on, Gately," the chief said, getting all red-faced. "And the next time I find you driving with just one drink in you I'll lock you up."

Gately spat from the truck. Screw the chief. There wasn't a thing Old Man Brown could do to him.

At thirty-eight, Leonard Gately was a most unhappy man, although he would not have admitted anything so shameful, not even to himself. Born in New Haven (where his English immigrant father was a club steward) he could not find acceptance in the village of Yorkport, much as he tried. A veteran of the early years of the Vietnam War—he had served with valor in the notorious Green Berets—he had grown rich through real estate. Yorkport was a rich town; property values there were about the highest in the state. A virulent right winger, he hated blacks, fags, Italians, Jews, Democrats, liberals of any stripe. In fact, he didn't like the Irish much either, except those of the extreme Right: Reagan, Connally, Buckley. Far from being a stupid man, he was well if erratically read in works by extremist writers. However, right now he had a skull-blinding hangover and a case of good Beck's beer was much in his mind. He actually lived on German beer, iced to the freezing point, and thick rare-cooked porterhouse steaks. But now, on this lovely summer day, he was fresh out of both.

Fifteen minutes before, after he fell out of bed, he had cursed wildly when he fumbled his way to his enorous refrigerator and found it empty.

Many years removed from military service, he still peppered his talk with GI slang. Even the best food was "chow;" getting up in the morning he referred to as "rolling out of the sack." Such talk reminded him of the good old days in Nam, but a bullet in the knee had ended his military career. He limped slightly and was proud of it.

The great rambling house he lived in stood high on the hill known as Copp's Hill, and was modeled after a hunting lodge in the Black Forest. It had been built in the mid-1920's by a millionaire admirer of Hitler, then having rather a bad time of it, his legions scattered, the world indifferent to his radical ideas. In a way, it looked like a castle of wood, with strange pagan carvings and figures, symbols of the new Nazi religion. Over it flew the American flag of Gately's own design: a screaming eagle holding a rifle. When he first bought the house it had been his firm intention to loft the swastika banner of the Third Reich, but his friend Colonel Mike Burns (USA. Ret.) had talked him out of it. It would not do, the gallant old soldier explained, to have their organization, Sentinel, associated with Nazis and Klansmen, even though their support might be welcome at some time in the future.

Gately had read about this strange house when he was a boy in New Haven, smarting even then in the knowledge that his English-born father was a servant who waited on the young gentlemen of Yale. The magazine article had been occasioned by the death of Willis Bannerman, the eccentric tycoon (foot powder) whose summer place it was. The text of the article was caustic, but the youthful Gately was not aware of that. In fact he liked the title of the article, HEIL BANNERMAN! He thought it snappy and to the point; the embryonic fascist vowed that some day he must have this house, or a house just like it. And now, twelve years after his discharge from the army, the house was his.

For all his shrill support of Hitler, old Bannerman wasn't really a Nazi, just a greedy Republican businessman, a reactionary terrified of losing his great fortune; and so inside the house, in the high-ceilinged livingroom (The Great Hall) there were no swastikas or other Nazi regalia, no display of weapons or shields, just a stuffed bald eagle, one killed in violation of federal law. The eagle wore an Uncle Sam suit made up by a skilled tailor in downtown Boston.

Gately bought the house and furnishings and changed nothing, but he festooned the walls of The Great Hall with SS battle flags, dirks, swords, maces, firearms from every period, all bought at Kaufman's army-navy store on West 42nd Street, in New York City. The enormous swastika flag which hung over the fireplace came from Kaufman's, too. Late at night when Gately was in his cups, the stereo boomed out German Army marching songs and patriotic medleys from the work of John Philip Sousa and George M. Cohan. Sometimes, stirred by the simple fervor of the canned music, Leonard Gately would cry into his tankard, adorned with the heads of snarling boars and other wild beasts. And at such times he would mourn the glory that was gone, and the glory that was to come.

Above all, Leonard Gately longed for glory. He wasn't quite sure what kind of glory, but he knew he must have it someday. LIVE FREE OR DIE was his favorite slogan, and he admired neighboring New Hampshire very much for putting it on its license plates. Freedom from what he would have found hard to explain. Well yes, he did know after all: faggots, niggers, etc.

And he hated to pay his income tax, state and federal.

Before leaving for the village he had made a careless attempt to clean up The Great Hall, a mess from the party—the bash—the night before. It had been a small bash but a good one. Always the same three people came to drink up Gately's booze and help him eat the steaks: his best friend, Darryl Bates, the girl Bates was humping at the moment, and Gately's ex-wife, Suzie. Bates wrote continuity copy for a radio station in Boston. Bates's girl of the moment, Angela, worked for the same soul station. Suzie Gately lived on alimony. Suzie lived in fear of her life, and with good reason, and she got her bloody money, as Gately called it, on condition that she come to his parties. Otherwise, her ex-husband swore, he would have the divorce case reopened and get a dozen witnesses from all over to prove that she had lied in her teeth.

Gately was proud of all the damage they had done the night before. A stout chair had been broken by someone with superhuman strength. Gately knew he hadn't done it, so it must have been his ex-wife, a frail woman with bleached hair and a pert nose twice broken. In the downstairs bathroom (one of five) the toilet bowl had been given a hairline fracture. Broken glasses were everywhere. There had been a feeble attempt to rip one of the doors from the kitchen cabinet; now it hung on one hinge. Have a good time, Gately always said.

After he swept up, sort of, he went to look for the others. A man of lusty nature, he broke into Bate's bedroom shouting, "Give it to her good, Darryl!," but there was no one there. Nothing but the rumpled bed and a pair of torn panties.

Suzie was absent too. Suzie the bitch! He'd give it to her good for sneaking off so early in the day. She knew God damned well he liked a piece first thing in the morning. They'd all gone to the beach, of course. Well, fuck the beach! What was there but ten thousand niggers and Jews? He knew he wasn't telling himself the the truth about the niggers, for even on the Fourth of July you couldn't find three niggers on the five-mile Yorkport beach.

Sweeping the broken glass into a corner he wondered why the Jews and foreigners didn't stay where they belonged—Coney Island, Atlantic City—and eat their kosher sandwiches and drink their chicken soup.

But he didn't like the beach at any time. Too passive, no place for a man with things to do. Aware that he was still holding the broom, he broke it over his knee and threw the pieces away with a great oath. By right, the two bitches should be cleaning the house. No work for a man. What he needed was four of five cold Beck's and a big steak to set him up.

Now, still angry, he slowed his speed as he entered the village proper. That asshole, Chief Brown would be hanging around the town square keeping his eye on the traffic. Cars and campers blocked his way and he cursed, hating the out-of-town license plates, especially those from New York. He wished he had a tank so he could run right over the bastards, smash them, crush them; enjoy their screams of pain and terror. That would be a funny bit, all right. Darryl would like that one. Darryl was the only guy around who appreciated his humor. Great guy, Darryl Bates. Darryl knew he'd be a great comedy writer someday. Probably he would. It was about time a few Gentiles showed up.

The traffic moved on by inches, in a fog of gasoline fumes. He saw Chief Brown watching him from the steps of the police station.

Hopkins and Daley were trying to untangle the four lines of traffic coming into the town. Finally, he got through the town square and turned into the alley beside his office, a miniature colonial house, a doll's house really. The office was two rooms: one for the two salesmen, Bass and Gorman, one for himself.

Elly Fisk, who did the bookkeeping and answered the phone, was kidding with Gorman when he stalked in. The other clown, Bass, was talking earnestly into the phone. "It's a fine piece of beach property," he was saying.

Elly Fisk scurried back to her steel desk when she saw him, but he didn't bawl her out for fucking around: a good commander had to know how to handle subordinates. But Gorman was different. He didn't like Gorman. He suspected Gorman of trying to set up his own real estate business.

"You're not too busy today," he said to Gorman. "Not busy, go to the beach, get a tan?" He knew he was being unreasonable; Gorman was a much better salesman than Bass; if not for that he'd kick his ass out of there.

"I was waiting for a call from Mrs. Foster," Gorman said. "It's a big sale, Lenny."

"You don't wait for calls, Joe. You make calls."

"Mrs. Foster gets mad if you call too often."

Gately sighed with impatience. His head throbbed. "You don't say the same thing every time you call, Joe. Call back and say you have some other question. Make up something. That's the way I'd do it, Joe."

Gorman reached for the phone and Gately stopped him. "Well, maybe you should wait a few hours before you call again. Meanwhile, try to unload that old place back on the mountain."

"The Hazlitt place?"

"None other, Joe."

"But it's falling down. It's rotten clear through."

"See it as a challenge, Joe. It's real traditional Maine, that wonderful old house. Say it's haunted. Assholes from the city like that kind of shit. The place has a history, right? Hang the sale on that peg." Gately smiled. "As any good salesman knows, all any old house needs is a good coat of paint. Run the ghost story up the flagpole, Joe. See if anybody salutes it."

"You're the boss, Lenny." Gorman started to look through his file cards.

Gately opened the door. "See you later, boys and girl."

He left the pick-up where it was and headed for the Village Market, which was two doors down from the post office. On the way he stopped at the bank to cash a check for two hundred dollars.

The teller, Colleen Rizzo, said, "How're you

today, Lenny?"

Gately stuffed the money in his pants pocket and gave her a wicked smile. She wasn't bad looking for a wop, originally from Providence. Nice boobs.

"You should have come over last night." Gately rolled his red-streaked eyes. "A good time was had by all. Darryl Bates, the writer, was there."

"Sorry I couldn't make it, Lenny. My aunt was up visiting. You know?"

"You should have brought her along."

"She's sixty-five, Lenny."

"We could have parked her some place."

Colleen Rizzo giggled. "You're a terrible man, Lenny."

"Maybe you can come over tonight?

Her smile faded. "I'll try. Be seeing you."

Fuck her, Gately thought as he left the bank.

At the post office he met his friend Colonel Mike Burns (USA Ret.) The two men shook hands and asked how was everything. Burns was a short, peppery, red-faced man in his late sixties. Now there was a real Irishman.

"This whole town is going to hell," Gately said in the brisk military voice he always assumed when talking to Burns. "Look at that street out there. Hippies and I don't know what. Would you believe it, some long-haired kid—need I add that it was dirty—got in my way, *tried* to get in my way, and said did I have

37

any spare change? I felt like throwing him in the traffic, but I remembered what you said."

Burns nodded. "Good thinking, Leonard. That's not the way—for now. Ha, Ha, you old dog, what were you up to last night? Mine eyes detect certain signs of morning-after."

Gately liked to be kidded by the colonel. "Well, you know how it is, sir."

"That I do, Leonard. And there's nothing wrong with a man having a bit of enjoyment. It's these bums and drug-takers I object to. By the way, have you seen this week's *Star*? There's another front page story about—I was about to call her a lady—but that would be an insult to decent women everywhere. I'm referring, naturally, to Mrs. O'Neal. Why in the name of all that's holy did she have to come here?"

"Well, sir, I guess it's a free country. No, I haven't seen the *Star*, but I'll get one at the market. Any more about that party she's supposed to be giving? There was something about it in the first story."

Colonel Burn's got redder than usual. "There's all too much, Leonard. You know what that fool Hayward wrote, and he calls himself an editor? I quote you now: 'The cream of New York's artistic world will be there.' *Scum* is more like it. *Mister* Linwood Duval will be an honored guest, if you please. Good God, Leonard, that pipsqueak is nothing but a pornographer and avowed deviate."

"Yeah," Gately said. "I saw him on TV swinging his handbag." Suddenly Gately was interested. "Did the paper say anything about local people going to this party?"

"Only the New York people were mentioned. But I dare say she'll find a few locals of her own ilk. No need to mention any names, but you know what I mean."

"Indeed I do, sir."

"Well, I must be off, Leonard. I trust I'll see you at the next meeting of Sentinel? We must remain strong."

"Wouldn't miss it for the world, sir." Gately nodded toward a too-handsome man of about forty who was talking to the clerk at the counter. "Know who he is? That's Zachary Danforth. You know? He's in the play this week?"

"Indeed." The colonel smiled bleakly.

"He used to be on TV and he's still in the movies." Gately, for all his wild, violent nature, was somewhat star-struck.

"Yes-yes," the colonel snapped. "Very well then, Leonard, I'll see you at the meeting.

After he got his mail, mostly from right wing organizations, Gately went to the market to get the beer and steaks. He bought ten quarts of liquor. Darryl sure could put it away when he was up from Boston for the weekend. Darryl called Saturday his drinking day; on Sundays, he eased off.

Leonard Gately got home at last and opened three bottles of Beck's and drank them while two steaks were broiling, and when the steak was ready he drank two more Beck's.

He spread the *Yorkport Star* and read about Tracy O'Neal while he ate and drank.

Whatever she was, she was a great looking piece of hair pie, he decided.

Yes, siree!

CHAPTER FOUR

The late afternoon sun glinted on the inlet of the North Atlantic known as Hard Luck Bay. Looked at from the wide terrace of the new house, the sea seemed like old silver. Gulls wheeled over the water and their cries had a lonesome sound. Tracy Callaway O'Neal and Lafe Tatum were drinking gin and tonics.

"I love it! I love it!" Tatum said in a voice that somehow made everything sound faintly amusing. "Oh, but listen, Trace. You'll have to do something about that wreck of a house out there on the point. It's like a thumb in the eye when you look at the sea."

Tatum, a waspish young man of about thirty, sang a few bars of "By the Beautiful Sea." He had a thin, intelligent face and quick eyes, and he wore jeans and soft leather boots and a silk shirt open to his belt buckle. Around his neck was a crucifix and chain of solid gold. His hair was cut very short and brushed forward in bangs.

Tracy sipped her tall drink and smiled at his antics. "I know you're right about the old house. It isn't exactly Andrew Wyeth, is it?"

"It's just a wreck. No-period period. Anybody live there?"

"A sweet old lobsterman lived there when I had the first house on this property. He was still there when we tore down the house and started this one. Now I'm told he's dead. Funny, his old house didn't bother me until I built this one."

Tatum, closing one eye, regarded the dead lobsterman's gaunt, unpainted house. While he did so, he whistled "Moonlight Bay."

"Well, listen now," he said. "The house you have now makes everything different, doesn't it? If you don't mind my saying so, Trace, your original house should have been demolished by shellfire. Living in a house like that, no wonder you didn't mind his. Most definitely that place has to go. Burned, carted away, or dumped in the sea."

"I wonder who owns it now? I know there's no one living there."

"You'll just have to find out, won't you?"

Lafe Tatum was one of the few people in the world who dared to be cheeky with Tracy O'Neal, and for all his homosexual posturing he was quite straight. But he thought it was good for business—people expected interior decorators to be gay, didn't they?—and so he played the part to the hilt.

Tracy was one of the few people who knew he was straight; was a devil with the women, in fact. Her patronage had made him rich, and everyone wanted Lafe Tatum to "do" their places ever since he "did" Tracy's triplex on East 63rd Street.

Theirs was just a friendship, naturally. Tatum would have liked very much to get into Tracy's pants and into her fabulous bank account; he knew that was not possible. They were the best of friends, but not of the same class. They were friends and he hated her guts. Sweet Jesus! The things she said, and where did she get that voice? The old crow!

"You want me to find out for you? The new owner, I mean. There has to be one. There always is. Actually, it's better if I try to make a deal—they'll soak you. Try to."

Tracy shook her head. "No, Tatey. This place is going to be my home—my *real* home— much more so than New York or Palm Springs. I want the local people to know that I'm no different than they are. I'll find out about the house."

Tatum had a tinkling laugh that he worked on a lot. "That's very neighborly of you, Trace. Perhaps some real estate firm is handling it now."

"Yes, there is," Tracy said. "I sent Mary down to look at it and she said there's a sign on the side."

"Jabez Bulltongue and Company, no doubt."

"No, Tracy said. "The man who has the company is named Leonard Gately."

Zachary Danforth, in the motel bathroom, shaving for the second time that day, stared at his face in the mirror. He knew he looked like Gig Young and it depressed him. At least Gig was out of it, gone with two bullets: one for his too-young wife, his sixth, and one for himself. Togetherness. Nothing like it. They had been friends of a sort and he remembered how good old Gig hated having to do the straw hat bit. Gig often talked about the meaning of life about the time he was starting on the second quart of the evening. "Tell me, Zack old chum. What is the meaning of life?" Gig said that a lot.

Three big drinks had stopped the shake in Danforth's hands, and he was able to shave with confidence. It wouldn't do to have the leading man go on with a dab of toilet paper on his chin. People would laugh, thinking perhaps it was part of the script. Well, why shouldn't the people here, the hicks, laugh at him? They laughed at him in New York and Hollywood.

The odd thing was, many people thought he was lucky. Seldom out of work, he was sought out by casting directors who wanted someone to play charming alcoholics, ironic piano players—the hero's best friend. He had played breezy newspapermen about ninety times. Flip with the lip, that was him.

He had to keep busy. Oh yes, he had ex-wives too, four of them, and they never let him forget it. Only by the Grace of God had he avoided getting tied up with a fifth. Lucky thing he got drunk and wandered off before the wedding. By the time he sobered up a week later she had married somebody else. Whee! That was a close one.

Dawn's voice came from the bedroom, lazy and petulant. "I miss you, Zachary," she said. "Hurry on out, please."

"Be right there, darling," Danforth said, patting cologne on his square, manly chin. He decided he had a good face for a man of forty; only the eyes were tired.

Dawn lay on the bed with her legs apart, a sheet pulled up between them. She was chewing the end of the sheet and smiling at the same time. It was a pose invented by Brigitte

Bardot in the dear dead days of yesteryear.

"You look very handsome, Zachary," Dawn Brodie said, holding out her arms. Dawn was eighteen and had a walk-on in the play, a comedy, because she attended the Yorkport Playhouse Acting School. The guy who ran the theater and the school would enroll any kind of student. It didn't matter if they were deaf, dumb and blind. Of course he wouldn't think of giving the dummies any kind of part in the playhouse. "Perhaps next year, when you're ready," Cal Cameron, the rotten son of a bitch, would say, thereby ensuring that the dummies would come back again with money.

But really, he had no complaints about Dawn. She did look something like the young Bardot, and he had been screwing her for the best part of a week. There wasn't a chance that she'd ever make it: she wasn't vicious enough. Didn't have that step-on-the-face quality. Perhaps she'd learn.

"I'd like another hit, darling," Dawn said in an idiotic moan. "I want my Cecil."

Did she now, with coke going at $2000 an ounce?

"I'll see what's left, darling," Danforth said, going to his suitcase. But in the glassine envelope there was nothing more than a trace of dust, and now that the cocaine was gone, Danforth found he wanted a hit himself.

From the bed Dawn said, "This is a terrible

46

situation, darling."

"Too right," Danforth said. "You think Cameron packs his nose?"

Dawn brightened up. "I *know* Mr. Cameron does. He puts it in an empy Vick's inhaler. Call him, darling. I know he likes and respects you." She made a pretty pout. "So what's the difference? You're the star."

Oh Jesus! The fucking star!

"What's the number over there, darling?" Danforth said.

"Let me think, darling. Oh yes, Mr. Cameron's private number is. . . ."

So she's been fucking him too, Cameron thought.

Watching him dial, Dawn cried out, "You're wonderful, darling. I've loved you since the first time I saw you in re-runs of *Uncle Zack and the Kids.*"

Danforth shook his fist at her. "Will you keep fucking *quiet*—darling?"

Cameron, millionaire play producer, answered the phone sounding irritable, as he always did.

"This is Cameron," he said.

"Cal, this is Zack Danforth."

"Nothing wrong, I hope." Cameron, after thirty years in the business, hated, absolutely hated, all actors. But those who filled his playhouse he could stand. Zackary Danforth had been packing them in all over New England.

47

"No problem play-wise. A personal favor. You got anything for a head cold?"

"Are you drunk, Danforth?"

"Absolutely not. You know I don't drink when I'm working." Danforth said. "What I mean is—sniff! sniff!"

"Oh that," Cameron said, thinking, The son of a bitch is trying to pad his wages with free coke. "You're asking the wrong guy, Zack. Don't use the stuff."

"I'd appreciate it, Cal. Perhaps you know somebody."

There was a pause at the other end of the line, then Cameron said, "Yeah, there's a guy in town might be able to help you. I can't promise anything, but if he's got it he'll bring it over. The guy's name is Freddy DiSalvo. Don't waffle with this man, Zack. He won't like it."

"You're a prince, Cal," Danforth said, and hung up.

"Looks good, darling," Danforth said. "Now clean up the place and go sit in the bathroom. You're not supposed to be here, darling."

Dawn kissed him on her way to the john.

Danforth put on his pajamas and waited, smoking one cigarette after another. In thirty minutes the buzzer sounded and he opened the door. A short, squat man of about sixty in loud play clothes stared at him.

"Gee, it's you all right. Pleased to meetcha,

48

Mr. Danforth. My five grandkids love you on the *Uncle Zack* show on the TV. Freddy DiSalvo is my name."

Danforth knew a hoodlum when he saw one. The man came in and they shook hands.

"Nice place you got here," the hoodlum said, looking around the plastic motel room.

"Thanks," Danforth said.

"I'll be there to catch your show opening night. I never miss opening night at the thee-ayter. How much worth do you want?"

"Five hundred."

"Sure," DiSalvo said. "In cash."

After Danforth and Dawn had their hits, Dawn lay back on the bed and he screwed her again. There was nothing like a hit to help you get it up. Danforth was content for the moment; the thought of having to go on in the fucking play didn't seem so hideous now.

Dawn rolled around on the bed, doing her cornball thing. "Everything is so wonderful, darling. I want to be somebody and do all sorts of wonderful things. But you know what I want most of all, apart from you?"

"You can't have another hit, if that's what you mean."

"No! No!" Dawn cried in her drama school voice, feeling her breasts at the same time. "I want to go to Tracy O'Neal's fabulous Fourth of July party. I told you about it the other day. You can fix it so we can go. I know you can."

49

"I'm just an actor, kid. These are society people." Danforth sighed. "It can't be done."

"But you'll try, won't you, darling?"

Danforth had been to a million parties; the thought of going to another one, even this one, made him tired.

"I'll try, darling," he said.

It's nice to meet a gentleman for once, Freddy DiSalvo thought as he drove his silver Rolls Royce (in the $100,000 class) away from the Yorkport Motel. Guy had the cash right on him in nice clean hundreds. Shook my hand like a man. "Pleased to make your acquaintance, Mr. DiSalvo," he said. What's more, he said it like he meant it. No wonder people all over like the guy. Wait'll I tell the kids I met the star of their favorite show on the tube. Shit! I should of asked him to autograph something. Now they'll think I'm bullshitting them. I'll bet Mr. Danforth didn't know I knew he had a cunt in there. The whole place smelled of hot pussy. Well, that's all right. A guy like that is under a lot of pressure and needs some relaxation. Maybe I'll catch him after the show and bring something to him to sign. I know the guy won't mind, not being a jerk-off like some of the actors who come through this town. Nice town. I got respect in this town. They know I keep my word—always have—I don't fuck around. . . .

50

Freddy DiSalvo made a long tour of the town because he had nothing else to do. For many years he had been a courier for the Boston-Providence organization, and in all that time he hadn't lost a dime belonging to his people. For twenty years, ever since he was twenty-two, he had driven millions, perhaps billions, of untaxed cash from one end of the country to the other. They knew him in New York, Chicago, Miami, Los Angeles, Las Vegas as "Mr. Wheels." Later, as a reward for his integrity, the Boston-Providence organization gave him his own territory in the towns of Boston's North Shore, and when he retired in 1979, Mr. Patriarca himself came all the way to Revere Beach, the most lucrative part of his territory, and gave a dinner for him. Other important Mafiosi came from the length and breadth of New England to pay their respects. Solly Fishbein, the most respected Jew in the organization after Meyer Lansky, found the time to drive down from Montreal. For an almost illiterate Italian boy, Vilfredo (Freddy) DiSalvo had come a long way since his beginnings in Providence in 1920.

Actually, he didn't need the money that came in from his dope dealing in the Yorkport area; to him it was something to keep busy, and he didn't deal to just anyone: a customer had to be a class person, a discreet person, someone with professional or social standing.

If the local police knew of his drug activities they didn't let on, and so he was able to obtain a permit for a concealed weapon when he applied for it. There was no need to deny him. He had never been arrested in his life; he had never been charged with anything. On the application he have his reason for wanting to carry a .32 Beretta automatic pistol: "I habitually carry large sums of money on my person." Which was perfectly true.

Several respected people vouched for him.

DiSalvo was carrying the Beretta now as he made one final swing around the town. It was a nice little community, he thought. No crime, no niggers, and, to tell the truth, very few Italians. It wasn't that he was ashamed of being Italian—far from it—but he didn't want a lot of low-class guineas coming in and steaming up the place with cheap pizza parlors and shoe repair shops. He liked Yorkport just as it was.

A man at peace with himself, Freddy DiSalvo felt no impatience at the traffic jam that persisted in the village square, where the four roads met. The old ordinances had been rescinded and the brightly lit main street was thronged with girls in bathing suits. Freddy DiSalvo looked at them with longing but also without bitterness. Young stuff. People were lining up at the two movie houses for the eight o'clock show. One of them was showing a revival of *Godfather 1*. Freddy DiSalvo smiled because he knew better.

What he'd do now was make a big veal stew and open a bottle of vino and settle down for the night.

The only thing that annoyed him as he finally drove through the village square was the sight of Leonard Gately carrying a case of beer from the Village Market.

Fucking ding-a-ling!

The butler was English and he stared at the two cartons of Perrier water Bruce Whipple was carrying.

"Young man," he said gravely, "deliveries are made at the rear of the house. There's a sign and a light. You won't have any trouble finding it."

"Look, man," Bruce said in a loud voice. "I'm doing this on my own time. You want this stuff or not?"

"In that case. . . ."

"What's going on, Shaw?" Tracy O'Neal asked, opening the door all the way. "Oh, it's you, Bruce—you came all the way out here with the Perrier." She waved the butler away and told Bruce to come in. "You mustn't mind Shaw. He doesn't understand that things up here aren't the same as they are in New York. Less formal, that is."

"You bet," Bruce said.

But he tried to flee when she started to lead him into a vast dining room in which there were at least thirty people awaiting dinner in formal attire. Some had beards and shining bald heads; one extremely tall man wore a monocle. Bruce was vaguely familiar with some of the faces, as if he'd seen them in magazines or on his portable television set. There was one short, pudgy man whose name was right on the tip of his tongue. He was sure he'd seen him on television many times, usually on late-night talk shows, always saying outrageous things.

Bruce said in alarm, "Gosh, Miz O'Neal, I can't go in there. Look at the way I'm dressed."

He was wearing wash-and-wear pants, white tee-shirt, and his University of Maine windbreaker. But at least I'm clean, he thought, if that means anything. He had rushed back home to take a shower after the Perrier came.

Tracy took his arm and propelled him forward like an officer driving his men toward the machine guns of the enemy.

"Don't be silly, Bruce," Tracy said. "I think you look perfectly sweet. Let's not have any reverse snobbery."

The thunder of conversation that seemed so incredibly loud to Bruce began to fade as he made his entrance.

"I won't introduce you to everyone just now," Tracy whispered. "Just those you'll be closest to at the table. Is that all right with you?"

"You bet," Bruce said.

Some of the people there nodded casually at Bruce, then turned away and began to talk, it seemed to him, all at the same time. Tracy halted Bruce in front of the pudgy man.

"Bruce, I'd like you to meet Linwood Duval. Linwood, Bruce."

"Hi there, Brucie," Duval lisped, offering a damp, limp hand that felt like a soft-boiled egg.

"Holy Cow!" Bruce almost fell over. This is the guy that's always saying that bad sutff on TV. Like how he's a fairy, and doesn't care who knows it.

"Hi there, Mr. Duval." Bruce gulped.

"What's this *Mister* silliness, Brucie? Call me Linny."

"You bet . . . Linny."

Duval looked slightly puzzled. "Was that a question, Brucie? For some reason it didn't sound like one."

A burly man of about fifty-five with curly hair and jug ears shouldered Duval aside and danced around the astonished Bruce in boxing stance, jabbing at Bruce's face and stomach but stopping just short. He spoke his blows: "Pow! Wham! Thunk!" Still in motion (though he was rather old to be doing it, Bruce thought), he said, "My name is Ormond Bailey

55

and I'm famous all over the world. You ever find yourself stranded in Tibet, tell 'em you know Ormond Bailey and they'll treat you square. I took on Hemingway and beat him at his own game. Who else is there to beat? Answer me that, kid?"

"There's me," the pudgy man lisped. "I'm famous too, Brucie. When I was your age—you're eighteen, aren't you?—I wrote a divine little book. I'm just teasing—of course you know the name of it."

Bruce shook his head. "Fraid I don't, Linny."

Suddenly Duval turned nasty, the way he did on television. "And why not, Brucie-Goosie?"

"Well, you see, Linny, I take business at college." Sweat was running from Bruce's armpits. Why the heck hadn't he gone out with Mary Beth tonight instead of standing her up to come here?

"They don't allow you to read in this business college?"

"Let the kid alone, Duval or I'll deck you in the first minute of the first round." The burly man danced around Duval, going "Pow! Whack! Thunk!"

In desperation, Bruce looked around for Tracy, but she was nowhere in sight. Taking no heed of the burly man, Duval sidled up to Bruce and lisped, "You young rascal, you're fucking her, aren't you?"

Bruce turned red. "Gosh no, Linny!"

"I believe you, Brucie. Want a blow job?"

"Gosh, I don't think I do, Linny, if it's all the same to you."

"You really mean that, Brucie? I give good head."

Bruce wanted to run. "I'm sure you do, Linny. The thing is, I have this girlfriend and everything."

"What does the 'everything' part mean, Brucie?"

"It doesn't mean anything special, Linny," Bruce said in desperation. "To each his own, right?"

"Now why didn't I think of that," Duval said. "All right, if you don't want a blow job, what do you want?"

Duval, standing on tiptoe, whispered in Bruce's ear while Bailey continued to throw out rights and lefts.

Bruce's face turned red. "Gosh, Linny," he said. "I never even *heard* of that stuff."

Tracy appeared, shook a warning finger at Duval, and dinner was served.

CHAPTER FIVE

The few party records that Leonard Gately owned were in such bad shape that Darryl Bates bemoaned the fact that they didn't have something they could dance to without all that hissing and scratching.

"Old buddy," Bates said. "We can't get it on with German marching songs."

"Hey there's some old shit in the closet under the stairs," Gately said. "I never looked through it, but I think it's all 78's from the Fifties. Take a look, will you, good buddy?"

"Will do," Bates said.

He came back with a box of 78's and started to blow the dust off them. "Hot shit!" he said. "Golden oldies. These are worth a lot of money, did you know that?" Bates held up one dusty record. "This is 'Johnny B. Goode' by Chuck Berry. And here's 'Chattanooga Shoeshine Boy.' Real bouncy stuff, Lenny."

"Nigger shit," Gately said.

"Come on, old buddy. It's good to dance to."

"I hate that shit."

"Well, naturally you do," Bates said. "It's only natural that a guy like you would hate nigger shit like that."

It was a kick to play straight man for a great guy like Darryl. "Why is dat, Mistah Bones?" Gately asked in a wretched imitation of a Negro voice.

Darryl Bates winked. "Cause you ain't a nigger!"

The two men fell around laughing. Angela, the girl from the radio station, did her best to laugh. Suzie Gately didn't laugh at all. Gately started at her, but Bates pulled him back.

"Let there be peace in the land," Bates said. "Be a buddy, buddy, and fix me somethin' tall and cool whilst I set a few platters on de spindle."

"Get in the mood," Gately yelled at his ex-wife.

In a moment the sounds of "Cheatin' Heart" filled the big room.

"Very, verrry tasty," Darryl Bates said, taking hold of Angela. After gulping another drink, Suzie Gately danced by herself. She was crying. Defying her ex-husband with her eyes, she began to sing.

Uncapping a Beck's, Gately thought what a bitch she was. She wanted a divorce just because he knocked her around a few times. Well now she had it, and how did she like it?

"Your cheatin' heart will make you weep," Suzie Gately sang.

"You'll walk the floor and try to sleep."

Nigger music, Leonard Gately thought. Absolute shit. But he tapped his foot when "Rock Around the Clock" began to shake the house. That Darryl was some dancer, all right. Better than the dumb bitch he was with. But as Darryl said, "When I'm not with the hole I love, I love the hole I'm near." The son of a bitch sure could write good lines.

Earlier in the evening Darryl had told him (for his ears only) that he had finished a screenplay that was being given serious consideration by one of the biggest Hollywood production companies. (No, Darryl said. He was not at liberty to divulge the name of the studio right now, but he would say the first letter of the name was P. Darryl dug him in the ribs. Matter of fact, he said, the last name is P as well. So that made it Pee Pee.) Sure, Gately thought. Paramount Pictures. The dirty dog!

Darryl was a pretty good-looking guy. No wonder the broads went for him. The guy got more ass than a toilet seat. Gately wondered what the screenplay was about. Something funny probably. It had to be with Darryl writing it.

Now the music was "Jealous Heart."

"What's all this heart shit? Sounds like Mass General." Gately found himself laughing at his own joke. Not bad. Not bad at all. He'd have to tell that one to Darryl. Give it to him free.

On the floor, Suzie Gately was dancing with a glass in her hand. Some of the liquor spilled on the dirty floor.

"Watch it," Gately yelled, trying to be heard above the thump of the music. But Bates had turned up the stereo as far as it would go.

Gately grinned when he saw Darryl whispering in Angela's ear. Then she moved away from him and began to take off her clothes. There wasn't much to take off, just a zippered dress with nothing under it. No shoes. Gately began to get an erection.

Darryl has something good there, Gately thought. "Spoon stuff", we called it in the army. He knew Darryl had been banging her for about a month. You had to hand it to the broad. She always looked great. She was blond all over and could prove it. Darryl said she'd do anything. Take it any way you wanted to give it to her. A sensational cocksucker, Darryl said.

Earlier in the evening they had screwed Angela. Later Darryl screwed his bitch of an ex-wife. Then he'd screwed her himself. All in the family, Darryl said.

Gately looked at his diver's watch. 10:15. If the bitch from the bank showed up, he'd screw her too. She might not like it but she'd get it. "The Stripper" started. That one he liked. One time he went to a dirty show in Saigon and they played it when the little girls came out.

"Hold it, Darryl!" he bellowed, making turn-off movements with his hands.

The music stopped and Bates looked puzzled. "Too loud for you, buddy?"

"Like hell, buddy," Gately said. "How's about we make this a real party?"

"Show us the way, oh master," Bates said.

"The way is for the girls to mix it up," Gately roared in his false-hearty voice. Gately, running to fat in his late thirties, was a great admirer of flamboyant actors with big voices. Fat shouters.

"Take it off!" he roared at his ex-wife. "Remember what I said about the money."

Once again Darryl Bates was the peace-maker. "Easy does it, Big Daddy." He pushed Angela toward Suzie. "Let's have a good time, kids. Come on, Suzie, you gorgeous creature. Remember, it's all in fun."

Suzie hesitated and Bates came over and took the glass from her hand. "Let me fill this up for you, my dear," he said.

After Suzie drank it all without taking a breath she no longer cared. Her clothes dropped to the floor.

"Whoops!" she said when Angela put her
hand between her legs. Suzie kissed her on the
lips and she responded, but when Angela tried
to press her down to the floor, she pulled away,
trying to make a joke of the whole thing.

"The Stripper" clicked off and "Sentimental
Journey" came on. Smiling, Angela took Suzie
in her arms and they began to dance slowly.
Gately, very drunk, was crashing around in the
kitchen filling his party stein with three bottles of beer.

Bates watched the girls with a smile. Unlike
Gately, he could wait to see them do their
thing. There was nothing you couldn't wait for.
The dancing was going good and "Sentimental Journey" was working its nostalgic charms
on poor old Suzie who, loveless and despair-
ing, was trying to please the madman who had
been her husband. Gately was a turd, but he
had his uses.

The two women moved around Gately's var-
nished, uncarpeted floor, their bare feet making a soft, swishing sound on the thin film of
beach sand.

"Beautiful! Just beautiful, ladies," Bates
said, smiling the cocked eyebrow smile that
he had copied from some long-gone movie
star. "I wish I could decide which of you to vote
for."

"You dirty dog," Gately said proudly, raising

his monstrous beer mug in salute.

Bates went to the kitchen and got big drinks for the girls. He held the first glass to Angela's mouth and she drank it while continuing to move. Some of the liquor dripped down her body but she didn't mind and neither did Suzie.

"Oh wow!" Angela gasped. "Good!"

Suzie sang, *"Got mah room and got mah reservation . . ."*

She wouldn't let Bates feed her the drink, so he gave her the glass.

They all watched her drink.

She drank all of it, swaying on her feet.

"That's a good girl," Bates said, winking at Gately. Two men of sophistication. Gately winked back, but when his eyes returned to his ex-wife his fatty face twisted into a grin of derision.

Suddenly Suzie Gately was very drunk. She cocked her head to one side when it began to rain. The rain beat against the windows and Suzie said in a Maine accent, "Looks like we're in for a bit of foul weather. 'Taint a fittin' night for man nor beast."

"Chattanooga Choo-Choo" started up.

"The hell with that one," Suzie Gately said, putting her hand on Angela's shoulder to steady herself. "Stop the goddam music, Darryl."

Bates grinned at Gately. "What's the matter

64

with it?"

"I can take it or leave it alone, Darryl, old buddy. You ever in the service, my man?"

"Sure," Bates said. "The Salvation Army."

"How'd you like it?" Suzie asked Angela.

"I'm with you," Angela said. "Us goils gotta stick together."

Suzie hiccuped. "Too fucking right." She began to sing along with the music.

"I thought you didn't like that song," Gately snarled, bunching his fist.

Suzie, flying high now, left off her solitary dancing. She smiled at Bates and pushed Angela good naturedly. She even smiled at her ex-husband.

"What was that you said, Lenny?"

Bates got between them just in time.

"You said you didn't like that song," Gately said.

"I love it," Suzie Gately said.

"That's not what you said."

"Didn't I? How about you, Lenny? You like it, lover?"

"It's a nigger song."

"Then I love it."

"Looks like it's our dance," Angela cut in before Gately could strike his ex-wife. By now Angela was nearly as drunk as Suzie. "You come here often?" she asked, grinding into Suzie.

"More than I should," Suzie said.

"You're a real cute kid, you know that?" Angela said, winking over Suzie's shoulder. "Only you look kind of tired. Whatcha been doin'?"

"Fucking." Suzie would have fallen if Angela hadn't held her up. "Jus' fucking."

"You ought to lie down for a while."

"You think so?" Suzie said stupidly, not knowing now where she was. She was no longer aware of her ex-husband's menace. She didn't know she was being a party poop. Drunk and staggering, all she knew was one thing: she wanted to lie down.

"So tired," she mumbled.

"You should lie down definitely," Angela urged.

"You're so right." Suzie began to totter.

"I have wall-to-wall," Angela said softly.

Lying on the dirty floor, Suzie wore a happy smile. "Nice and soft," she sighed.

"I knew you'd like it," Angela said.

From the sidelines Bates gave Angela the Churchill Victory Sign. "Good girl," he said.

Only Gately was impatient. "Get on with it, for Christ's sake."

Bates nodded quickly and his eyes began to shine as his girlfriend pulled Suzie's legs apart and began to work on her.

"Lovely," Suzie moaned. She knew something wasn't right, but she didn't care. It was better than what she did to herself in bed early in the morning. It was good. It was wonderful. Images, voice, lights, music grew strong in Suzie's mind. It was all sensation and nothing else.

If Gately hadn't spoken it might have gone on and on.

"Look at the dirty bitch,'" he sneered.

It was just enough to roll back the clouds from Suzie's mind. At last she knew what those sensations meant, and it made her mad.

"Damn you!" she screamed at Angela, grabbing her by the hair. Angela screamed too, but with pain, as Suzie raked her body with her nails. Angela tried to pin Suzie to the floor. Over Angela's shoulder, Suzie saw Gately pulling off his heavy garrison belt. She saw Bates trying to stop him. The belt swung up and came down and Angela gave a sharp cry. Bates threw himself on Gately, but the belt came down again. The next time Bates jumped on Gately's back he was gripped and thrown, landing with a crash halfway across the room. And then Gately seemed to know what he had done, because he ran to pick Bates up. Bates spat in his face and Gately didn't hit him.

The belt dropped from Gately's hand.

"Jesus, buddy! I didn't mean to do that. There's the belt. Take it. Flog me with it, buddy." Suddenly, Gately tore open his shirt, exposing a hairy back and chest. "Please, buddy, don't look at me like that. We've been friends for so long. You're the only real friend I have in this town."

Bates managed to get to his feet. His left knee nearly buckled under him when he put his weight on it, but he managed to stand. Angela and Suzie were getting dressed as fast as they could, sensing that Gately might go berserk at any moment.

"Hurry up, Angie," Bates said, flinching with pain.

Tears were running down Gately's meaty face. "Listen, buddy. You can't leave like this. You got to pay me back for what I did, then we'll be even. We can be good buddies again."

Bates raised his hand to strike Gately, but didn't do it. "Why don't you cut out the faggot shit, good buddy? Because that's what you are. A big fat faggot!"

Gately balled his fits, but didn't move.

"What're you going to do, faggot? Kill me? How do you want to do it? Commando style, with the knife? Bare hands? Piano wire? You know where I heard all that military bullshit? In the movies when I was about twelve. That's what you are, good buddy. A twelve-year old faggot playing with real guns. No wonder the people of this town don't like you. Who could like you?"

Bates limped across the room until he was standing directly in front of Gately. Gately was about six inches taller and fifty pounds heavier than Bates. Bates was drunk, but that wasn't all of it.

"Here's your chance, shithead. You don't want to take it, fine with me. So now I'll tell you a secret, good buddy. I never liked you for a minute. There was free room and board here. The best Scotch, the best steaks, the use of the office car. That's why I hung out with you, faggot. If you thought there was some other reason, that just shows how a faggot thinks."

Bates turned but Gately let him go.

"So long, faggot," Bates sneered.

And then Leonard Gately was all alone.

CHAPTER SIX

Along about midnight, Patrolman Steve Daley brought in two hippies he'd caught screwing in the sand dunes. The boy was black, about nineteen or twenty, with a sullen face and a fuzzy head of hair. What did they call that? Chief Brown thought. An Afro?

The black wore a .50-caliber machine gun bullet on a leather thong. Some necklace, Caleb Brown thought. The girl, all curls and ringlets, couldn't have been more than fifteen. She looked Italian or Greek, something like that.

"He was screwing the ass off her," Daley said, grinning. "They didn't even hear me coming up on them."

"Okay, Steve," Caleb Brown said. "You caught them and they're here. You two kids, what're your names?"

"None of your business," the boy said. "We don't have to tell you a thing. Maybe you never heard of the Miranda decision?"

Caleb Brown sighed. "I want your names, your right names. I can turn you over to the state police if that's what you want. Believe me, they'll get your names. So you can talk to me or to them. You decide. If you go to the county jail the charges will stand. You'll go before a judge and there won't be any bargaining."

The girl spoke first. "I am the Truth."

"Come again," Caleb Brown said. "You are the *what*?"

"That's my name."

"Is it now? And what's yours?"

"Akomi Baraka."

On the other side of the room Steve Daley was drinking coffee from the urn with a big grin on his face.

Caleb Brown pointed at the boy. "You there, you could waste a person's time awful easy. Well you won't waste mine, sonny boy."

"I'm not your sonny boy."

Daley was young and had a bad temper. He slapped the kid before Caleb Brown could stop him.

"That'll do, Steve. No more of that."

"You don't have to take that shit from a lousy nigger and this greaseball whore with him."

The girl was startled. "Oh, no," she said. "You see. . . ."

She was trying to smile.

Caleb Brown said. "Go back to work, Officer Daley."

Daley said, "He sort of pushed me when I arrested them. That's resisting arrest, Chief. Let me call the staties and send them to county."

"I'm going, Chief," Daley said when he saw the look on Caleb Brown's face.

"That guy don't seem to know what he's doing," the boy said.

Caleb Brown was tired and the Fourth of July was still three days away. He didn't want to think how tired he'd be then.

"You don't seem to know when to talk and when not to," Caleb Brown said.

He heard the patrol car driving away from the station. Usually he was the one to make the last tour of the town, but at the height of the summer season—and this was it—he let someone else do it. There were three summer temporaries as well as the regular men.

Caleb Brown did not like hippies. There were plenty of people he didn't like. Some of the moneyed summer people were beyond his understanding. They painted, molded things in clay, and they wrote poetry that made no sense, not a lick of sense, no matter how hard you tried to dig into it. Some of them walked along the beach, collected driftwood, old beer bottles worn by the action of the sand and tide, even shiny stones. Some took chunks of driftwood home, nailed it to a board and gave it a name. One artist—if that was the right name for him—had a hunk of driftwood called "Creation of the Moon."

Caleb Brown asked the girl what she wanted.

"A cup of coffee."

"I guess so," Caleb Brown answered. He asked the Black if he wanted one too. He shook his fuzzy head.

"What're you going to do with us?" he asked.

The girl giggled.

Caleb Brown told them to be quiet. He had to make up his mind. The last two summers the village had been thick with hippies. This present one was the worst so far. Back in the Fifties, which seemed bad enough at the time, the police had trouble with the Beats, so-called. Looking back now, the Beats didn't look so bad. You never heard of them begging in the streets or stealing women's purses, something that had happened a few miles down the road. A woman driving up from Boston picked up these two hitchhikers, aged about seventeen, she told the police. She thought they didn't look so bad. Anyway, her own brat of a kid, a girl, was on the bum too.

Poor foolish woman, she even bought them hamburgers, all they wanted to eat. At McDonald's, where they had the hamburgers, this idiot lady opened her handbag and gave each of them five dollars. An hour later she let them off at the Portsmouth traffic circle—they said they were going up to the Green Mountains—and the Portsmouth traffic circle was the best place to hitch a ride. They thanked the lady and said goodbye and all, but five minutes later when she stopped for gas, she found they had stolen her bag, with all her money, credit cards, house keys and United States passport.

As he grew older, Caleb Brown was more and more given to reverie, and he often smiled when he thought of his friend Jack Durkin's suggestion that he take his pen in hand, so to speak, and write his memoirs.

Jack, retired now to Florida, was an editor on the old *Brooklyn Eagle*, and he always said that everybody had a book in them, especially the chief of police in a small town, someone who knew all the secrets of such a place. Well, yes, he did know all the secrets, or most of them, and some of them he had hushed up for the general good.

He knew about Freddy DiSalvo and his dope dealing, but what the hell, the whole country was taking dope of one kind or another, and if you wanted to keep your job you didn't step on too many toes. After all, how different was dope dealing from running booze back in Prohibition days? Selling and drinking booze was against the law, but everybody was doing it just the same.

Oh yes, he knew plenty of secrets. He knew about the elderly millionaire and the Vietnamese orphan he had "adopted," but maybe the boy was better off getting buggered than he would have been back in the jungles or wherever in hell he came from. At least he had three squares a day and a warm place to sleep, and what happened when the lights went out was none of his, Caleb Brown's, business. It made no difference what people did as long as they didn't do it in the street and make the Yorkport police department look bad. That was the trick of being a small town police chief: you looked the other way when that was the smart thing to do. No matter what they said, there was one law for the rich, another for the poor. It wasn't fair, but that was how the system worked. Go against it, and the system broke you like a stick.

Still and all, it wasn't a bad life. It was better than pulling lobster traps at five o'clock on a winter morning. It was better than plowing or sanding the roads during a snowstorm. It was better than driving for some cranky old woman who might decide to get romantic after a shaker of martinis. That had happened to a friend of his, and the man said it was the worst experience of his life, but he had to go along with it or lose his job. No, all things considered he was doing all right for himself, and all he had to do was hang on for a few more years and then he could retire on half pay and maybe open a lobster shack, something like that, and become a village character spinning yarns for the tourists. If you knew what you were doing, and he did, you could make enough money in the summer months to take it easy for the rest of the year.

Caleb Brown became aware that the black boy was talking to him. "What's that you say?"

"How's about letting us go?" the boy said. "We'll be on the first bus out if you let us go."

"That's not for you to say," Caleb Brown said. "Statutory rape, contributing to the delinquency of a minor—I could charge you with that. You broke the beach curfew by being in the dunes after dark. That's one more charge."

"Big deal," the black boy said.

"Big as I want to make it," Caleb Brown said, wondering how Patrolman Daley would take it if he turned them loose. It was no secret that Daley wanted his job—not that he blamed him for that—but on the other hand it wasn't smart to let a subordinate get something on you, something he might use against you, maybe by means of an anonymous letter to the town manager or the board of overseers. Since the beginning of summer there had been a number of burglaries that everybody took to be the work of kids like these two and it wouldn't do to be regarded as soft-hearted. Indeed, there were some people in town who wanted to run the hippies out the way the Cape Cod cops had done some years back. That old nut, Colonel Burns, was always calling for "drastic action" to control the dopers and the long-hairs. That wasn't legal, of course, and he wasn't going to have the civil liberties people on his ass just to please Burns. Even so, he was going to have to think this over before he let the little bastards go, which was what he wanted to do because there wasn't much to be gained by taking them to court. That would mean paperwork and still more paperwork. The girl's parents would have to be notified. So would the juvenile authorities. Daley was too hot-tempered to make a good witness, and that would mean having to go to court with him so he wouldn't blow up when some black attorney started needling him. Daley had been in the Marine Corps and didn't like blacks.

Caleb Brown found himself looking at the girl. She gave him a shy smile and shifted in her chair. Lord knows she looked harmless enough. She was sort of dopey looking—a little "short," as they said in Maine—but maybe that was from the dope. They had no dope on them when they were brought in, and that was the only thing to be said for the whole messy business. If there had been drugs, there was no way he could not book them and send them to county.

The girl looked as if she hadn't eaten a decent meal for God knows how long. It was said that these idiot kids lived on nothing but brown rice and Gerber's baby food. Gerber's was their big favorite because the jars were tiny and could be palmed in a supermarket without much chance of getting caught. And the sweet mush counteracted the bitter aftertaste of marijuana.

"You hungry?" Caleb Brown asked the girl. He was under no obligation to feed them— that was county business—but the girl was so woebegone that he felt a tug of pity. Besides, there were ham and cheese sandwiches going stale in the refrigerator.

"I'm not hungry, I don't want your food," the black boy said.

"I'm very hungry, officer," the girl said.

"There's ham and cheese," Caleb Brown said, and got up to get a sandwich. The light was still blinking on the side of the coffee urn. "Help yourself to coffee, what's left of it."

The black shook his bushy head when the girl held up a plastic cup as a question.

"What harm can it do?" the girl asked. "A sandwich and coffee?"

"What the fuck's the matter with you?" The

black looked as if his cause had been betrayed.

Caleb Brown clenched his big fists, thinking, it's so damn hard to do these kids a favor. "Listen to me good," he said slowly, trying to keep the anger out of his voice. "Any more talk like that and I'll chain you to a steam pipe."

"You been chaining up my people for four hundred years." The boy rattled off the words as if he'd said them many times before.

"Not me," Caleb said. "None of your people ever got chained up in the State of Maine. Maine was about the first state to raise a volunteer regiment in the Civil War. My great-grandfather was in it."

"Big deal," the Black said.

Caleb Brown shrugged. He was close to sixty and he was tired. "They didn't think it was any big deal. They just went. What's your name?" he asked the girl. "The one you were born with."

"You don't have to talk without a lawyer being present," the boy said. "That's the law."

Caleb Brown said, "You won't like it if it gets as far as lawyers. Let her answer the question."

"Jodi Christopher, that's Greek," the girl said, ignoring the boy's angry eyes.

"From where?"

"East Boston. My father runs a produce stand there."

"Christopher's Fruit and Vegetables. Sure. That's not far from the exit to Logan Airport."

"That's right. You know it?"

"Know where it is, that's all. How long since you been home?"

"Nearly a year. You're not going to call my father, are you?"

"No," Caleb Brown said, deciding that it wouldn't do any good. The girl's father might drive to Maine to fetch her back, and then again he might not, but what difference did it make what he did? The kid would just run away again.

"What are you going to do?" she asked. "Please let us go and we'll never come back to Maine."

"That's the idea, miss," Caleb Brown said. "I know what you look like and so will the state police when I tell them. There won't be a police officer in the state won't know what you look like. Do your thing on the other side of the state line. Is that what you call it these days? Do your thing?"

"Jesus Christ!" the boy said.

"Shut up, you clown," Caleb Brown said. "If it wasn't for the girl here, I'd get you a year in the Thomaston Jail. They built Thomaston a hundred years ago, more than that. It doesn't have carpet in the cells. Now what the hell is your real name?"

"Please tell him," the girl said desperately.

"I just want to get away from here."

"Larry Pearson," the black boy said.

"You sure? I can always find out."

"That's his name," the girl said. "I swear it is. Now will you let us go?"

"Not till early bus time," Caleb Brown said. "And I'll be right there to see you get on it. Don't come back—ever. Not a year from now, not ten years from now."

Caleb Brown was thinking that he sounded like one of those Southern sheriffs you saw on TV. *Listen, I run a nice quiet little town here and I want to keep it that way.* Etcetera, etcetera. Well, what the hell, it was true, wasn't it? The kid was probably tough enough to survive the life he led; the girl didn't have a chance. No psychologist except in the most homespun way, he could see the short, miserable life that lay ahead of her. If the boy didn't turn her into a hooker, she'd end up dead of an overdose, or in a nuthouse. Anyway, something bad. It was a hell of a thing, but it wasn't his business. All he wanted now was to see her gone.

He checked his watch and saw that it was less than two hours to bus time. The sky was fading from black to grey and more cars were passing through the town. People coming home from parties, other people going to work. It would be good to get this thing over with, then drive home to a big breakfast. He and Katy would have breakfast together, though she would have had her third cup of coffee by then.

Katy was an old State-of-Mainer—a Maniac—and they would talk about the night's doings at the station, and he knew she would cluck her tongue when he told her about the Greek girl. Katy, whose idea of a big time was Saturday night bingo, knew little of the outside world except what he told her, but she liked to hear about things that were beyond her understanding. When she warned him not to get shot in the line of duty, he always said he had no intention of getting shot, and then she'd say, "Well, Caleb, see that you don't." Katy was scared to death of bank robbers, and to tell the truth, so was he. In recent years there had been a few bank robberies in Maine, pulled by out-of-state hoodlums, but so far Yorkport's only bank hadn't been touched. Caleb Brown didn't think he was a coward, but he had no idea what he would do if he had to face a gang of desperadoes from the city. In all his years as chief of police, never once had he fired his service revolver at another human being, and (knock wood!) he would serve out his time without having to pull a trigger or take a bullet himself. If the bank bandits came, then let Daley and Hopkins handle them. Daley was young and thought he was Wyatt Earp or John Wayne or somebody. He, Caleb Brown, wanted to live to be a wise old man.

In a little while he looked at his watch and said it was time to go. Now that the moment of freedom was at hand, the black boy kept his mouth shut, for which Caleb Brown was grateful. Walking down the main street of the still quiet town, he asked the girl where they were planning to go.

"Boston, maybe New York," she answered. "Somewhere."

They sat on a bench until the Greyhound arrived. Two elderly tourists got off, and that was all. Caleb Brown waited until the bus pulled out: the last thing he saw was the black boy scowling at him from the back window. That was the way to get things done, Caleb Brown thought. Nice and quiet. No fuss, no mess. He felt the lifting of his spirits that always came when he knew he had his job under control. After all, nothing really bad ever happened in Yorkport.

CHAPTER SEVEN

Sitting at the battered oak table in the Great Hall, Leonard Gately remembered little of the night before. That always happened when he switched from beer to vodka. The first hour of the party was clear enough in his head; after that everything became blurred and then black. There had been some kind of a mix-up with Darryl, but what about he didn't know. He had an unclear idea that he hit or pushed someone, probably his ex-wife. The bitch never did anything but start some kind of trouble.

Still, it must have been a rough scene because Darryl was gone and so were the women.

The company car that Darryl used all the time was outside the house next to the pick-up. His ex-wife had her own car, so they must have left in that. He felt sure they'd be back. Darryl was the one he cared about; the women didn't matter a tinker's dam.

Gately went to the phone to call Darryl in Boston, then hung up without dialing. Let Darryl call him: he wasn't about to crawl for anybody, not even Darryl. If the guy couldn't take a little horseplay now and then, he wasn't a real friend. You took the rough with the smooth if you were a real friend.

Rubbing his reddened eyeballs, Gately went to see if the ice he had dumped in the kitchen sink had melted yet. He ran cold water in with the ice and splashed it in his face and over his head. Then he dried off with a handful of paper towels and combed his hair with his fingers. He fumbled six aspirins from a bottle and washed them down with a bottle of beer and waited for the pain of the hangover to diminish.

Now he returned to the table in the Great Hall and sat nursing another beer while he tried to piece together the events of the night before. It was no use. Maybe it would come to him later. Sometimes it did.

Gately hoped he had gotten rid of his ex-wife for good, unwilling to admit that the only reason she came around was because he insisted and that she was too weak to resist. Once she was gone, he and Darryl could be buddies again.

Unopened mail was scattered all over the table and he collected it into a pile, looking for something that would take his mind off the business with Darryl. He separated the mail into three stacks: bills, junk mail, and the mail he wanted to read.

There was a letter from the Yorkport Country Club turning him down for membership for the second time. A year before there had been a fight when he went to the club as Mike Burns's guest. It pissed him off that they were still mad at him after a whole year. He drank another Beck's and sifted through the pile of letters.

A begging letter from an elderly aunt in England was thrown away with a curse, not because he begrudged the old biddy a few bucks, but because he didn't want any connections with the unpleasant past.

Gately's heart quickened as he opened the letter from the Reverend Amos Trask, leader of the Christian Alliance, Inc., which had its headquarters in Dallas, Texas. Amos Trask's Saturday morning television show was Gately's favorite (next in his esteem were *Charlie's Angels* and *Wonder Woman)* and it was a very bad hangover indeed that would keep him from the set. Reverend Trask didn't have the money or the support that Jerry Falwell had, yet Gately preferred him to Falwell because he seemed to be more basic, more aware of the dangers that threatened the United States of America. Of course he couldn't come right out and say what he wanted to say, not even on syndicated television, but his meaning was clear just the same. It was necessary, Gately knew, to use certain code words to get his message across to his listeners. A youngish man with silver hair and a booming voice, Reverend Trask had been a preacher since the age of twelve. No crony of politicians, as he often said himself, Reverend Trask trusted no one but the "good Protestant people of America." There would come a time, Reverend Trask said, when mealy-mouthed politicians would have little to say about how the country should be run: the "people" would decide.

Gately had been expecting a letter from the Christian Alliance for almost a month. Now it was here at last and his irritability disappeared as he read.

"Dear Mr. Gately:

"First, let me thank you for your generous contribution of one hundred dollars. Moral support is ever welcome to us, yet as you know, and your generous contribution proves it, it takes money to combat the forces of internal and external subversion. Therefore, it is most heartening to hear from such a thoughtful and concerned person as yourself.

"Your comments on the state of this country are exceedingly well taken, and if you have no objection we would like to publish your letter in its entirety, in the September edition of our newspaper, *Christian Power.*

"We were especially interested in your observations as to the truly menacing influence of the Hebrews in the real estate business, and while we were well aware of its existence in the large cities, we were shocked to learn that it extends even to the beautiful State of Maine. Believe me, Mr. Gately, the time will come . . .

"Need I say more?

"You will be pleased to know, in spite of the slanderous charges hurled against the Christian Alliance, that the movement has never been in 'better shape.' We have endured much calumny, but we shall do more than that—we shall triumph.

"Fine Christian men and women from all over the country are flocking to our standard. Together, we shall defeat the Satanic/ Communistic forces that would make slaves of us all. We are putting the evildoers on notice that no longer can they expect to 'get away' with their drugs, pornography, their murders of unborn infants. After all, what are these things but a cloak for Godless Communism?

"The tide of affairs is turning, Mr. Gately, and the outcry for Law and Order is making itself heard. Our enemies call us reactionaries, and we glory in it. Two thousand years ago, Christ's enemies reviled and mocked him, tortured and crucified him, and yet He rose again to lead the world.

"As we shall.

"We hate nothing but Evil, Mr. Gately. The 'good' Jew, the 'good' Negro, the 'good' Roman Catholic can be our friends. All we ask of them is that they accept the reality of their position in our American society.

"God did not intend the Colored to mix with the White. It was not His intention that these radical Catholic priests should disrupt the social order of our country. And the Jew must learn that clean-minded Christians will no longer stand by while he strangles our country's economy with his underhanded financial manipulations.

"Let me use harsh words and say that 'All who oppose us must be crushed.'

"With God's help, and the help of good Christians everywhere, our great goal will be reached. If not today, then tomorrow.

"Tomorrow belongs to us, Mr. Gately. There can be no turning back.

"All future contributions will be welcome. (They are tax deductible, of course.)

God Bless You,
Amos Trask"

Wow! What a letter, Gately thought after he read it again. What he liked best about Reverend Amos Trask was that he didn't rant and rave like some of the nut preachers in the South, yet there wasn't one thing he said that wasn't absolutely true. Let them say what they liked about the reverend, the guy didn't fuck around. And he didn't send form letters like some of the others: his reference to the kikes in the real estate business proved that. The signature was genuine, too. It hadn't been rendered with one of those writing machines the politicians and movie stars used.

Gately felt so good that he wished he could have shown the letter to his friend Colonel Mike Burns, but that wasn't possible because of the stuff about the Catholics. Burns was a Catholic and it always surprised Gately when he thought about it. There was nothing Catholic about the colonel, although it was a fact that he went to early Mass every Sunday. Not only that, he drove twenty miles to attend Mass in the nearest big town during the winter months, when the R.C. church in Yorkport was closed for lack of parishioners. No church-goer himself (his parents had been Methodists), Gately could never understand how an intelligent man like the colonel could possibly believe in all that Roman Catholic shit. Foreign shit. Holy Water. Statues. Incense. Confession. Faggot priests. It didn't make sense for a good guy like Mike Burns to be connected with shit like that.

Gately knew there was a conflict of interest in his respect for Burns and his admiration for Reverend Trask. It was something he would have to work out as he went along. He felt sure that good guys like Mike and Amos would get along all right, if they sat down and had a heart-to-heart talk. Like, for instance, there were a lot of things Mike Burns didn't like about the "new" Catholic Church: hairy-faced young priests playing guitars at "folk" Masses, priests running for political office, nuns wearing mini-skirts and fucking monks and so forth and having babies. Mike Burns even went so far as to say that those nuns killed down in El Salvador had no reason to be there in the first place, and why didn't they stay in their blasted convents where they belonged? Colonel Mike was proud of his sister, the Mother Superior of a convent in Maryland, and he always referred to her as a "credit to the Irish-Catholic Church." Was there, after all, a difference between the Irish Church and the Italian Church? Gately didn't know, but he hoped there was.

In the old days, in the 19th century, the micks dominated the Catholic Church in America: these days it looked like the wops and Polacks were taking over. That was bad because at least in the old days, a hundred, a hundred and fifty years ago, the mick priests and bishops and cardinals kept the Irish ditch diggers from turning to Socialistic ideas. A lot of the starving Irish fuckers wanted to go West with the Swedes, most of them still good Lutherans and true-blue Americans, but the Micksers, not a strong people, really (though there were exceptions) did not have the *cojones* (that meant "balls" in the language of Mexico and other banana splits—here Gately barked out a laugh at his own leaden wit) to shake loose from the priests, so they stayed in the cities and became the Democrats most of them still were.

However, there wasn't one Democrat bone in Colonel Mike Burn's body. Mike always said Democrats were nothing but closet Communists who didn't have the courage of their convictions. Mike could go on about the Democrats for hours, tearing into the whole welfare system and saying as how Franklin D. Rosenfelt (Mike never called him by any other name) was the first American to give people numbers via the Social Security fraud. Mike drew a military pension as well as Social Security, but he hated Big Government like poison. America wasn't going to the dogs, Mike said. It had been there for a long time.

Leonard Gately thought about the woeful state of the country while he drank another frosty Beck's and inspected his enormous breakfast steak in the broiler. The telephone rang and when he picked it up it was Elly Fisk calling on the direct hook-up from the office. She sounded excited.

"Yeah, Elly," Gately said, his head still throbbing from last night's hangover.

Elly spoke quickly. "You won't believe this, Lenny, but I have Mrs. O'Neal—Tracy O'Neal—on hold for you. She just called about that old fisherman's house down on Hard Luck Point."

"You didn't quote her the listed price, did you?"

"No way, Lenny. You always say charge them what they can afford. This lady can afford."

"Good girl, Elly," Gately said. "She called asking for me?"

"For you," Elly said. "You want me to put her on? She's been holding on the line."

"Let her hold—okay, put her on."

"Is this Mr. Gately?" Tracy O'Neal asked in her breathless, husky voice.

"This is Leonard Gately. My secretary said you're interested in the Harkins property."

Gately thought, Wow, I'm talking to a billion dollars!

Tracy O'Neal said, "It's got your sign on it. I'd like to buy it if the asking price is reasonable."

Gately thought, You'll pay through the nose if you want it badly enough, but what he said was, "It's a prime piece of real estate, Mrs. O'Neal. The heirs are asking a hundred-thousand dollars for the house and land."

"One hundred thousand?" Tracy O'Neal sounded startled. "Just for that old house?"

"The land is more valuable than the house, Mrs. O'Neal. It's right on the sea, nearly two acres of prime building property. A developer from Boston is interested in putting up a motel. I can't give you his name, of course, but right now he's willing to go over eighty thousand."

Tracy O'Neal said, "But surely we have enough motels along this beautiful coast?"

"I agree with you, Mrs. O'Neal, but the old man's heirs don't even live here and have no interest what goes on. They don't care who gets the property as long as they get their asking price. Which is a hundred-thousand. How much were you willing to pay?"

"Not more than thirty-five thousand, Mr. Gately. I think that's a very fair price."

Like hell, Gately thought. "I'm afraid the heirs won't think so. They're firm at a hundred-thousand and there's nothing I can do about it. I can suggest a price, but the final figure is up to them. By any chance can you meet the developer's offer of eighty?"

There was a developer, but he had offered exactly half the figure quoted by Gately. The heirs, two elderly ladies, the dead fisherman's sisters long resident in Florida, would be glad to take fifty. "I wouldn't wait too long, Mrs. O'Neal."

"Well, I'd have to see the house before I do anything else," Tracy O'Neal said. "Can you send one of your salesmen? Or better still, can you come yourself? We can have lunch after we look at the house."

Gately thought, She's trying to bribe me with lunch. The bitch is trying to trade one lousy lunch for thousands of dollars!

"Certainly I can come over," Gately said. "What time is good for you? . . . Eleven thirty? That's fine with me."

Gately was so elated after he hung up that he called Colonel Burns to tell him the news.

"That's most interesting," Burns said in his hard flat voice. "Now it's up to you, Leonard. Prove to her that she can't have her way all the time, not here in Maine. You're going to have lunch with her, is that a fact? Take care she doesn't work any of her tricks. I've heard stories about that woman that would make your hair stand on end."

Gately barked out a laugh. "Don't worry,

Colonel. It'll take more than a lunch and a few smiles to make me come down in my price. Sometimes a smart country person knows more about business than these outsiders."

Gately always referred to himself as a "smart country person," in contrast to "sneaky city trash."

"That's the right spirit, Leonard," Colonel Burns said. "Keep me informed, will you? I may have a few words to say about Mrs. O'Neal at the next meeting of Sentinel. We'll all be most interested in how this lunch of yours goes. Keep the faith, boy."

As a rule, Gately dressed in army officer's suntans. These and yellow work boots gave him a virile appearance, he liked to think, but now he decided that he ought to dress in more businesslike clothes. A few minutes later he changed his mind and settled for a clean pair of suntans from the enormous store he kept in a chest. Then he carried a fresh beer into the bathroom and trimmed his fierce Green Beret mustache. He drank the rest of the beer and soaped his big body under a hot, then a cold shower, singing a dirty song with many verses that he had learned in the army. This lunch with Tracy O'Neal was going to make him the talk of the town. She hadn't sent a letter through a lawyer, and she hadn't dispatched one of her other flunkeys to try to make a deal. No sir, she had called herself. And no bullshit either. She was a tough cookie, that one. Gately smiled. Sure she was, and so was he.

Gately drove the pick-up and left the Marlin rifle where it hung in plain sight in the rear window. That would give them something to think about when he pulled into the parking lot of the big house. All he'd seen were the foundations when the builders started work, and he wouldn't have been there at all if it hadn't been for an inspection of the old Hayes house. But now he could have a close-up look at the O'Neal house. He wouldn't be like some of the locals who tried to see it from a distance. Now he was invited.

It took Gately no more than fifteen minutes to reach the narrow county road that went down to Hard Luck Bay. First, there was a long stretch of salt marsh brown in the summer sun. Gulls soared and banked, occasionally dropping down to the water like fighter planes. Beyond the marsh the sea glittered and far out, a sailboat ran before the wind. The road to Tracy O'Neal's place had been hard-topped, the tar rolled smooth. Farther down, the road that branched off to the Hayes property was weedy from disuse.

Gately had never seen Tracy O'Neal in person, and he hoped she wasn't going to be one of those forty-year-old women who look great in photographs, but turn out to be all face lifts and make-up that only a camera can hide. He knew that she had nothing to hide when he parked the pick-up and she waved to him from the wide, flagged terrace facing the sea. She wasn't just as good looking as her pictures: she was better; the sight of her lovely tanned legs in the briefest of tennis shorts made him think of other things besides money. Christ, he thought, imagine having a billion dollars and looking like that into the bargain.

Tracy O'Neal came down the terrace steps to greet him, her hand extended. A skinny faggot in a jogging suit and striped sneakers stayed where he was at a glass-topped table. The faggot wore his hair brushed forward in bangs, the way Marlon Brando did in those old mumble movies when he had hair. Gately didn't like the fruitcake from the word go.

Tracy O'Neal took Gately's hand in a firm tennis player's grip. "So glad you could come, Mr. Gately. I'm sure you're a busy man." She didn't seem to find his dress extraordinary for a real estate man, a breed whose clothing tends to have echoes of the Eisenhower era. Nor did the rifle seem to distress her, though the faggot viewed it with mild concern once he got a good look at it.

"Would you like a drink before we go down to the house?" Tracy asked. She glanced up at the sky and laughed. "It's just past noon, so there's nothing wicked about it."

"Sure," Gately said, not knowing how to respond to this kind of small talk.

"Mr. Gately, I'd like you to meet Lafe Tatum, a dear friend from New York. Lafe's an interior decorator."

That figured, Gately thought. If not an interior decorator, then a hairdresser. He wondered what else the faggot did for Tracy O'Neal other than decorate her houses. He had heard so many stories about this woman that anything was possible.

Tatum shook Gately's hand without getting up. "Gately," the faggot said, using the last name in the British manner.

Tracy O'Neal handed Gately a tall glass with beads of moisture on its frosted side. "Is gin and tonic all right with you? I think it's the best summer drink of all."

Gately tasted the drink and pronounced it to be just right.

"Well then, why don't we take our drinks and go on down," Tracy O'Neal suggested. "You want to come along, Tatey?"

"I think I'll stay here, Trace. All that running has knocked me out."

"Then we'll see you later," she said.

They sipped their drinks as they made their way down the rutted road to the old fisherman's house. The house hadn't been painted for years and its warped boards were cracked in places. It was a two-story house built in the tall, narrow style of the early 1900's, and the porch faced the land rather than the sea. Gately unlocked the door and they went into the darkened interior.

"Old Hayes didn't like electricity so he never had it hooked up," Gately said. "I'll get a few lamps going so you can see better."

There were three small rooms on the ground floor, three on the second. The furniture was hard-used and none of it matched. In the kitchen there was a wood stove and an old fashioned blond oak icebox with a drip pan underneath.

"Will you look at that," Tracy O'Neal exclaimed.

"A real antique," Gately said. "They tell me in the cities they make those into bars and so forth."

They went upstairs to look at the other rooms. Gately had hired two local women to scrub the place out, but it still smelled musty.

"Of course I'm just going to tear it down if I buy it," Tracy O'Neal said, gently cutting in on Gately's sales pitch.

"I figured you would," Gately said, very much aware of her presence in the gloomy old house. She smelled a lot sweeter than the fat motel operator who seemed to have been born with a wet cigar in his mouth. He wondered what it would be like to screw a billion dollars. Why the hell not? he asked himself. She'd had plenty of cocks in her, if you could believe the stories, so why not his? Maybe she'd like to have a real man in her for a change. And if she got to like it—wow! Gately was a rich man, but he wanted to be richer. There was so much more he could do, if he only had the right capital behind him. . . .

They went outside and walked over the property as he told her some of the stories associated with the Hayes family. Tracy O'Neal listened attentively while he told her about the timber bark that had sunk in Hard Luck Bay during the big nor'easter of 1902.

"So much history," Tracy O'Neal said. "That's why I'd hate to see a motel in this particular place. One question I've been meaning to ask you. How can this man build a motel if the property isn't commercially zoned?"

Gately had been expecting that. "He thinks he can get it rezoned."

"You think he can?"

Tracy O'Neal stumbled on a root and Gately kept her from falling. For a moment he caught the scent of the delicate perfume she used.

"You all right?" he said.

"Fine," she said.

"I don't know what to think about the rezoning," Gately said. "This man seems to think he can swing it, but you never know how it's going to go in a small town. If they don't like you, get their backs up, they can give you a very hard time."

Tracy O'Neal said, "I hope they do. Oh I'm sorry, I shouldn't have said that. It will mean a loss to you."

"That's all right, Mrs. O'Neal. The place won't go begging if you don't buy it."

"Please call me Tracy. All my friends do. I'd so much like to buy the property, but I'm afraid I can't go any higher than thirty-five. My accountants just won't allow it. You know how they are."

"Yes I do," Gately said. "And I'll do the best I can for you, but you may have to go higher. I'll call the heirs and see if I can take them down. I may not be able to catch them for a day or two, but I'll get back to you on the asking price."

Tracy O'Neal placed her hand on his arm just for an instant. "Thank you, Mr. Gately— Leonard," she said. "But let's not talk any more business today. Let's go back to the house and have lunch. Tatey must be over his exhaustion by now."

Fuck Tatey, Gately thought.

Lafe Tatum had changed into a white linen suit by the time they got back. Gately thought it looked like one of those ice-cream suits all the foreign agents wore in old movies set in the tropics. Looking at Tatum's lithe elegance, he decided maybe he should slim down a bit. Too many bottles of Beck's, too many thick steaks cooked in butter.

Gately settled his bulk under a striped umbrella, and with a tall glass in his hand, he thought the world looked pretty good from where he sat. He had the feeling that if he played his cards right he might luck onto something tasty here. The faggot was knocking the drinks back, and he told several stories that Gately only half understood, but after he finished his second drink he decided that this limp-wristed creep was no real competition. But, remembering Mike Burns's warning, he vowed not to be suckered in by these people.

While they were waiting to be served lunch they were joined by a girl in her early twenties who reminded Tracy O'Neal that she had to get some checks signed and put in the mail.

"Thank you, Mary," Tracy O'Neal said. "Leonard, I'd like you to meet my secretary and friend, Mary Galligan. I don't know what I'd do without her."

Mary Galligan had some kind of New England accent Gately couldn't place, but he knew she didn't come from money. Maybe she had gone to Boston College or the University of New Hampshire. She was pretty in a perky way, well built too, and she spoke in a snotty way that wasn't quite the real thing.

"Nice to meet you," she said, sipping at her gin and tonic, trying to appear relaxed without too much success.

"I was saying to Linwood Duval the other day . . ." Tatum said in his bored voice. "By the way, Trace, where is Linwood? Where *is* everybody?"

Tracy O'Neal laughed. "Some of them were on their way back to New York before you tumbled out of bed this morning. Linny and the others decided it would be a kick to go to the public beach. You know how Linny is when he gets carried away. What were you going to tell us about Linny?"

"I forget," Tatum said. "Linny says so much."

Tracy O'Neal laughed again. "Don't be naughty! Linny is a good writer and a dear friend."

Gately, in spite of the steaks he'd eaten that morning, was hungry again and he wished the fuck they'd bring out the food. It came in a minute and was served by a silent black man with hooded eyes. The only time he looked up was when he served Mary Galligan. Gately caught the glance that passed between them and he thought, What have we here? Was the nigger fucking the secretary? If so, was the nigger mad at having to serve lunch instead of taking part in it? Personally, he wouldn't mind throwing a hump into the secretary, but all he'd get out of that was a hump, and he was getting plenty of that as he was. He noticed that the faggot hardly spoke to the secretary. That might be just snobbishness—faggots were the worst snobs in the world—or was there something else? They were all sucking up to the lady with the bucks, but it's hard to like people that you have to suck up to.

"Have you lived in Yorkport for a long time?" Mary Galligan asked Gately, and that annoyed him because he didn't think his outsider origins showed any more. After working on his Maine accent for years, he didn't believe he sounded any different from the natives.

"Lived here a good part of my life," Gately said, concealing his irritability by a forced laconic manner. "Can't say I was born here, but all my folks were, for generations. Not in Yorkport, though. Down East about a hundred miles. So I guess that makes me native enough."

"You certainly sound like one," the faggot said.

Gately liked the faggot a little better for that. Or was the faggot trying to make fun of him? You never knew with these bastards. No wonder people hated them.

There was cold white wine with the lobster salad, but this was a meal for people who ate sparingly, and Gately decided to throw a steak on the fire the minute he got home. He wondered if he had made a mistake by telling the lie about his family being old State of Mainers. What the hell. How could she check if she ever bothered to do it? His parents had been dead for years. He blamed the secretary for the lie, as he blamed so many people for so many things.

Gately knew better than to wear out his welcome, and as soon as lunch was over he announced that he had to be getting back to the office. "Man wants to buy a mountain in the back country and start a ski resort. He'll bring in his snow-making machines as soon as we come to terms. Winter months are kind of dead around here. It would give the economy a boost if we had a ski resort going, even a small one."

The faggot was back to the gin and tonics. "That's very civic minded of you," he said.

"What's good for Yorkport is good for me," Gately said.

Tracy O'Neal smiled at Gately. "You men are so good at business."

The faggot hiccuped. Gately felt like punching him in the mouth.

"When it comes to business you don't know which end is up," Lafe Tatum said.

"That's right, Tatey," Tracy O'Neal said with a smile that was as hard as a diamond.

CHAPTER EIGHT

"Is that you, Sandy?" Tracy O'Neal said when Sandor Antonescu came to the telephone.

"Trace darling," Antonescu said, holding the phone in one hand, a drink in the other. "What have you been doing, you bad girl?"

Sandor Antonescu wasn't as rich as Tracy O'Neal—few people were—but he was many times a millionaire and they knew each other from New York, where Antonescu spent part of the winter in his perfect little townhouse on East 72nd Street.

Tracy O'Neal said, "I tried to call you last week, but your housekeeper said you were away."

"I was visiting a sick friend," Antonescu

said. The truth was that he had been in a "farm" for rich alcoholics in Vermont. Now he felt better and was back on the booze and other things. "Someone told me you just moved into the house beautiful. I got the invitation you mailed from New York."

"It's going to be a lovely housewarming, Sandy. The whole gang will be there—Linny Duval, Osmond Bailey, Lafe Tatum, Denny Callaway—everybody."

"Sounds divine," Sandor Antonescu said. "You do give the most perfect parties, Trace. Life would be a desert without your parties."

"Listen, Sandy, why I'm calling. The caterer from Boston just called to tell me the catering union, whatever you call it, has just gone on strike and there's no way he can do my party on the Fourth. I asked him if management could handle it, but he said no. I think he must be afraid of gangsters or something. Is there anyone you can think of locally? Somebody competent?"

Antonescu had a drink while he thought about it. Then he said, "There is somebody, Trace. A fellow named Lacey Putnam. Our little ambitious Lacey has been around, all right. Not a local boy. From California, I think . . . How did he come to Yorkport? Do you remember the name Joel Benford? An old silent movie star. Benford had a summer place here and Lacey was his secretary-companion. Yes, it was like that. Before he worked for Benford, Lacey was with a party planning service on the Coast. Benford died here three years ago, leaving Lacey not a cent, though he always expected to inherit a bundle. So Lacey stayed on and went into catering and party planning. They say he filched a few paintings from Benford's house before the lawyers moved in . . . Don't worry about that. Lacey's doing all right for himself these days. Use the little sod by all means. He's next to illiterate, but he talks a good line."

"Have you used him, Sandy?" Tracy O'Neal said.

"No, but I've been to parties he catered. My friends were quite pleased with him. He's in the book under Catered Affairs."

"You've just saved my life, darling," Tracy O'Neal said.

"Anytime, darling," replied Sandor Antonescu.

It was afternoon now and Sandor Antonescu was utterly bored. He ached with boredom. Boredom hung like a cloud above his elegant head. After lunch he had spent an hour watching young lovers having sex in the sand dunes. The powerful binoculars he used were the best money could buy. Everything he owned and used was expensive and in exquisite taste. Good taste. Yes. That was it.

Watching kids screwing was a beastly bore. It seemed to him that the grubby little beasts had absolutely no imagination when it came to sex. First there was that dreadful fumbling. The little bastards made all sorts of agonized faces, as if they never had done it before. The boys always ended up between the girl's legs. So much for that tired routine.

As a child, Antonescu had wanted to play the violin. And he had learned to play, not very well but with great passion and soul. It had grieved his mother when he dropped his musical studies at the age of ten. His father, who owned a chain of immensely profitable funeral parlors, thought it just as well. Even so, Sandor Antonescu had many years later purchased a Stradivarius during a trip to Berlin.

Now, bored with spying on the kids, he unlocked a large wall safe and took out the priceless fiddle. With a dramatic flourish he tucked the violin under his chin and proceeded to play a medley of weepy Slavic folk tunes. It really wasn't a medley, since Antonescu was unable to play any of the tunes all the way through. When he experienced difficulty, he switched to something else. Classical pieces were beyond him.

Bored by the folk tunes, he attempted to play "La Compasita," which called for a certain amount of intricate fingering. However, the playing did not go well and he had to fight hard to keep from smashing the Strad against the fireplace. Actually, he might have broken the Strad if other people, people who counted, were present. *That*, without a doubt, would give them something to talk about. So far as he was concerned, "Man Bites Dog" wasn't news any more. But "Man Breaks Strad" certainly was. He promised himself that he would keep the Strad-breaking for some really special occasion—the Christmas party perhaps. No, his birthday party would be better.

Sandor Antonescu was a man who played many parts and wore many costumes. On this particularly boring afternoon he wore the gorgeous blue uniform of an Algerian Spahi. His white silk shirt was ruffled and collarless and on the front of his military jacket were pinned rows of colorful decorations and jingling medals. Feeling that American decorations were too lightly bestowed, he wore none. Neither did he wear any decorations from Mexico or the banana republics.

Among his foreign decorations were the Victoria Cross, the *Croix de Guerre* (French), the *Croix de Guerre* (Belgian), the Iron Cross, the Imperial Russian Star, The Order of King Carol (Rumanian.) The last named was more prized than any of the others.

None of these awesome decorations had been bestowed upon Sandor Antonescu. He had bestowed them on himself—and why not? If a plebian little twit like Napleon could crown himself Emperor, then why should he, Sandor Antonescu, not lay a few medals on himself? He deserved them.

Antonescu had switched from brandy to his favorite tipple, a drink of his own invention—a Bucharest Mule. Brandy, all right in its way, simply was not strong enough to get him through the day. It was not potent enough to give him that zombie-like evening drunk without which life would have been unbearable. For that he needed his beloved Bucharest Mule, the ingredients of which were known only to himself and a few special friends. Swigging from his jeweled tankard, Antonescu sought to drown his awful sense of boredom. Let others suck on their Scotch and sodas, their gibsons and gimlets, their nauseating martinis. He would take his Bucharest Mule every time. After all, it was so *Rumanian*.

He put his drink down and decided to be honest with himself for a minute. It was time to play something easy. So he played "Down in The Valley" on the $100,000 Stradivarius.

With much elbow action and elaborate bowing, he got all the way to the end of the doleful tune. Menuhin couldn't have done it better, he decided. Encouraged, rather proud of himself, he had a fling at "Spanish Eyes" before he discovered that the fucking thing wasn't as simple as it sounded when you hummed it. There was a hump in the middle that he couldn't seem to get over.

So he returned to "Down in The Valley," but it wasn't so good the second time around. Furious, he thrust the Strad back in the safe and picked up his drink. He began to laugh. Perhaps he should wear a deerstalker cap and Inverness cape when he played the violin. Sherlock Holmes always dressed like that, but Holmes wasn't a very good musician either, if Watson was to be believed.

Holmes was some kind of junkie, wasn't he? All those hypodermics lying around. Antonescu wished he had the nerve to pick up on heroin. But he didn't, so cocaine would have to do.

"Which reminds me, old boy," Sandor Antonescu said aloud. "It's time for a snort."

Opening the safe again, he took out an elaborately decorated Chinese box full of tiny glassine envelopes. This was his joy supply and there was enough to last him for weeks.

Using a tiny scissors, he cut off the end of one of the envelopes. He put the envelope to his nose and sniffed heartily. There was an immediate tickling sensation in the back of his nose. It was necessary to fight off the desire to sneeze. Antonescu held his aristocratic nose and the sneeze reflex passed.

He sat in his high-backed chair and waited.

Ah yes, there it was. It came and it was beautiful. There was a sense of whiteness, a winter landscape without cold. Snow glistened on the trees, bells tinkled, and there was laughter. There was an immense happiness, a langorous knowledge of universal peace.

Sandor Antonescu smiled benignly, nodding in a fatherly way to the teeming masses of the planets. He was a good and great man, he knew. Sometimes misunderstood, it was true, but wasn't that the lot of all great men?

He sat perfectly still, eyes closed, a look of contentment on his ravaged face. His throne was a lonely place, he realized, but *someone* had to rule. Someone had to take it upon himself to create order in this vast and unruly world.

They had begged him to rule because all other rulers and systems had failed. He had been reluctant to abandon his musical career, yet in the end he could not bring himself to turn a deaf ear to the pleas of humanity. Mankind needed him and he must serve. There was no shirking duty, so he had kissed his beloved Stradivarius and put it away for the last time. No more would the concert halls of the world echo to the sound of his immortal violin. . . .

"Oh balls!" Sandor Antonescu cried.

Cocaine highs never lasted long; he was coming down. There was no use trying to go on. He got up and walked to the enormous, thermal-paned floor-to-ceiling window and stared down at the sea. If only something would happen. A tidal wave—anything. Anything to get rid of this awful boredom.

He wondered if the house would withstand a tidal wave. The architect who designed it, the builder who built it, swore it would survive just about anything. They hadn't mentioned tidal waves.

Sandor Antonescu rummaged through his eccentric scholarship in an effort to learn if ever there had been a tidal wave on the coast of Maine. If there had been, he hadn't heard about it. Suddenly he longed for a tidal wave. Yorkport was a lovely town, but it did get dull.

He returned to his high-backed Nottingham chair and pressed the electric buzzer set into one of the arms. Mrs. Briley appeared, placid, cynical, easy of manner, impossible to surprise after twenty years with Sandor Antonescu. He tossed the empty tankard and she fielded it expertly.

"My cup runneth empty," Antonescu said.

The letdown that followed a cocaine high was the worst problem associated with the drug, worse even than the rotted nose it gave the heavy user. It was great while you were zooming up the high. It was great when you got there. It was great for the short time you stayed there. But the fucking thing didn't last long, and then you were racing downhill to the slough of depression. In minutes you were earthbound again. For a beginning user, the high lasted for a relatively long time. Antonescu had, however, been using coke for many years, and now at fifty he had developed a certain immunity to the drug, just as he was able to drink large quantities of alcohol without passing out.

Mrs. Briley returned with the brimming tankard and he commanded her to switch on the lights. The housekeeper busied herself while Antonescu pondered the problem of what to do about his boredom. He considered the possibility of buggering some nice young lad. There was, as always, some merit in the idea, yet there was boredom in it, too. Sandor Antonescu had buggered many young lads, not all of them nice; many were, in truth, rather nasty. He had buggered young lads all over the globe. Bugger one, bugger all.

Why was it, he wondered, that male prostitutes never had hearts of gold? It was a convention of fiction that female whores always had hearts of gold. They were always helping the hero to escape the cops or the robbers. So why not men?

He drank deeply from his overproof drink and could find no answer.

Pleasure itself was a bore, he decided. There had to be something better than—or beyond—

buggering. There had to be. Otherwise life was a farce.

Once you set a limit on pleasure, it quickly grew stale. So there could be no limits. The pursuit of pleasure was, in its way, the last frontier. Soon men would land on Mars, and taking into consideration the infinite distance of space, there was no place to go after that.

A day without excruciating pleasure was unthinkable to Sandor Antonescu. His nerve ends raw with longing, he dismissed Mrs. Briley and stalked dramatically about the enormous living room. He glared at the ancestors he had created. On the surface, he had everything to live for. Perhaps that was the trouble with him. He could not be content with everything. He wanted more.

Once again he thought of Greg Delaney and quivered with exitement. Mister Hard-to Get Greg Delaney. The more he thought of Greg Delaney, the more he drank. As the big drink took effect, he recalled the time he had offered Delaney the great privilege of sucking his cock. At the party that marked the opening of the Yorkport art gallery he had, after many drinks, whispered the invitation to Delaney when they happened to be standing in front of a seascape by some latter-day Winslow Homer. Delaney had laughed and walked away—and that was the end of it, or so it seemed. Yet now, whenever they met, in the post office, in the bank, Delaney avoided him and there was nothing between them except an exchange of unsmiling nods. Well, no, *he* smiled but Delaney didn't.

Greg Delaney must be in his late twenties now, still a reporter for the *Yorkport Star* and hadn't won any Pulitzer Prizes. He wasn't so young any more and therefore should have been outside the range of Sandor Antonescu's interest, and yet some of the old fascination remained. Like hell! A lot remained.

"Mad about the boy," Sandor Antonescu sang in a creaky tenor.

Greg Delaney, not yet thirty, had become a roly-poly choir boy, his unwrinkled face as smooth as a baby's bottom. (Horrible thought!) And yet there was a look of decline. His pretty face, his Cupid's mouth, now had the look of a wax figure exposed to heat. Greg Delaney's face, though still pretty, was beginning to slide. It was one of those tragedies.

Sandor Antonescu clasped his hands together in prayer. "Dear St. Noel," he intoned. "I just want one chance at that boy's ass. After that I'll cast him aside like a worn out shee—oo."

(Noel Coward was Sandor Antonescu's favorite saint.)

Why hadn't Greg Delaney done as he had asked? Handsome still at fifty, Antonescu knew he had been extraordinarily good-looking at the time of the art gallery opening, eight years before. The other fags at the opening (Yorkport was fully integrated in a sexual way) had climbed all over themselves trying to please him, trying to swing on his joint. Of course, Greg Delaney wasn't a homosexual. Then what was he? Antonescu was certain that Greg Delaney didn't know *what* he was. He had been married to that silly bitch for years. That didn't have to mean anything. A lot of fags got married as a cover—oh men of little faith!

Sandor Antonescu considered snorting another hit of coke and decided against it. Fighting his depression with one Bucharest Mule after another, he kept Mrs. Briley running back and forth to the kitchen. Mrs. Briley never complained. There was nothing to complain about: she was the best paid housekeeper in the State of Maine, perhaps in all fifty states.

Sandor Antonescu smiled. One crack at Greg Delaney was all he wanted before the fellow's cherub features melted for good, before his once lean tummy thickened even more. Antonescu whacked his own tummy and found it hard. No flab there, by God!

He was beginning to get drunk. There was nothing like it: the first moment of the day when the realization hit him that once again he was going to get drunk. As the evening wore on he would be drunk, then very drunk, then drunk as a skunk. Usually, in the wee hours, his drunkeness approached the comatose stage.

Having begun to think about Greg Delaney, he couldn't let go. He was like a dog with a bone-on, he thought with mild amusement. But what was he to do? He couldn't very well accost the fellow in the street. Not after having been turned down once. Both Delaneys had jobs but were extremely poor by Sandor Antonescu's standards and they didn't move in the same circles. So there could be no chance meeting. He could give a party and invite them, but that would appear suspicious. Anyway, if he did that, Delaney wouldn't come. The meeting would have to take place on neutral ground, so to speak—but where? It would have to be a place where Delaney *and* his fucking wife would want to go. By all accounts Delaney's wife—what was her name? Carol?—was an ambitious, social-climbing bitch who edited some shitty little poetry magazine—*Ambush,* that was it—and wanted to get on in the world.

Click! A lightbulb, a cartoon lightbulb, came on above Sandor Antonescu's head. Tracy O'Neal's party—where else! Clapping his hands together, Antonescu could not have been more delighted with himself. It was perfect. Simply perfect!

He buzzed for Mrs. Briley and commanded her to fetch a plug-in telephone.

"Thank you, my good woman," he said when she brought it in and plugged it in by the side of his "thinking chair." Dismissing her with a grand gesture, he was pretty sure that she would be listening in on the extension in the kitchen, no doubt accumulating blackmailable items for use in her old age. Well, they would see about that when the time came. There was a long fall down the cliff to the sea. An elderly lady could easily miss her step.

Sandor Antonescu dialed and waited for the telephone to ring at the other end.

"Mrs. O'Neal," he said when the butler answered the phone. "Tell her it's Mr. Antonescu calling.

Tracy O'Neal was a little breathless when she came to the telephone. "I was playing tennis with Tatey Tatum," she said.

Antonescu had nothing to say about Tatum; he didn't like his fag act. But then perhaps he was a fag pretending to be a fag. He'd seen that, too.

"Did you call Putnam about the catering?" he said.

"Yes I did, and he's very nice. Thank you, Sandy. And thank you for being concerned. That was sweet of you."

"Actually that's not why I'm calling, Trace. A favor, sweetheart. There's a very nice boy— well, not exactly a boy, but boyish—that I want to meet. Re-meet, that is, and I don't seem to be able to arrange it."

"Ah," Tracy O'Neal said.

"Ah indeed."

"Is he someone local?"

"Local enough, which means that he's lived here for about nine years, ever since he got out of Dartmouth. He's a reporter and article writer for the *Yorkport Star*, Maine's answer to the *Village Voice*. He wants to be a novelist, but the publishing world isn't ready for him yet."

"Is he?" Tracy O'Neal asked.

"I think he might be persuaded," Sandor Antonescu said. "I'd like to persaude him. We had a brief encounter—well, not *exactly* a brief encounter—some years ago and he's been standoffish ever since."

"You're a naughty fellow, Sandy."

"I try to be, Trace. What I'd like you to do is invite him to your party."

"But how can I do that, Sandy? Won't it seem strange if I invite someone I don't even know."

"Not if you invite him as a member of the working press. You've always said you want to do something for the locals, so invite this local. You know how to make it sound right. The dear boy will jump at the chance when he hears Duval and Bailey are going to be there. Big writers, big New York connections. One more thing, Trace—he's married. Say you'll do it, darling."

122

"What's his name?"

"Greg Delaney. I've just looked up his number and here it is . . ."

"Got it, Sandy. Now I'd better go. Tatey is making faces at the window."

"Give him my love," Sandor Antonescu said. "You already have mine."

When he hung up he said to himself, "I hope the little twit breaks a leg."

Caleb Brown looked at Dwight Endicott with weary astonishment. "What do you mean, somebody stole your house? I'm tired, so say it slow so I'll get the full meaning of it. Maybe you said somebody stole your *horse?*"

"You know damn well I ain't got no horse," Dwight Endicott said peevishly. "What in hell would I be doing with a God damned horse? I said somebody stole my *house*, made off with it while I was in the hospital. You ought to know I was in the hospital. You drove me there yourself when I came down with the DT's."

"You sure you got over them, Dwight? I never knew you when you couldn't get hold of a jug."

Dwight Endicott was Caleb Brown's age; they had gone to school together a thousand years before. Dwight was a carpenter by trade, a pretty good one, too, when he wasn't hocking his tools to buy liquor. He had been an alcoholic since he was sixteen; only death would put an end to his thirst.

"You want to smell my breath, is that it?" Dwight said. "I ain't had a drink since you locked me up in that hospital. You can bribe the attendants in there if you got money, but I didn't have none. They gave me bus fare back to town, and I walked the rest of the way out to my house. Only it wasn't there, Caleb. It was gone—vanished. Somebody loaded it on a truck and took off with it. You're supposed to be the chief of police, so what are you going to do about it?"

Caleb Brown got up from his desk and put on his cap. "First I'm going to see if your house is really missing. My question to you is, Why would anybody in their right mind want to steal your house? It isn't any bigger than a tool shed."

"It's still my house, the only house I got."

"It's still just a tool shed with a bed, a table, a chair, and a stove."

"Maybe the bastards that stole it needed a tool shed," Dwight said.

Caleb Brown took Dwight by the arm and propelled him toward the door. "Come on, you old souse, I want to see for myself."

They drove the four miles out into the back country where Dwight made his home just beyond a smooth boulder with JESUS SAVES painted on it. Here the road was unpaved and the chief's cruiser rattled and creaked as it went over the bumps. Caleb Brown braked to a stop and they got out. That far back in the pines it was hot and the air had a sweet resiny smell. A stream gurgled over rocks on one side of the road.

Dwight pointed a shaky finger. "See, what did I tell you, it's gone. It wasn't much, but it was all I had. Now what the hell am I going to do?"

All that remained of Dwight's tiny house was the loose cinder-block foundation on which it had been placed. "Look at those tire marks," Dwight said. "They backed up in a truck and put my house on it and just drove off. Well, ain't you going to make impressions of the marks like they do on TV?"

"That's state police stuff, Dwight."

"Well, call them then."

"Not a chance," Caleb Brown said. "I'll do what I can to get your God damned house back, but I'm not going to make a fool of myself. You know God damned perfectly well you've got no right to be here in the first place. That shack of yours was put up on state land, and that's against the law. You're a squatter, but all right, all right, if the state hasn't evicted you, it makes no difference to me where you live."

"That's one hell of a way for an old friend to talk."

125

"Dwight, I'm not just an *old* friend, I'm your *only* friend, so I'll talk any way I like. You're a pain in the ass from start to finish, so don't go telling me my job. In the old days they'd tag you for a habitual drunkard and put you away for a long time. You know many times I've picked you out of a snow bank to keep you from freezing to death."

"That's your job, Caleb. A mighty soft job if you ask me. I'm a citizen and a taxpayer and I got the right to police assistance any time I need it."

Caleb Brown sighed. "You sure as hell need some kind of assistance. And what's all this taxpayer business? You never paid a dollar in taxes in your life."

Dwight stood his ground. "What about my house, is what I want to know?"

"I said I'll try to find it, you halfwit. Now get back in that car and I'll see what I can do to put a roof over your head. It gets cold at night and you can't sleep out in the woods."

Caleb Brown opened the door on the passenger side, but Dwight balked at getting in. "Where are you taking me, Caleb? I ain't going to some charity, if that's what you're thinking."

Caleb Brown pushed Dwight into the cruiser and slammed the door on him. "We're going to see Reverend Hardesty," he said when he got in on the other side. "Maybe he can put you up for a while. If I don't find your house you'll have to start building another. I'll pay for the lumber, so don't go crying about that."

Dwight said, "I know how much I owe you and I'll pay back every cent. I have it all written down in my book."

"Don't worry about it," Caleb Brown said.

Dwight refused to be let off the hook. "I do worry about it. I wouldn't want to die owing money . . . Who the hell is Reverend Hardesty?"

Caleb Brown eased the car over a hole in the road. "If you weren't in a fog all the time you'd know who he is. Reverend Hardesty took over the old church up on the river road. He calls it the Church of Nazareth and all are welcome there. Even you may be welcome. I don't know if Reverend Hardesty is a Baptist or a Methodist. Maybe neither. Makes no difference to me what he is. He's a decent Christian man that's trying to help those that need it."

"I'm not much for this Jesus Saves stuff," Dwight said gloomily. "What does this Hardesty cutter do? Make you sing hymns before he gives you a bowl of bean soup? That's what I had to do that time I was bumming around in Boston."

"Too bad you didn't stay in Boston," Caleb Brown said. "What made you come back, anyway?"

Dwight gave out with a wheezing laugh that

turned into a fit of coughing. After it passed he said, "Was fixing to break a liquor store window with a brick when this cop comes along and starts to arrest me."

"What stopped him?"

"Cop was from up here in Maine so he let me go provided I got out of the city. Us State of Mainers got to stick together."

"Don't I know it," Caleb Brown said wearily.

He drove along the river road and over a wooden bridge to where the church was. Up on the roof a solid-looking man in overalls and work boots was nailing new shingles in place. He waved and came down a ladder when he saw the cruiser. Two boys and three girls, all in their mid-teens, stood on the steps of the church and stared with sullen faces. A middle-aged man with a booze-bloated face of a derelict stood by himself with a paint bucket in his hand.

Caleb Brown shook hands with the man in overalls. "How is the world treating you, Reverend?"

"No complaints, Chief," the minister said. "We're getting it done little by little. We should be finished before it starts to rain in October."

"Good," Caleb Brown said. "Reverend, I'd like you to meet Dwight Endicott, the man with the original hollow leg. He's the most contankerous drunk in this or any other county, but he'll be sleeping in the woods if you can't find a place for him. While he was drying out in the hospital somebody stole his home. If you decide to take him in, this man will test your Christian principles right down to bedrock."

Caleb Brown turned to Dwight. "Did I leave anything out?"

"Not a thing, not a thing," Dwight said with heavy sarcasm. "Thanks, Caleb, you described me just right."

Reverend Hardesty shook hands with Dwight. "You look like you could do with a drink, Mr. Endicott."

"That's the last thing he needs," Caleb Brown said.

"If he needs it, he needs it," Reverend Hardesty said. "I'm not here to reform people, Chief, just to help them if they need it. I try to show people the right road, but I don't drag them down it by the scruff of the neck. Stay as long as you like, Mr. Endicott. Mr. Moultrie—he's the gentleman with the paint can—will show you where we keep the liquor. Tell him I said it's all right."

Caleb Brown drew the minister aside. "I have to warn you, my friend Dwight will try your patience to the limit. He's everything I said he was. He's a good carpenter and you may get some work out of him. But I doubt you'll get very much. He'll never stop drinking no matter what you do. So if you feel you can't handle him I'll take him away from here and put him somewhere else."

"We'll see," Reverend Hardesty said.

"How are the hippies doing?" Caleb Brown asked.

"Not too bad. One of these days they'll wander off without as much as saying goodbye. They'll end up starving and drug crazy in some other place, but for the moment they're here and as safe as I can make them. What else is there to do?"

"Not much I guess," Caleb Brown said reluctantly. "Well, I have to be getting back. Just remember, if Dwight gets to be too much for you, get word to me and I'll come and drag him out of here."

"We'll see," Reverend Hardesty said.

CHAPTER NINE

Both Delaneys were in a rotten mood. It was a lovely summer day and their small rock garden was bright with flowers of many kinds, but they were in a bad mood. Their house was small too; Carol Delaney didn't like it. At one time it had been their dream cottage; now Carol called it "a tacky box."

"It should be in Daly City, California, with the rest of the tacky little boxes," Carol said. She had read about Daly City in *Time*.

"What's wrong with the house?" her husband, Greg, said. "It's nearly paid for, isn't it? It's ours. You're the one who wanted to live in Maine. I didn't. Now I do."

"That was over eight years ago," Carol said.

"We were just out of college then. People don't always know what's right for them at that age. People grow over the years. We've outgrown this house."

"You know better now, is that it?"

"I know I'm a different person."

"So am I. I thought I wanted to go to New York then. Get a part time job and work on a novel."

"You've been working on a novel, two or three novels. Greg, we're stagnating here. Your job on the newspaper, it's going nowhere. You write the same old stuff and get a tiny raise every year. At least in New York you'd be getting union scale."

"And I'd be covering rapes, child murders, arson in the South Bronx, Mayor Koch's latest foolishness. No thank you. Look, I think I have a good shot at managing editor when Hayward retires."

Carol, blond and irritable, refused to be per-suaded. "Hayward is about fifty-five. He's the publisher's brother-in-law and year after year he's raised circulation. He'll still be editor when he's seventy."

"Unless he dies," Greg said.

"Is he ill?" Carol said.

"Not that I know of."

"Then what the hell are you talking about?"

"Suggesting a possibility, that's all."

The TV dinners in the oven were starting to

burn and Carol ran from her typewriter to the smoky kitchen. "Damn! Damn!" she cried. "If I don't get out of here I'm going to go crazy!"

Using a pot holder, she yanked the ruined TV dinners from the oven, threw them in the sink and ran water over them. The smoke in the tiny kitchen got worse. Carol began to cry.

Greg Delaney didn't move from the living room where he had been re-reading one of his stories in the *Yorkport Star*. It was about a visiting professor who claimed that the Vikings had landed in the Yorkport area rather than in Newfoundland. Greg liked the light, skeptical tone of his writing. He thought it was just right. He didn't look up as Carol, teary eyed, returned to her typewriter where she had been laboring over a poem for the next issue of her "little" magazine, *Ambush*. It called itself a quarterly, but in fact it appeared only when there was enough money to get out another issue. It was listed in *Ayer's Guide to Periodicals,* but its fame had spread no further than that. Sometimes it was a sixteen-pager, more often an eight, yet Carol kept it going year after year, determined to force her way into the bigger world outside Maine.

A tiny person physically , she was "possessed of great fire," in her own words, and in the days when the *New York Times* still ran short poems on the editorial pages, her work had appeared several times. Now that market was dead too. She'd never made it in "Metropolitan Diary."

During the week she sold advertising space for the *Star*, making the rounds in an old VW convertible. Instead of receiving a regular salary, she worked on commission; in recent months her income had dwindled due to her lack of interest in the "boring, boring job." It galled her to have to smile at sexist lumber merchants and chauvinist restaurant owners just to earn a few dollars. Some thought she was cute; others were put off by her superior manner, her boarding school voice. As a girl she had spoken in brisk, clear tones: now her voice had grown shrill, filled with complaint.

In college (Wellesley) she wanted to write like Emily Dickinson, only freer, of course, with greater energy. That hadn't worked out. Then struggling toward the new frontiers of poetry, she had been interested in certain poets no one ever heard of. The craze for the mediocrities, Rod McKuen and others, sent her dashing back to the older poets.

Allen Tate hadn't managed to satisfy her. Neither had John Crowe Ransom. Frank O'Hara was somehow too close to the Beats like Ginsberg. All the way back she went: MacNeice, Spender, Auden, Jeffers, Stevens, Williams, the Lewises. All the telephone poles of modern poetry flashed by her on her backward journey. Back all the way: Crane, Eliot, Pound,

Millay, Masters, Robinson. Yeats failed her. They all failed her.

And now she was stuck in Yorkport with a husband she could learn to love again, if only he had more money. Another thing: Greg was at home too much, the house was too small. Yeats had his tower, Emily Dickinson her pristine 19th century room, Jeffers the phony castle in Big Sur. And she wondered if any of them could have written a line if they had had Greg Delaney around all the time.

She glanced over at her husband, who was reading his silly newspaper story for the third or fourth time. Such ego. Such mental masturbation. She glared at the poem she was trying to write. It was about herself—most of her poems were—but even that had grown stale for the moment.

"Go on to something else," she said aloud.

"Huh?" her husband said.

"Oh God!" Carol said.

Her next poem would be about New England, she decided. She was a New Englander, wasn't she? So why shouldn't she write about her native region. (Of course, she would have preferred to write about New England in New York City. Robert Lowell had written some of his best New England poems in an English manor house.) One did not have to live in a place to write about it. In many ways it was best to be far away from one's roots—in exile, so to speak. Good poetry was forever.

Like diamonds.

"I'm going to write a new poem called "Fried Clams," she told herself.

Her husband looked. "You want to go for fried clams?"

"Shut up, Gregory," she snapped. She always used his full name when she was truly mad at him.

The title was ironic; therefore the poem must have nothing to do with fried clams. Perhaps she should call it "Steamed Clams." No, the original title was better. "Steamed Clams" was too wholesome, too "healthy," whereas "Fried Clams" conjured up images of tacky tourists in play clothes, stringy-necked mothers with bickering children waiting to be served at roadside stands. It evoked the acrid smell of frying fat. Cans of orange soda rattling down the slot in vending machines. My God! The things Americans put in their bodies!

After searching for inspiration, Carol typed:

> *Hissing tires on asphalt*
> *Smell of frying fat*
> *Cans of Coke with pop-tops*
> *More and more of that.*
> *Daddy in his play clothes*
> *Mommy in her Sears*
> *Waiting for their junk food*

Filled with inner fears.

Was it any good? Carol wondered. It rhymed, but what was wrong with that? Rhyme was coming back, in moderation, of course. The thing to do was to let it cool for a while, then come back later and see how it tasted. Anyway, she was off to a start, and that was all that mattered. To get something done every day. A day without a poem was like an egg without salt.

She unrolled the sheet from the typewriter and locked it in the drawer of the desk, where Greg couldn't see it. She knew he snooped through her work if she didn't lock it up. What was he looking for? Did he think she was writing about the lover she didn't have? Well, there had been a few lovers; none lately. Most of the men around Yorkport were so *boring.* There had been a short thing with Leonard Gately a few years before, during her Ezra Pound period, when she was mildly interested in fascism. Not fascism exactly. More like primal man. But Gately had been too *physical,* even for a primal man, and so she had dropped him after a particularly violent scene. They hadn't spoken since. You might call them enemies.

Dissatisfaction overcame her once again, now that the joy of creating something beautiful had passed. "Greg," she said. "I wish we could leave here and move to New York. Don't give me that look. I mean what I'm saying. It would be good for both of us. Please, Greg, I want to move to New York."

"Using what for money?" her husband asked.

Carol said in her reasonable voice, "We could sell the house, pay off what's left of the mortgage. That would pay for an apartment and keep us going until we found jobs. You could get a job on a newspaper—don't make a face—and I could work in publishing."

"Just like that? You know how many people in New York are looking for jobs?"

"I don't know and I don't care. New York is the place to be. It's where things happen."

"Like muggings. I don't want to live with gates on the windows and ten locks on the door."

Greg Delaney had just seen a re-run of *Death Wish* on cable television.

"It's not as bad as all that," Carol insisted. "You make too much out of everything. If New York is so bad, why do millions of people choose to live there?"

"Most of them can't get out. We're out and we're going to stay out. Eighteen thousand people were murdered in New York last year, and it's going to get worse all the time. I don't want to be a victim."

Carol said, "You don't want to be anything."

Greg said, "That's a nice thing to say."

"It's the truth, but you don't want to hear it."

"I'm listening. I'm here. You got any more nice things to say?"

Carol hesitated, unsure of how far she could go. "Well . . .," she said, but didn't go on with it.

"Well what?"

"Oh Greg, why do we have to fight? We're two adult people, so why can't we talk this out?"

"We're talking it out. It's all we ever do."

"No, it's not. We go round and round, but nothing gets settled. All I want is what's good for both of us, especially you. You're in a rut and don't even know."

"I like the rut I'm in. It suits me."

"Well, it doesn't suit me. This town depresses me. I want my own space. I want us to grow, together and individually. Nothing ever happens here. Forgive me, but I think that's the reason you haven't been able to write. Every year is the same as the one before. In summer the tourists descend on us like locusts, but there's no life here. In winter the place is like a funeral parlor. Dead! Dead! Dead! Snow and ice and rain and fog.

"That sounds like the postmen and their appointed rounds," Greg said, rattling his newspaper, wanting to get back to his story about the professor and the Vikings.

"That's just dumb," Carol said furiously. "Here I am talking about our *lives* and you try

139

to make dumb jokes about it. We're in a *crisis,* Gregory, and you don't even seem to know it."

"I know you want to move to New York. What happens if you don't like it there? What will we do? Move to Key West? L.A.? This house will be gone and so will my job on the *Star.* They won't take me back. Hayward has enough job applications to fill a file cabinet. Answer me: what happens if you don't like New York?"

Carol smiled, sensing a crack in her husband's resolve. "I'd never get tired of New York. How could I? There's so much to do and see. The Village. SoHo. The galleries on 57th Street. Did you know that every New Year's Day they give a nonstop reading of Gertrude Stein's *The Making of Americans* in some coffeeshop. Famous people read. Bowery bums can read. Anyone can read. *We* could read."

"At least you could have put us before the Bowery bums. Anyway, it's not a coffeeshop, it's an art gallery."

"Then you know about it?"

"Who doesn't? It's in the *Voice* every year."

"But doesn't it excite you?"

Greg said, "Not a bit. I don't like Gertrude Stein."

Carol said, "Who cares about Gertrude Stein? It's the *occasion,* don't you see? People getting together to do a creative thing. What do people do in Yorkport on New Year's Day, the few that are left? I'll tell you what they do.

They nurse their hangovers and tell each other: 'Boy, did I get bombed last night.' Or, 'Did you hear that Oscar Tibbetts ran his truck into the toll booth on his way home from a party?' Very witty, don't you think?"

Greg said wearily, "People do that everywhere. What's so different about Yorkport?"

"A lot," Carol said. "If I have to spend another year in this place I'm going to die. You're killing me, Gregory. I don't know what else to say."

"Don't be so dramatic. Tell you what we'll do. I have two weeks' vacation coming in August. We'll go to New York instead of Vermont. New York is like Calcutta in August, but we'll go anyway. We haven't been there for three years. We'll go in August. Then you can go crazy in SoHo, all the rest of it. Is it a deal?"

Carol stamped her foot sitting down. "It is *not* a deal, Gregory. I hate it. I *hate* it when you try to patronize me like that. Let the little wife do her tourist things, then take her back to the country for another three—maybe ten—years of absolute boredom."

"Oh, come on," Greg said.

Carol's shrill voice became threatening. "*You* come on, Gregory. I'm sick and tired of your indecision. If you can't see what's right for us, then. . . ."

"Then what, Carol? You've said a lot. Say the rest of it."

"Not now," she said, backing down a little but still angry. "Think about what I've said. That's all I want you to do. *I'm* going to the library."

Motionless at the living room table, Greg Delaney listened to the sound of the VW going away from the house. It was old and made a noise like a sewing machine.

It was getting serious, he knew; there was no way to talk her out of it. There was nothing new about it, of course; for more than two years she had been hinting, then harping about moving to New York. But she hadn't gone so far as she had today. Money was a good part of it; if only he earned more money they could move to a bigger house, take trips, get her a better car, a charge plate at Bonwit's in Boston. The paper paid him two hundred and fifty dollars a week, and after taxes—they had no children—that didn't leave very much. They could live on it, but not with any kind of style. And that was what she wanted most: to live with style. She made some money selling the ad space, but she spent most of that on the dumb poetry magazine. It was an extravagance, she admitted; it kept her sane, she said. Knowing that she was Wellesley, a local private school for girls had offered her a job at more money than he made on the *Star*. Not interested, she said. After having spent a good part of her life in girls' schools, she didn't want any more of it. Naturally, he respected her position, yet some irritability remained when he thought about it. With the girls' school salary added to his they could be living very well indeed. What did Freud once say: "Does anyone know what women want?" Words to that effect. No matter how he said it, Siggy was right. What did they want? What did Carol want? Did she know?

Right now she thought she wanted to live in New York, but he'd be damned if he'd make the move to please her. New York wouldn't satisfy her. Nothing ever would. He might lose her if they stayed in Yorkport; in New York the end would come a lot sooner. Once she found herself in New York, it would be all over. Yorkport didn't have the kind of men she liked, while New York was full of them.

He knew about her affair with Gately, if you could call it that. The word "affair" didn't seem to go with Gately, who was simply an animal. Everybody in Yorkport knew about the thing with Gately, mostly because Gately spread the word himself. Greg Delaney cringed at the idea of Gately and Carol. Carol was so small, Gately so big. But he would have hated Gately anyway: Carol was just one more reason. Gately was a fascist swine, a sadistic loudmouth with too much money. It was ironic that a creature like Gately should have so much money, while many people with intelligence and sensitivity should have so little.

Greg Delaney was afraid of Gately, as any sane man ought to be. Occasionally, they met in the bank, post office, supermarket, and Gately would say things like, "When are you moving over to the *New York Times*, old buddy?" Or, "I hear *Time-Life* is after your ass." At such times he wanted to come back with, "How are things in the Ku Klux Klan?" but he didn't because it was beneath his dignity. Besides, he wasn't sure that Gately might not throw him through a window or stomp him with his stupid boots. The man was a psychopath, so anything was possible.

A few months before Hayward had asked him to do a story on Sentinel, the nut group headed by Colonel Burns, but he had backed out of it, not because of Burns but because of Gately. Hayward, an old fashioned Maine Republican quite unlike the Sun Belt kooks, hadn't forced the issue, thanks be to heaven. If he wrote the story and Gately got drunk enough, there was a good chance of being killed or crippled. That Gately would be sent to jail for a very long time was no consolation. Greg would still be dead or walking on crutches.

But why was he spending so much time on Gately? Actually, he wasn't. Gately wasn't a problem any more. Carol was. If only he could get one of his novels published, she would, be able to say, "My husband the novelist." She'd like that even if the books didn't make much money. It would hold her for a while. However, all three novels had been rejected by seven publishers, two in Boston, five in New York. One lady editor in New York—he guessed she was very young—sent him a personal letter instead of a standard rejection slip. She praised his intention, but suggested that he try something more "commercial."

There had been a few magazine sales, none to national magazines. *Maine Monthly*, published in Camden, paid him fifty dollars for a short piece on the wild lumber towns of the 1840's. He hoped to go on writing for the M & M, as some people called it, but they dropped him after a lot of readers wrote in informing the editor that he had gotten some of his facts wrong in the first article. After that his only income from freelance writing was the $500 he got for writing the family history of some people named Perkins in Bangor.

Not much. Not enough to make Carol proud of him.

If only Hayward would die. That was too harsh. So he amended it to: if only Hayward would make some serious mistake that would force him into early retirement. That was better: he liked Hayward, whose title was managing editor, but was the real editor. The publisher, billed as editor in chief, wasn't any kind of editor but simply a man with opinions. There was only one other staff member who might have a chance at Hayward's job. Fat chance, Greg Delaney thought. They'd never pick Davies over me. Or would they? What worried him was the possibility that they might bring in an outsider to take Hayward's place. What would he do if they did?

Greg Delaney didn't get to answer the question, because just then he heard the *varoom* of a sports car as it pulled up to the house, and when he went to the window he saw a girl with a headscarf getting out of a beautiful old Morgan with an envelope in her hand. He opened the door before she reached it. She was even prettier than the car.

She smiled. "Are you Mr. Delaney? Greg Delaney of the *Yorkport Star?*"

Greg Delaney said he was. "Is there something I can do for you?" With that car and that accent she wasn't there to tell him about next Wednesday night's baked bean supper at the Baptist church.

"My name is Mary Galligan," she said. "Tracy O'Neal's secretary. Mrs. O'Neal is. . . ."

"I know."

"Mrs. O'Neal wants to invite you and your wife to her Fourth of July party. You wrote the story about the house, didn't you?"

"Sure did," Greg said. "Is that why she's inviting me?"

"Yes, it is," Mary Galligan said. "She liked the story—no gush."

"I try not to."

"Will you be able to come? I know it's short notice, but you can blame that on me. I forgot to mail your invitation along with several others. That's why I'm bringing it in person."

"I'd be delighted to come," Greg said, taking the invitation envelope from her. "I'm sorry. Won't you come in for a moment? Some coffee? Perhaps a drink?"

She laughed. "What have you got?"

"I can fix you a rum and coke with plenty of crushed ice. Or just coke."

He held open the door and she came in. "Don't leave out the rum," she said.

Greg Delaney didn't drink much, hardly at all, in fact, and half a bottle of Myer's Jamaica Rum was left over from Christmas. She was a classy gal and he was glad it was a good brand. She didn't say anything about his house, and he was glad of that, too.

"Good," she said, tasting the tall drink. "How do you like working for the *Star*?"

"It's all right. The work is easy and it gives me time to write. I'm halfway through my first novel. It'll be another six months before I finish it." Greg Delaney sighed, then grinned. "Then will come the rewriting."

"I'll be sure to buy a copy when it comes out," Mary Galligan said.

Greg Delaney protested, "No need to do that. I'll send you a copy."

"Thanks. I'd like that. Be sure to sign it."

"Galligan. That's Irish, isn't it?" As soon as Greg said it he felt stupid.

"How did you guess?"

They laughed together.

"Delaney isn't exactly Lithuanian," Greg said. "Anyway, it gives us something in common. Have you been with Mrs. O'Neal for very long?"

"Two years. Before that I was a legman for a society columnist in Washington. That's how I met Mrs. O'Neal."

"You aren't writing a novel, are you?"

This time her smile was forced. "Not a novel."

Something in the way she said it made Greg want to change the subject. He sensed she was unhappy and wondered if the stories about Tracy O'Neal's pettiness, her stinginess, were true.

There was a moment of silence that he filled by saying, "I like that Morgan of yours. Is it as fast as it looks?"

Mary Galligan had finished her drink. Greg had barely tasted his. "I bought it at college. Time payments, but I had to have it. No, it's not as fast as it looks. It's fast enough for me and it's hard sprung so you have to buy an air cushion. Have you ever ridden in one?"

Greg said no.

"Would you like to go for a spin sometime?"

"I'd like that very much."

Mary Galligan stood up. "Then give me a call sometime. I'll be here until September."

"I'll do that," Greg said, not quite sure he was going to—but probably.

He saw her to her car and she was driving away when Carol braked the VW to a stop. Mary Galligan was gone by the time she got out of the car and came down the walk to the house with an armload of library books.

"Who's your girlfriend?" she said nastily.

Greg said, "I knew you'd catch us sooner or later." Then he grinned.

Carol came in and dumped the books on the table, rattling the glasses. The bottle of rum was on the kitchen counter. So was a bowl of crushed ice, now melting.

"Drinks and everything," Carol said. "How romantic. *Love in the Afternoon.* Which one are you? Gary Cooper or Audrey Hepburn?"

Greg knew she didn't mean any of it, just being unpleasant. "I'm Hepburn," he said.

Carol drank some of her husband's unfinished drink. "All right, Gregory, who is she, and what was she doing here?"

"Her name is Mary Galligan and she's Tracy O'Neal's secretary. She came to invite us to the big Fourth of July party."

"Don't be such an idiot. I'm not in the mood

149

for it. Why was she here?"

Greg was enjoying this. "You mean you don't believe me?"

"No."

Greg pushed the invitation across the table. "There's proof."

"My God! You're telling the truth," Carol said. Then her excitement faded slightly. "Oh, she's probably inviting everybody at the *Star*."

"No, she's not. I asked about that. Nobody but us. Not Hayward, not even the publisher."

"But this is marvelous," Carol cried, eyes wide again. "You know some of the people who are going to be there? Linwood Duval. Ormond Bailey. Lots of others."

"I know, dear. I wrote the story. That's why I—we—were invited." Greg Delaney polished his fingernails on his lapel, grinning all the time. "Tracy O'Neal happens to like the way I write. In fact, she's mad about it. She would have come herself, but she's too busy reading all my old stuff in the *Star*. 'Mary,' she said to Miss Galligan, 'get over to Yorkport chop chop and don't take no for an answer.' Those were her very words."

Carol was too delighted to sneer at him. "I've read everything Linwood Duval's ever written and I'm going to tell him so."

"Easy, girl, don't crowd that guy. He can get pretty nasty."

"Beeswax," Carol said, dismissing the no-tion that she and Duval might not be flying on the same beam. "Linwood is nasty to people who don't understand him. I'm sure he's perfectly nice to people who do."

Greg took the glasses to the kitchen and came back. "Then you really want to go?"

Carol cried, "Are you crazy? Of course I want to go."

Suddenly she threw her arms around him, kissing him wildly. "Oh Greg, my darling, you've made this happen! I love you so much. So much. So much!"

CHAPTER TEN

Lacey Putnam was in seventh heaven. His blue eyes sparkled, his slim figure quivered with unsuppressed excitement. He seized his lover, Jeffrey Rodriguez, around the waist and waltzed him all over the stainless steel kitchen. Both men wore macho mustaches. They were new style homosexuals, short haired and muscular, unafraid and unashamed of what they were. They were healthy and if not exactly happy, then happy enough. At the moment, Lacey couldn't have been happier.

"We've got it made," Lacey cried. "Today Yorkport, tomorrow the world. What a break! What a break!" Lacey released his lover and junior partner and clasped his hands in supplication. "Dear Sweet God, don't let anything go wrong. Don't let Tracy change her mind. God, sweetie, don't let the strike be over before the Fourth. Do this for me, Pops, and I'll light a candle. A box of candles. I'll turn Catholic, Episcopalian, anything you like. Just name it, God!"

"You're wigging out, lover," Rodriguez said, his big teeth very white, very big against his Los Angeles-Mexican face. "You're forgetting that Mrs. Stein is going to be very mad at you. You were supposed to do *her* party on the Fourth. After all, she's been our best client since we started here and she never tries to jew us on the price."

Lacey danced by himself, doing long tango steps. "Who cares? *One. Two. Three. Dip.* Who cares what Mrs. Stein thinks, what she does? Have you ever seen *her* name in the society columns?"

"Sure I have. Will you stop clowning for a minute?"

Lacey slid to a graceful stop. "All right, so she's in the columns now and then. A very now and then. You didn't know she has to pay a big bribe to get a mention. Well, did you?"

Rodriguez shrugged. "What difference does that make? She's very rich and she's very nice. She's thrown a lot of money our way."

"Nice old ladies finish last," Lacey said.

"Okay, I feel kind of bad about letting her down, but what can we do? We don't have the staff to handle two big parties. Maybe she can call McDonald's or the Colonel."

"That's vicious," Rodriguez said, frowning while Lacey did his Fred Astaire imitation. "And how do you know Tracy O'Neal will use us more than once?"

Still tapping, Lacey said, "Once is all we need. It's like saving the President's life. Zap—you're famous. You can name your price. Tracy's party will be in every paper in the country, in the world." Lacey, still tapping, blew a kiss at his junior partner. "And we'll be right there with her. This is a star-making part, as they say in Hollywoodland. How do you think Cary Grant got to be a star? By working hard and eating his Wheaties?"

"I know the Mae West story."

"Mae saw Cary and liked what she saw. Instant stardom. The same thing is going to happen to us. Forget the strike. Nobody's going to know or remember that's the reason she hired us. She didn't mention any strike, but you know me—I checked it out. All the world will know is that the super-fabulous Tracy O'Neal called Putnam & Rodriguez. Out of all the caterers and party planners in the world, she picked *us*. Makes you feel almost humble, doesn't it?"

"She sure went on about the cost," Rodriguez said.

"Everybody knows she's tight with a buck. I'll tell you a secret, *amigo.* I'd do the party for free just to get the publicity. You can't put a price on what she just handed to us. It's just like the Ruby Keeler bit, dig it? The star of the show falls down a manhole and the kid goes on in her place."

Lacey sang, " 'Next day on your dressing room they've hung a star . . .' "

"That's from the wrong show."

"It's all show biz, baby. Seriously, Jerry, this has got to be absolutely right. This is our big chance, just like Ruby, and if we screw up we'll stay in the chorus for the rest of our lives." Lacey kissed his fingers like an actor playing a chef. "Eet az to bee jus' zo. Anything else is disasterville, *comprende?*"

"What can go wrong?" Rodriguez asked. "We've been doing parties for three years. We did bigger ones in L.A."

"You worry me, Jerry," Lacey said. "What can go wrong? *Anything* can go wrong. The whole staff has to be checked and then checked again. Just one jerk can ruin the whole schlemozzle. A guy takes a drink, smokes a joint, and we're back with our noses pressed to the window. I want some substitutes on hand in case somebody fouls up. Check them, too. Check the refrigerated trucks. Check everything."

155

"Aye, aye, sir. Anything else?"

Lacey clapped his hands together. "Re-hearsals, that's what."

"Just like on Broadway?"

"But of course," Lacey Putnam said.

"I don't care what you say," Cal Cameron said. "I want a complete run-through. The fact that you played four weeks in four towns is none of my business. What is my business, is the Yorkport Theater. I built it, I made it into one of the best—if not the best—summer play-house in America. So don't tell me they can do the show in their sleep. I don't like people do-ing shows in their sleep. They go to sleep, the paying customers go to sleep."

"You're the boss, Cal," Noah Shawley said. Shawley was the director of a revival of '23 Ski-doo, a romantic comedy about to open at the Yorkport Playhouse. The company was four weeks out of New York: they had made the swing up through Connecticut, Massachu-setts and New Hampshire. Maine, which was a late starter because it stayed cold into June, was last.

Julie Ferguson was the leading lady, Za-chary Danforth the leading man. They didn't speak offstage, but played well together; audi-ences could easily see them in love. It was an old play, and frothy, but none of the original book had been cut. They played it in the jittery style of the Twenties, and actors less skillful than Ferguson and Danforth might not have been able to bring it off. It was a gamble in a small way, nothing like opening a new show on Broadway, but reputations were at stake and actors who bombed on the circuit would be remembered when booking time came round next year.

The Yorkport Playhouse was, apart from the plays produced there, one of the best appointed in the country. Fully air-conditioned since the early 1960's, the large theater stood in beautifully landscaped grounds, and it was easy of access, being situated on the main road between Maine and New Hampshire. It was owned by Cal Cameron, who had taken over the original Yorkport Playhouse, an amateurish venture that had had some critical success in the Twenties and Thirties. Cameron had the old building, a converted barn, demolished: the new building was erected in 1950. Over the years it had earned an enviable reputation of being well run; the technical facilities were superb.

Dawn Brodie, standing near Zachary Danforth, whispered something to him and Cal Cameron, ever irritable, whirled on her, his thin mustache twitching. Cameron looked something like the distinguished Broadway actor Arnold Moss; he had the same sardonic stare, the booming voice.

Fixing the terrified Dawn with his celebrated stare, he shook the theater with: "DO YOU MIND?"

Instead of keeping quiet, Dawn said, "Not a bit, Mr. Cameron."

Cameron smacked his forehead and turned back to Noah Shawley. "You've got to liven this thing up," he warned. "You didn't see me, but I caught this show twice before you got here. Speed it up even more. By that I don't mean all the scenes, just the slapstick pieces. Slow down the love scenes. They're supposed to be funny, but they're tender, too. That's the boy, Noah. I knew you'd see it my way."

Cameron, a menacing figure, went down and sat in the empty theater, waiting for the run-through to begin.

Julie Ferguson was by herself at the opening of the play, so Danforth was able to talk to Dawn, backstage in his dressing room.

"Help me with my line, please Zachary," Dawn implored, looking at herself in the mirror.

Tired from too much of everything, Danforth said, "All you have to say is, 'Telegram for you, sir.' That's it, period. Say no more, no less. You're one of the maids in the house, but you don't have a name in the script. You're not Irish or Swedish or South American, just *the maid.*"

Dawn was desperate: this was her first appearance before a real audience. She had been in plays at the theater school attached to the playhouse, but that didn't count. At the theater school nobody ever showed the slightest interest in what anyone else did.

"But how do I get inside the part, darling?" Dawn said. "What's my motivation?"

"Your motivation is that Cameron will kill you if you don't do it the way you've been told. I'm telling you the same thing now. You're one of many maids in a Long Island mansion. The time is 1923. They could hire a lot of maids in 1923. A telegram comes and you happen to be the maid delegated to take it in to the master of the house. He's in the library with the lady of the house. I'm the master of the house. The library door is open so you don't have to open it. That makes it easier for you because opening a door onstage isn't as easy as it looks."

"But you will teach me how to open a door, Zachary?"

"Later. Listen to me. The door is open, but you knock politely and wait. Don't knock and walk in. Just stand there and I'll say, 'Come in.' It'll be an offhand remark, no big deal. You just walk in and say, 'Telegram for you, sir.' You hold the telegram out to me and I take it. By then you're walking out."

"Why don't you say 'Thank you?' "

"Because it's not in the script. Marlon

159

Brando might decide to say, 'I'll meet you tonight by the hollow oak tree,' but not me. I play by the book. It's safer and nobody gets mad at you."

"But if you said, 'Thank you,' then I could say, 'You're welcome, I'm sure,' and that would give me an extra line."

"Don't think about it," Danforth warned. "You want to go over your line again?"

Dawn's long blond hair had been coiled up and covered with a lacy maid's cap. "No need, Zachary, I know the line. But I've been thinking, looking in the mirror here, that I look kind of Scandinavian, the blond hair, blue eyes, and all. I can do a nice Norwegian accent. You know, Liv Ullman, or I *Remember Mama*."

Before Danforth could stop her, Dawn spoke her line in what she took to be a Norwegian accent:

"TELL-AY-GROM FUR YEW, SUR."

Danforth winced with mental anguish. "Don't you like it?" Dawn wanted to know.

Danforth said, "I keep telling you it's not in the script, in the book. *No accents*. You're a maid. You don't have a nationality." Playing his trump card, Danforth warned her, "Mess this up and you'll never work in show business again. You'll be poison in Hollywood and on Broadway."

Dawn bit her knuckles. "You're frightening me, Zachary. I'll do it right, I promise."

Danforth was thinking it was too bad they didn't have time for a quickie. There was something about Dawn, and it wasn't just her great figure, that turned him on. He guessed it was her stupidity: getting in bed with her was like getting in bed with a life-sized Barbie doll, and her conversation, if you could call it that, might easily have come from one of those tape loops they implant in the chests of talking dolls.

"I'm on in five minutes," Danforth, the professional, said. He had been half listening to the dialogue on stage.

Now that her mentor was leaving, Dawn grew panicky again. "We haven't worked on my walk, Zachary. How do I walk?"

Danforth wanted to scream. "Make it a little stiff. Short steps, okay? You don't have to look graceful. You're just a maid."

Dawn smiled. "I'll make them remember me."

"Please don't. Please," Danforth begged. "You'll get bigger parts you can do that in."

"Zachary," Dawn said sweetly. "Have you done anything about getting us an invitation to Tracy's party? You promised you would."

"I said I'd try."

"Well, have you?"

"I'm working on it," Danforth said, hating her a little.

As the rehearsal continued, the meeting of Sentinel was called to order by Colonel Mike Burns in his modest year-round house on a quiet village street. There were only ten people present, including Burns and Gately, but as the colonel said so often, there was no reason to be discouraged by small numbers: a handful of dedicated men could sway the course of events, no matter how powerful their enemies, how ferocious their foes.

There was only one woman present, a fifty-ish schoolteacher who had been forced into retirement because of her determination in the matter of public prayers in a local school. Warned many times that she was in violation of a Supreme Court ruling against such prayers, Miss Elizabeth Hatcher had stood her ground to the last, only to find that she had no ground to stand on. Now she lived on her pension and what she earned from privately tutoring backward high school students who wanted to get into college. Fierce as Colonel Burns in her political attitudes, she was a tireless worker for the Yorkport chapter of Sentinel, and from the pine paneled basement of her ranch-style house poured a torrent of mimeographed broadsides attacking everything from smutty jokes on late-night talk shows to Elizabeth Taylor's love life. Never married— though she'd had her chances, she said—she was prepared to devote the rest of her life to setting the country straight.

Colonel Burns, though she made him uneasy, acknowledged her formidable presence by complimenting her on the number of envelopes she had stuffed for the movement during the past month.

"One of the great fighters for freedom," Colonel Burns called her.

Miss Hatcher smiled: she knew she was.

The low-ceilinged living room of Colonel Burns's house was decorated with all sorts of military gear: regimental flags, swords, rifles; autographed photographs showed the colonel shaking hands with prominent right-wingers from many parts of the country. There were even a few from Canada, mostly Quebec-French separatists who wanted to break loose from the oppressive Federal alliance.

One of the most outspoken members present was Ira Molson, a stringy, beer-bellied carpenter who had worked on the new O'Neal house and was ready to tell them a thing or two about "that woman." And while the colonel droned on about old business and new business, Molson fretted in his chair, wanting to get on with it.

Leonard Gately, quiet for once, looked around at the other Sentinel members in the room. Ira Molson was an idiot and Miss Hatcher was an old battleaxe. Then there was Ollie

Masterson, once a famous syndicated cartoonist, now dropped by nearly a hundred newspapers that had once published his work. Wealthy enough to disregard the admonitions of the syndicate chief, Masterson now devoted his time to drawing cartoons for extremist publications. An art student in Paris in the 1920's, Masterson still wore the wide-brimmed black hat and pointed beard affected by some writers and painters of that period. He looked like Erza Pound at his craziest.

They all looked a little (or a lot) cracked, Gately thought, feeling a twinge of disloyalty. Naturally this did not apply to his good friend, Mike Burns, who was as sound as IBM stock. Gately realized that he had been affected, in a subtle way, by his lunch with Tracy O'Neal. It wasn't that the lunch had changed his political opinions—far from it—yet he had been forced to admit that the lady had class.

He knew the colonel would call him to speak on the subject of Mrs. O'Neal, and he wished to hell he hadn't said anything about the old house she wanted to buy and tear down. That had been a lapse in judgment; there wasn't much he could do about it now, so the best he could do was to say as little as possible.

The colonel always opened the meeting with a prayer, and he did so now. Then he launched into one of his little jokes, to show the world that the members of Sentinel had a

164

sense of humor.

"I just heard Mrs. O'Neal went shopping the other day and bought herself an assistant supermarket manager. Handsome youngster—most of you know him. Name of Bruce Whipple. Believe it or not, friends, Mrs. O'Neal invited young Whipple to her so-called fabulous party. I got that from Bruce's father himself, so there's no doubt about it."

Gately sat up straight in his chair. What the hell was Mike saying? Bruce Whipple was an idiot who couldn't walk and chew gum at the same time. If Tracy O'Neal was inviting locals to her party, then why hadn't she invited him?

"Looks like she's taken to robbing the cradle," Mike was saying. "I tried to tell Bruce's father to keep his son away from that crowd. You know what he said to me? 'Why should I? Maybe it'll help him in his business career.' It's all true, friends. Every word of it."

Ira Molson kept raising his hand and finally the colonel recognized him. The ranting carpenter had done some free work on the colonel's house and couldn't be put off any longer.

"Yes, Ira?" the colonel said, knowing damn well what he wanted.

"What we talked about last week," Molson said. "As you know, I worked on Mrs. O'Neal's house and I'd like to say a few things that have been on my mind."

"Go right ahead, Ira."

165

The carpenter scratched his head and glanced at a scrap of paper in his work-calloused hand. "One of the city men I worked with told me Mrs. O'Neal sometimes raises money for charities and such by letting people stay in her houses and charging them. That to my mind makes a house a hotel and not a private house. What I'm saying is, if she's going to run a hotel she can be charged with running a hotel without a hotel license. Furthermore, the property is zoned for residential, not business."

Colonel Burns, looking slightly pained, said he didn't think they could get her that way.

Miss Hatcher spoke up. "Why can't we have a lawyer look into it?"

"Good thinking, Lizzie," Ollie Masterson said.

Colonel Burns nodded and made a note and told Molson to continue.

Molson said, "I know for a fact that some of the men she brought from the city were non-union."

"You want to get the unions after her, is that it?" Burns said.

"Anything to make trouble for her," Molson argued.

Burns shook his head. "I'm afraid I'm going to have to oppose you on that, Ira. One of the strongest planks in Sentinel's platform is the abolition of labor unions in the United States.

How would it look if we take the side of the union members against Mrs. O'Neal?"

"Why does it have to come out that we're part of it?" Ollie Masterson asked in his fluty voice.

"Too risky," Burns decided. "You can put it to a vote if you like. I'll still oppose it. Those who vote yes raise their hands."

Molson, Miss Hatcher and Masterson raised their hands.

"Those opposed." Burns raised his hand in support of the No's.

Leonard Gately lowered his hand and began to scribble a note on an office memo pad. All this bullshit with Molson was likely to go on for half an hour, and he was getting sick of it. In the note he apologized to the colonel for having to leave early, but there was a man passing through from Portland that he had to see on urgent business. He folded the note and passed it to Burns and walked out. Ira Molson and Miss Hatcher glared after him.

Outside, he stood by an open window and listened to Miss Hatcher denouncing him. The colonel said she was out of order—no member of Sentinel should attack another's character—but she went on anyway. Gately walked away. If the deal with Tracy O'Neal fell through, he would have plenty to say about her, and he'd say it better than that fool Molson. Right now he wasn't about to say anything *about* Mrs. O'Neal that might get back to her. Anybody who did something that stupid deserves to lose a commission. The next meeting of Sentinel was a week from tonight, which might not be nearly enough time to clinch the deal. If he didn't wrap it up by then, he would just skip the meeting and make his excuses to Mike Burns. But he'd have to be careful not to make Mike suspicious, to think he was deviating in the slightest way from the God-given principles of the movement.

Pleased with his plan of action, Gately drove home, but when he got there loneliness closed in on him. The big house was silent: at this hour it usually reverberated to the turned-up sound of the stereo. Steaks would be broiling, drinks would be pouring, Darryl would be cracking jokes a mile a minute.

Gatley knew that beer was not going to do it, not tonight. So he opened a fresh quart of 103-proof vodka and sloshed at least a triple into his boar's head beer mug, added some bitter lemon and quaffed it all at once.

As the drink took effect his hand began to stray toward the telephone. He wanted to call Darryl, at least try to find him, and say he was sorry for whatever it was he had done. Maybe he would later. No, that was wrong. He wouldn't call Darryl. He was the one with the power.

Let Darryl call him.

What Gately didn't know was that Darryl Bates was less than three miles away, in a motel at the northern end of Yorkport. Angela, still nursing the weals left by Gately's belt, was with him. Both had called in sick; the radio station employed many people; they wouldn't be missed, they hoped. Gately's ex-wife had left town with only a vague idea of where she was going. Bates decided that was just as well. Poor old Suzie was close to collapse.

Now, lying on the double bed with a cold towel wrapped around his damaged knee, Bates asked Angela to go to the service room to get some more ice. "Don't they have anything in the soda machine that goes with vodka?" Bates asked.

Angela said, "Sprite was the best I could do. The rest is Pepsi, Tab, Mr. Bubble."

"You should have remembered the grapefruit juice when you went to the liquor store."

"I can go to the market in town. Be back in fifteen minutes."

"Forget it," Bates said. "Remember to take the keys out of the car when you came in? You leave the keys in a rental and it gets stolen, they hit you for the whole thing."

Angela reached into her pants pocket and held up the keys. "See, Darryl?" she said.

"Go get the ice and the soda," Bates said, reaching down to feel his throbbing knee. There wasn't much wrong with it: still, it hurt.

If it had happened any other way, it wouldn't have bothered him much. But to be thrown around like a rag doll by that lunatic—that was something else. He knew Gately was potentially dangerous, but he had never expected to be set upon himself. At the station he was paid $400 a week, which wasn't too bad outside New York, except that he had to pay out more than $800 a month in child support. That left him short all the time, and that's where Gately came in. A generous man for all his faults, Gately was always good for a fifty, a hundred, and he always said, "When you get to be a bigshot comedy writer, then you pay me back. Till then, old buddy, don't worry about it." Bates didn't know how much he owed Gately by now. Eighteen hundred? Two thousand? Could be more. Too bad he hadn't socked him for a couple more thousand. Nothing he borrowed was ever paid back.

Darryl Bates smiled: it was a good rule. Of course, if the Mafia held him out the nineteenth floor window and hinted that he ought to pay up, then he probably would. But he didn't borrow money from the Mafia or anyone connected with the Mafia.

He knew that he was giving up a good thing in breaking with Gately. Having the run of Gately's house, the use of the company car, was worth a couple of hundred a week, at least. The cheapest motel room in Yorkport went for $30 a day during the season; the fancy ones down by the beach charged $100. So when you added up room rent, the car, food and booze, it couldn't be less than $200.

Angela came back with the plastic bucket of ice. While she was making fresh drinks, she said, "You could still get him for assault."

"Don't be so dumb. How would I explain it? You see, officer, there were these two naked broads making it on the floor and this other guy started whacking them with his belt. Me, Superman, rushes in to rescue the ladies and I get thrown across the room. Sounds good, wouldn't you say?"

"Not the way you say it. There has to be a way to get him. No big bastard like him hits me with a belt. What're you going to do, Darryl?"

"I don't know. A couple of things I've been thinking about. One is all the guns he has. I don't mean the ones hanging on the walls. They're all legal or he wouldn't hang them in plain sight. What I'm talking about, guns that he doesn't show to anybody. You know what an automatic weapon is?"

"I hate guns," Angela said.

"It's a weapon, any weapon that fires and keeps firing as long as you keep your finger on the trigger. Submachine guns, automatic rifles. If Gately has anything like that he could be in very serious trouble. In Massachusetts you get life for possession. I don't know about

Maine. It has to be a long sentence."

"Then why don't you call the FBI?"

"Treasury handles illegal possession."

"Whatever. What's holding you back?"

"I'm not sure he has such guns."

"That's not the real reason, Darryl."

"Smart girl," Bates said. "I wanted to kill Gately when it happened. Now I'm thinking of the money I'm going to lose by staying mad at him. I don't have the money to rent a summer place, not with cardboard cottages going for a thousand a month. About the gun thing, what I mean is, we send Gately to jail and there goes the freebies."

"But how can you make up with him after all the things you said? You said to his face he was a big fat faggot. I didn't know that. Is he?"

"I think he is, but I don't think he knows it himself. All that gung ho junk. The guns and daggers. Beating on his chest like King Kong. I read half the Nazis were faggots. Look at the law and order Southern judge Nixon kept trying to get on the Supreme Court. The guy keeps getting arrested in men's rooms for bothering other guys. It figures Gately is a fag and can't face it. Or doesn't know."

"Sounds weird," Angela said. "Too weird for me. You can go back if you like. Nothing could make me go through that again. Why don't we drop the whole thing and go back to Boston?"

"I like my weekends and vacations here. It's

a classy place and I'm a classy person."

"But what about what you called Bately? The fag thing? How can he forget you said that?"

Bates laughed. "Because I'm sure he doesn't remember it in the first place. Most of the time he blacks out or gets everything ass backward. I'll know when I see him."

"How's the knee?" Angela asked.

"Gately's going to hurt a lot more before I get through with him," Darryl Bates said.

He lay back, thinking about how to do it.

CHAPTER ELEVEN

Senator John Morrison Callaway, brother of the late president, arrived in Maine by way of the Washington-Boston air shuttle and a chauffeured limousine. Now he sat talking to Tracy. The big house was quiet. Most of the guests were out for the day, at the beach or wherever their idle fancy took them.

A dark wiry man with thinning hair, John Callaway had been a United States senator ever since he was old enough to be legally elected, which was thirty-five. Now, twelve years later, he was sometimes mentioned as a Presidential candidate, but he resisted all attempts to draft him for the office, explaining that the Senate, the most exclusive club in the world, was where he wanted to stay. His was a safe seat; it would take a scandal of major proportions to get him out of office. Now and then some political upstart took a swing at him, but to no avail. A widower—his wife had been killed in a skiing accident in Stowe, Vermont—he lived quietly; a townhouse in Georgetown, an apartment on Beacon Hill. Unlike certain senators, he never neglected his political base, which was Boston, where he was as popular with the Cambridge liberals as he was with the hardhat Irish in the South End. Neither a true conservative nor a true liberal, he walked a middle line, veering to the right or left when it suited him. Above all a pragmatist, he had no stated political philosophy, or if he had one, he kept it to himself. As head of a powerful committee, he got along well with the Southerners in the Senate; he was famous for his compromises while managing to avoid being labeled a wheeler-dealer. A millionaire, he could afford to be honest, but he was unscrupulous, even ruthless, in the way he used people to gain his own ends. He never questioned his judgments: always the end justified the means.

That he had remained Tracy's close friend was a matter of confusion to some people. They had so little in common. Cultural events bored him; serious plays put him to sleep, and though he dutifully supported many of Tracy's projects, he had no interest in any of them. Most of her friends appalled him; nonetheless a firm bond of affection remained between them. Some of Tracy's friends made jokes about him, as people joke about the people they fear, but no one, not even Linwood Duval, dared to joke about the senator in Tracy's presence.

Not a few Washington ladies had their eye on the senator, but he remained unmarried. There had been little love between the senator and his late wife; theirs had been an old-fashioned marriage of convenience. As a senator he needed a wife; for her part, she needed a millionaire husband. The marriage had worked well enough, but now that his wife had been dead for six years, he saw no reason to tie himself to another woman for any reason. His long-lived and utterly discreet affair with the wife of a Virginia gentleman farmer, an elderly and amiable alcoholic to whom sex was nothing but a distasteful memory, was known only to a few intimates, including the husband, who was pleased that his handsome, fortyish wife had chosen a man of means and good sense. It was a workable arrangement for all concerned. The senator liked to keep things in order.

Now he sipped a Scotch and water that was mostly water and listened to Tracy's plans for the house and for the Fourth of July party.

"Do you really like the house, Johnny?" she asked. They had been on the terrace, but a light summer shower forced them indoors.

"It's a lovely house," he said. "It's what you've always wanted and now you have it. The people on the Cape feel slighted that you didn't build there."

"They never liked me that well on the Cape," Tracy said.

"No, it was Dan they didn't like," the senator said. "Some of them. They thought the Callaways should have waited another hundred years before moving into the White House."

"You still don't want that for yourself? With the Southerners behind you, you could make it. Of course you'd have to get married again."

The senator smiled. "I don't want to get married again, so there goes the White House, I guess. Anyway, I don't want the job. There's no real power, not finally. They can tear you down any time they like. The Senate is safe if you know what you're doing, and I do. I don't want to be a business man and the idea of retirement bores me stiff, so the Senate is where I'll stay as long as the voters will have me."

Tracy laughed. "Don't try that humility business with me, Johnny. I know you too well. You'll stay in the Senate as long as you decide to stay. I don't think the voters have much to say about it."

"Never forget the voters, Trace. A lot of poli-

177

ticians have done that, and where are they now? Gone like the snows of yesteryear. You have to stay in touch all the time. That's how it's done. Never turn on old friends unless they embarrass you in public. Never go back on your word without a very good reason. Politics is like show business, right? Well, a senator is like a good solid character actor, a dependable supporting player. The President, on the other hand, is like a new star, a sort of roman candle, all noise and glitter. Everybody watches the President, waiting to see him fall over his feet, hoping he'll screw up so they can tear him limb from limb. If he falters, then fails, he's out on his ass for good. Like the faded star who spends the rest of his life explaining what went wrong with his career, the failed ex-President writes books. They all do it. But the senator—the sound character actor—keeps on working as long as he's able to walk and talk."

"And you're a good character actor?" Tracy said.

"Pretty good," the senator said. "I think I keep getting better."

A maid came to the door. "Mrs. O'Neal, there's a call for you if you want to take it. A Sarah Bannard. I don't know if a Missus or Miss. She didn't say. It's on line two."

Tracy shook her head, then she changed her mind and said she'd take the call. "I'll take it here," she said.

"Crazy woman," she said to the senator. She pushed a speaker button and said, "How are you, Sarah? I heard you were back for the summer."

Sarah's distinctive voice came from the speaker. "It seemed like a good idea at the time."

"How was your winter?" Tracy winked at the senator.

"We spent most of it in Tangier," Sarah said. "You never saw so many German tourists in your life. Whole planeloads of Germans. It used to be Italy, where the people absolutely loathe them. Now it's North Africa. Next year I think we'll go to Germany. There can't be many Germans left there. Where did you go last winter?"

Tracy winked again. "Stayed home most of the time. New York. A few short trips to catch the sun. Sea Island. Scottsdale. Jamaica is too dangerous these days."

"How true," Sarah said.

Tracy pointed to the speaker and mouthed, *She's been drinking.*

"We must get together for drinks one of these afternoons," Sarah said. "Oh, I almost forgot. Buffy Winship in Palm Beach said to say hello."

"Buffy's a great gal," Tracy said.

"Or something," Sarah said indistinctly.

"What was that?"

"You're right. She's a great gal. Well, I just wanted to call and everything."

"That's very nice of you. And we will get together for drinks. I'll call you."

Sarah said something that might have been anything. Then her voice cleared up and she said, "Bye now."

"I'm ready to swear she said 'Fuck you,' " Tracy said to the senator. "Did it sound like that to you?"

"Not so much the words," the senator said. "But the tone was there. Yes, it might have been that. Who is she?"

"Sarah Bannard. From Atlanta."

The senator showed interest. "Not old Jack Bannard's daughter? Bannard Distilleries?"

"That's the one and one is enough. You know her?"

"Not personally."

"Just as well for you. She's all right, even pleasant, when she isn't drinking. But she's a holy terror when she gets started. I don't know her all that well, but I have heard stories about her."

"That was a pretty guarded conversation," the senator said. "Might I ask if she's coming to your party?"

"I haven't invited her," Tracy said. "Why should I? That's why she was calling. Fishing for an invitation. I don't want her and I don't

180

want her bull dyke friend either."

"Ah yes. I'd forgotten she was like that. Still, you have many friends with unconventional lifestyles."

"Goodness, it isn't that. Why are you so interested, Johnny?"

"Well, for one thing old Jack Bannard was one of Dan's earliest supporters in the South. Not so much money support because that's limited by law. Other support—quiet support—that counted more than money. Old Jack twisted a few arms, called in a few debts political and otherwise."

Tracy said, "Then you think I should invite her?"

The senator shrugged. "Jack Bannard was behind Dan from the start. Maybe he thought having an Irish President would be good for the whiskey business. Whatever his reasons, he came through for Dan, even pressured a few bigshot clergymen when the Catholic issue came up. Besides, there are plenty of Bannards left in Atlanta and a fellow never knows when he's going to need a friend."

Tracy smiled fondly. "You're not so bad at pressuring yourself. But you're right. A debt is a debt even if the man you owe it to is dead."

"It's your party, Trace," the senator said.

"Of course I'll invite her," Tracy said. "I'll call her back in a little while."

"Good girl," the senator said.

181

Sarah Bannard made another bullshot, the strongest so far, and sat in silent rage. Dee, filling out an order form in a L.L. Bean catalogue, knew better than to tease her about the call to Tracy O'Neal, the party that hadn't been mentioned, the invitation that hadn't been tendered.

"Fuck her," Sarah said, breaking her silence.

"Who are you talking about?" Dee asked, pretending to be busy. But she knew that was wrong, so she said, "Oh, you mean her? What do you care about her stupid party? I can't imagine why you even bothered to call her. We'll have our own party on the Fourth and it'll be a lot better than hers. We'll have our own friends over. You're a lot better liked in this town than she is."

"You sound like *Death of a Salesman*," Sarah sneered. " 'He's liked but he's not well liked,' Willy Loman said."

"Why go on about it?" Dee said, dusting off her hands as if dismissing Tracy O'Neal. "It's not worth thinking about."

"I'm thinking about it."

"Then don't."

"I will if I like, you bitch! I'll think about anything I want to think about. Who the hell does she think she is?"

Dee nodded. "That's right."

"Don't agree with me. I hate it when you agree with me and I know you don't."

Dee was beginning to lose her temper. "I only agree with you when you're right and you're right now. Tracy O'Neal is nothing—a nothing—and I'm sick of hearing about her. I told you not to call her and you did and now you're mad at me instead of her. Your family had money before her family even came to this country."

"No snob like a small town snob," Sarah said. "You manage to bring money into every conversation. Anyway, how do you know I wasn't invited? Maybe I was invited and you weren't. Have you ever thought about that?"

Dee threw the mail order catalogue on the floor. "You can go to hell, Sarah! That's what you can do. Here I am trying to be nice and you treat me like the enemy or something."

"Or something. I think I wasn't invited to the party because of you. Look at you. When are you going to go on a diet, for Christ's sake? I'll tell you what I'm going to do with you. I'm going to make you go on a fucking diet. If I had the time I'd go right down to the hardware store and buy a chain and lock for the refrigerator. Cheesecake and chocolate milk! What are you—knocked up? You buy diet soda and put sugar in it."

Dee assumed her martyr's pose. "That's right, Sarah. Take it out on me. That's what I'm

183

here for. That's all I'm good for, so go right ahead."

"I don't need your permission to do anything, old girl. Old fatass girl. You better lay off the Twinkies, kid. Cut back on the calories or I'll put you out to pasture like an old horse."

"You're just a drunken bum. You're such a drunk old bum they wouldn't even let you into AA."

Sarah swigged her enormous drink. "That's all you know, fatass. They loved me in AA. They were crazy about me in AA. In Santa Barbara I was the most popular person in AA."

"You were drunk all the time you were in AA," Dee said. "I had to drive you home, you were so drunk. You started drinking in the meeting and they asked you to leave. Hah!"

Sarah smiled. "Are we having a fight, darling? You know what Maureen O'Hara said to John Wayne? 'You're beautiful when you're angry.' That's what she said."

"You get everything ass backward."

"Not in *my* movie."

Sarah began to sing the old Chiquita Banana advertising jingle. " 'I'm Chiquita Banana and I've come to say . . .' "

She stopped. "I can't remember the rest of it, lover. Help me out, willya?"

"You're drunk," Dee said.

"That a fact now?" Sarah said. "Be a pal. Help me out with the last line. How does it go?

" 'Never never put banan-yas . . .' "

" 'In the ree-fridge-erater,' " Dee sang.

Sarah got up and kissed Dee, who pushed her away. "You're a wonderful person, you know that?" Sarah said. "What I'd ever do without you I don't hardly know. I often think it's wonderful having a wonderful person like you in my house. However, you may not be as wonderful as I think you are. How wonderful are you?"

"I won't dignify that with an answer," Dee said. "For two cents I'd move out of here."

Sarah clapped her hand to her forehead. "Is this the end? The end of everything. Say it isn't so. Divorces are so messy, don't you think? I know what we'll do for the sake of appearances. You go to Juarez if they still do divorces there, and tell the judge I'm queer. Wear a dead cigar into court. The Mexicans'll love that. Say you were tricked into matrimony with a Daughter of Bilitis. You know—a lez. You could very well end up as a centerfold in the *National Enquirer*."

"You're insane, Sarah," Dee said.

"Not a nice thing to say to a person," Sarah decided. "It's one thing to say a person is kooky, spacy, daffy, dippy, dizzy or daft. Off the wall is all right in certain circumstances. But insane is just a tad too strong, and I think you'll agree after you think about it."

"You *are* insane," Dee said.

"Not a bit," Sarah said mildly. "You're just mad because you haven't been invited to Tracy's fabulous party. I love that word 'fabulous,' don't you? Press agents would be dead if it weren't for 'fabulous.' Even small town newspaper columnists use it. Like so. 'Mr. and Mrs. Herman Burkhalter have just installed the most fabulous cesspool at their house in Know Knot Hills.' "

"You're just hurting yourself with all this crazy talk," Dee said.

"Would you deny me my fun? What's the use of having money if you can't have fun?"

"Now who's mentioning money?"

Sarah went down on her knees like Al Jolson. "I 'pologize, honeychile. I'm talking to you with the bee stung lips and frizzy hair. Be a good ol' gal and say you forgive me. I swear I'm going to throw myself off the bluff if you don't."

Dee said, "I don't know why I put up with you!"

Sarah's smile was bright. "For the money, honey. Lawd God, I did it again. Mentioned money."

"You and your Southern nigger shit. You're crazy out of your skull."

"I don't like California trash like you putting down our good Southern colored people. It's all right if I do it when you consider the circumstances of my birth and upbringing."

186

"More shit," Dee said.

"Gawgia On My Mind," Sarah sang in her gravely voice. Her blue spotlight voice, she called it. "I wish I could play the piano like Ray Charles. Remember the old Lenny Bruce joke about Ray Charles and Ray Hibbler bumping into each other during the march in Selma? Or was it Ray Charles and The Five Blind Boys?"

"You're a vicious person, Sarah. Making fun of blind people is a rotten thing to do and you're rotten to be doing it. I'm just telling you for your own good."

"A most puissant observation," Sarah remarked.

Dee eyed her with suspicion. "What the hell does that mean?"

"I like it because it sounds like pussy. It means powerful—trenchant, you silly twat. Didn't they teach you anything at that junior college in Pomona? You still have a Pomona accent, do you know that? You think you sound like Julie Harris, but you sound like Pomona and I wish you'd stop it. What's the use of all these expensive how-to-lose-your-accent teachers if you don't pay attention? Here I am scrubbing floors to send you to a speech teacher and all you do is throw spitballs at the blackboard."

"If you don't stop soon I'm going to go crazy," Dee said. "I swear to God, Sarah, I'll kill you if you don't stop! You're a human devil, a filthy rotten devil of a person. Can't you ever be nice?"

Sarah smiled. "With you, it's hard."

"You miserable bitch!"

"Sticks and stones."

"Corny shit."

"Then how about this?" Sarah said. "Jack and Jill went up the hill to fetch a pail of water. Jack went down and broke his crown, and Jill said—he's liked but he's not well liked."

Delighted with herself, Sarah threw herself on the floor and rolled around laughing.

"Have your fun," Dee said.

"By golly, I ain't had this much fun in a month of Sunday's" Sarah howled. "In a coon's age, in a dog's age I ain't had this much fun. I ain't had this much fun no-place, no-how. I'm like to die if I don't stop laughing!"

"You're like to die, then why don't you?"

"Not yet. Listen to this joke. It's a goodie:

"Italian Gigolo: 'I would die for you, my darling.'

"American Heiress: 'You keep saying that, but you never do it.'"

"Hilarious," Dee said.

"I like to think so," Sarah said, still shaking. "It's all in the manner of telling, don't you think?"

"This whole thing is infantile," Dee yelled, suddenly losing her temper, as Sarah knew she would. "You're acting like a retard. I swear

I'd like to have you committed."

Sarah looked up at her. "You won't get my money that way. You'd love to get me locked up. I'm not sure you won't try to murder me one of these days. How do you plan to do it, bitch? Weed killer in my soup?"

"You'll die soon enough if you keep on drinking a fifth a day. Just because you mix vodka with bouillon won't keep you from getting sick and dying like every other alcoholic. Just don't come crying to me when the doctors give you the bad news."

Sarah said nastily, "When I die everything goes to the Animal League. You won't get a cent. I want to make sure all the nice doggies are provided for."

"You're a liar," Dee shouted. "I've seen your will."

"How do you know I didn't make a second will." You don't know everything I do. You aren't with me every minute of the day."

"I'll sue you," Dee warned, white-faced with anger. "Times have changed, or haven't you heard? These days you can't just throw a person away. So don't think you're going to get rid of me that easily!"

"You're going to hire Lee Marvin's girlfriend's lawyer, is that it? That wouldn't work and you know it. You sue me and I'll sue you back. Don't think I don't know you've been taking kickbacks from travel agents. A few hundred here, a few hundred there. It adds up, my fine foxy friend."

Dee took a step closer to outright violence. "That's a damned lie! I've always been honest with you and all you do is make my life miserable. I can't help it if that bitch didn't invite you to her party. Why take it out on me?"

Sarah smiled pleasantly. "Because you're *here*, darling."

The telephone rang and Sarah answered it. "Why yes, Tracy," she said. "Oh, that's all right. I know you must have a million things on your mind. Of course we'll come to your party and later in the season we must give a party for you . . . Dee is fine. We're looking forward to seeing your house. Thanks for calling."

Sarah looked at Dee. "What do you think of that, smartass?"

Linwood Duval, back from the beach, was going good.

Still wearing the North African *jhabala*, conical Vietnamese hat and woven grass sandals, he said, "I don't know why I'm so modest, my dears. Nobody else is. And it's not because I'm ashamed of my pleasingly plump bod."

Tracy smiled. "Did they stare at you, Linny?"

"No. They thought I was Bo Derek, that

pneumatic little piglet, and wanted to show how sophisticated they were by *not* staring. They might have stared if I'd brought along a Victorian bathing box."

Duval inhaled rather than drank his gin and tonic.

"I can get a carpenter to run one off for you," Tracy said.

Duval sighed. "Don't bother, Trace. It wouldn't do any good. The world is getting harder to shock all the time."

Tracy said sweetly, "Poor Linny."

"Oh well, it's their loss," Duval said. "The world is full of *real* freaks and I'm just a *fake* freak. William Buckley thinks he's just a fake freak, but he's real freak. All the freaks in the world: Maggie Thatcher, Deborah Harry, Ed Koch, Dustin Hoffman—how can I compete? Did you know that some producer once called Dustin the luckiest Jewish midget in the world? And then there's our friend Ormond Bailey over yonder."

Looking up from the book he was reading, *Death in the Afternoon,* Ormond Bailey said, "You want a knuckle sandwich, Duval? Watch it or you'll get five in the snot-locker."

Bailey returned to Hemingway.

"Don't be such a big bully," Duval said. "What was I talking about? Yes. Freaks. A phony freak like me can't hold a candle to the real thing. Take Nixon—pul-*eeze*. I know for a fact that he wears a tie with his pajamas. Dick is so formal-freaky that he makes even his wife call him 'Mr. President.' Even when they're *doing it* once a month, Pat has to shudder and gasp and cry out: 'Oh, Jesus! I'm coming Mr. President.' He used to claim to be Irish, but now that Reagan is in, he claims he was misquoted. How come you ain't laughing, Ormond?"

" 'Cause it ain't funny," Bailey said.

Duval went on. "People say Reagan is a freak president, but I don't think so. Years ago I saw him in *Storm Warning* with Ginger Rogers and I knew he was presidential material. I could see right away that he was a take-charge guy. It was a Down South flicker, in the summer with everybody saying how hot it was—you get tense when it's hot—and there were all these Kluxers all camped up in their sheets (no brand names, please) and they were threatening to do something pretty rotten to Ginger's baby sister who had seen them doing a number on some pore Nigra man. Well now, this sister was married to Steve Cochran, a gorgeous beast of a man, if you recall how blue-jowled he was, and old Steve was a Kluxer himself so he's torn between love and duty. Then along comes Ron—he's the DA—and he says, 'This ain't right, this ain't fair. Under such unacceptable conditions there ain't nothing for me to do but push the kibosh on the Klan.' Which is what he did. He was married to Jane Wyman at the time, so you know what I mean."

"You seem to like Mr. Reagan," Tracy said.

"Deed I do," Duval said. "I like Nancy too. Nancy's a fine woman. So Pasadena. Very controlled. Did you see that newspaper picture of her being kissed by Sinatra at the Inauguration? Frank was giving her a *smeck,* but did you notice she was holding onto Ron's hand while he was doing it? Nancy likes Frank but he's a little too hot-blooded for her Newport Beach taste."

Ormond Bailey said, "Whoa there, Duval! A minute ago you said she was 'So Pasadena.' Now it's Newport Beach. Make up your mind— which is it?"

Duval sighed breathily. "Yes, Ormond, there *is* a difference but it's so slight you'd need a slide-rule to measure it. The old families in Pasadena don't like air-conditioning. That's the only difference I can think of."

"Bullshit," Ormond Bailey said.

"What about Mrs. Reagan and Mr. Sinatra?" Tracy said to Duval.

Duval said, "It's like I said. Nancy likes Frank all right and she'd like him a lot better if he stopped chewing Sen-Sen. Nancy knows Frank put them in the White House—if you can't either of you be a super-moviestar then why not the next best thing? You better believe she's one tough lady when she has to be. She proved that when she told Ron there was no way she'd let Frank re-name Pennsylvania Avenue in honor of Lucky Luciano. Frank was a mite peeved about that, but he's still tight with De Fustest Massa an' Missy. Frank has access to the White House any time of night or day—preferably night—provided he uses the back door. There's always a plate of spaghetti and meat balls on the back burner should Ol' Blue Eyes come a-calling. On Fridays, just in case, Nancy leaves fish cakes, now that Frank is a legit Catholic and buddy-buddy with the Pope."

Ormond Bailey's ancient New School liberalism came floating to the surface. "All these racial slurs, Deval. What do *you* eat?"

"Not you, Ormond," Duval said.

Ormond Bailey pointed. "Mississippi's that way, Duval."

"Well curse me an' curse my cat," Duval said. "Do I detect regional prejudice in that remark? Just because us Rebels lost the War's no reason to be down on us all the time! A barefoot lad like Nixon, I come to the big city with my little sheaf of writings under my arm. Oh, I never baked pies at four in the morning in Whittier, like Nixon, but fate has not been unkind to me. Hey, did you hear that Nixon just placed an order for fifteen suits from a London tailor and couldn't get it filled because the tailor refused to make an extra pair of pants with

194

every suit? That kinda stuff's gone out even in Brooklyn. Isn't that right, Ormond? Huffy! Huffy! Actually, Nixon's become quite sophisticated since he moved to New York for the second time. His musical taste has changed too. Nowadays when you lift his toilet seat it plays 'My Sweet Gypsy Rose'."

Duval continued with, "Ronald Reagan thinks El Salvador is a brand of coffee. And, boy, does he get mad when somebody interferes with his coffee! Actually, Ron isn't all that old when you think of the recent advances in science, and I see no reason why he shouldn't serve out a full second term if Warren Beatty would just stop bothering Nancy for a date. Oh, I know that rascal sure enough. 'Come take tea with me at the Plaza, what could be more innocent than that,' sez he? The Secret Service has warned him away and you'd think he'd give it over—just you don't count on it. Look at the way he swept Mary Tyler Moore off her teeth."

Once again Ormond Bailey looked up from his book. "You got a garbage mouth, Duval," Bailey snarled, doubling his hairy fists and sending out hard lefts in Duval's direction.

He started toward Duval but Tracy intervened, pushing him back gently into his chair. She picked up *Death in the Afternoon*, which had fallen to the floor, and after Bailey took it from her, she stroked his matted grey hair.

195

"Pay no attention to him, Ormond," she said. "Linny is carrying on because no one noticed him at the beach. What about you, Ormond? Did *you* have a good time at the beach? Tell me."

"I came close to decking a lifeguard," Bailey said, basking in the warmth of her interest. "Yeah sure, I had a pretty good time."

Duval cut in. "That's a barefaced lie, Trace. That was no lifeguard, that was his kid brother. Old Ormond changed his mind quick enough when the real lifeguard showed up. That's why we had to leave. The real lifeguard said he'd kick his ass up between his shoulders if he bothered the kid again. My! Such a lifeguard! Big as Big Foot. I had a chat with him while Ormond was lumbering back to the car. It turns out that he's no ordinary lifeguard but is Moose McGonigal, light heavyweight of the New England College League."

"Amateur night," Bailey said.

"Then why didn't you 'deck him,' as you say?" Duval said, winking all round.

Bailey opened and closed his hands and his smile was modest. "I didn't want the kid to look bad," he said. "How would it look if a guy my age decked a guy his age? He'd be through with the broads if I did that."

"At least you could have kicked sand in his face like in the old Charles Atlas ads," Duval said. "Or was it the other way round?"

196

Tracy pushed Bailey back into his chair and told him to behave himself. "You too, Linny," she said in gentle warning.

"Mercy me!" Duval said. "Everybody's ganging up on me. Seriously, Trace, you should have come to the beach. It was worth the price of admission, as they say—the parking fee. You should have seen all the French-Canadians. All the French-Canadian women wear pastel swim-suits—peach must be in this year, my God!—and all the French-Canadian men stick their cigarette packs inside the elastic, do you follow me? L & M, Camels, Lucky Strike Goes to War! Woooeee!"

"Calm yourself, Linny," Tracy said, smiling at his antics.

Lafe Tatum came in, sweating. "What's going on, Trace? Sounds like Linny's calling the hogs."

Duval made a face. "Hello, *you*," he said. "But you should have seen them, Trace. You can tell they're French-Canadians even if they don't say a word."

"How is that, Linny?"

"All their kids have little metal detectors like they sell on the second floor at Schwartz. Well listen, it pays for itself, doesn't it? A quarter here, a quarter there. A lost earring. Whatever they find helps to defray the cost of their American vacation. The French-Canadians are stingier than the real French. Four hundred years in Canada and they're still saving string. They do speak a kind of French, I suppose, but with that frightful clanging accent."

"Clanging?" Tracy seemed puzzled. "What a curious way to describe it."

"The only way," Duval said. "I've always wondered why the Canadian French never have produced anything. Art. Music. Literature. All strangers to them. So very much like the Welsh in that respect."

"The Welsh produced Richard Burton," Tracy chided him.

"Yes, they are guilty of that. The voice that walks like a man—Old Mister Cathedral Tones, Mr. Coal Miner's Daughter. Dickie Jenkins is his real name, did you know that, Trace? Well it's true. Trivia, trivia. The point here is: can trivia ever be pertinent? A contradiction, I suppose. However, Dickie Jenkins Burton would be down in a coal mine singing 'Men of Harlech' if not for the grace of God. He'd be scoffing fish and chips three times a day and glad to get it and at night his big thrill would be throwing darts at the local. No wonder everyone hates the Welsh. Evelyn Waugh hated them, said all they do is blow through shiny instruments—and SING! At this point in time I'm reminded of the old joke in something Brendan Behan wrote. See, there's this old literary sort of creep sitting by a peat fire over in Ireland and some bloody English tourist brings up Evelyn Waugh and the old creep sucks-on his bottle of stout and ruminates (that's the word):

" 'A hell of a nice girl, that Evelyn War,' is what the old creep says."

Duval was delighted with himself; it was clear that he hated Eddie Fisher's ex-wife's ex-husband. Duval sneered, "All Burton's American movies (never say 'film,' it's vulgar) were flops. And while we're at it, never say 'perhaps' instead of 'maybe.' "

Ormond Bailey was angry again. "What is this, a fucking lesson, Duval? Where is it written, you asshole?"

Duval said, "The best thing Burton ever did was when he played Rommel in *The Desert Fox*."

"Surely that was James Mason," Tracy said. "Yes, I'm sure it was."

"More trivia," Duval said. "Okay, it was James Mason, and I'm pretty sure he must be Welsh too, by the looks of him. Mason made a whole movie career out of beating women with canes before they brought him over here. Now he's in his dotage and they call that great character playing. I don't like him either."

Lafe Tatum asked, "What *do* you like, Linny?"

"I like *B.J. and The Bear*," Duval said. "And don't ask me if I like Maine. I might if I could speak the language, but I can't. I'll tell you

199

other things I like: those portraits of Colonel Sanders they used to have. I stole one in some town near Slippery Rock College where I was lecturing at the time. I like Robert Morley's awful striped shirts and Julie Christie's plebeian good looks and Robert Montgomery when he was playing Danny in *Night Must Fall.* I love lamb kidneys and laughter."

Linwood Duval began to cry. Tears fell into his gin and tonic.

"Next week *East Lynne,*" Baily sneered.

"Shut up, you bitch," Duval said. "All the time wanting to 'deck' guys. But we know what you really want to do, don't we? All you *macho* men give me a pain."

"Please, boys," Tracy scolded them. "This whole thing has gone too far. If you can't get along, why don't you stay away from each other? Actually, I happen to know you're the best of friends."

"Like hell," Bailey growled, inspecting the back of his hairy hands.

"I wouldn't be caught dead in the same plastic clothes bag," Duval insisted. His crying jag was past and he grinned maliciously at Bailey. "That was a nice cry," he said. "Turn on the waterworks now and then and you take off the pressure. Some of the toughest guys in the world cry like babies. If you don't believe me, you should go to a Mafia funeral. The guys that cry the loudest are the guys that killed

200

the guy in the coffin."

Duval stopped talking when the senator came in after a walk on Tracy's strip of private beach. "Hello everybody," the senator said. He didn't know Lafe Tatum. Tracy introduced them and they shook hands.

"Lafe decorated the house," Tracy explained.

"A fine job," the senator said. "Speaking of houses, Trace, that's a pretty beat-up place down by the point. Did that come with the property? If it did I don't see why you leave it standing."

"It's a wreck, isn't it?" Tracy said. "No, I don't own it, but I'm trying to buy it. An old fisherman lived there, but he died. Now the heirs—his sisters—are asking one hundred-thousand for the house and land. That's much too high, of course."

The senator whistled. "A hundred-thousand for that place. Ridiculous! Don't pay it."

"Naturally I won't. It's a nice piece of land, but I can't see that it's worth more than thirty-five. I suppose I'll go to forty-five, even fifty if there's no other way to get it. Thirty-five is what I offered to the real estate man, Gately. *He* says a motel developer has offered eighty, but I'm inclined to doubt it. But I don't want to see a motel every time I look out the window. That would be ghastly."

"Ghastly is right," the senator agreed,

though "ghastly" wasn't a word he used. "You'll have people walking all over your property if a motel goes in there. You could always build a high cedar fence."

"Oh no," Tracy exclaimed. "I don't want to feel like a prisoner. There's still a chance I'll get it at a reasonable price. The real estate man is going to call the heirs and then get back to me."

"What sort of man is he, this Gately?" the senator asked.

"The bluff and burly type," Tracy answered. "I suppose he's nice enough. You met him, Tatey? What did you think of him?"

"I didn't like him," Lafe Tatum said.

"Don't be unkind," Tracy said. "I think he's nice in his own way. At least he says he's going to try. Wouldn't it be wonderful if I got it for thirty-five?"

"Then you could give another party and burn the old house at midnight," Duval said. "What a lark that would be!"

"You have the craziest ideas, Linny," Tracy said.

Still smiling, she took the senator aside and whispered, "Can you find out how much the motel man really offered to Gately? That's Leonard Gately Real Estate, Yorkport. I know you have ways of doing things. I'd like to know today."

"I have ways of doing things," the senator

said, and they both smiled and rejoined the
others.

CHAPTER TWELVE

The next morning Leonard Gately was in his office when Elly Fisk knocked on his door and came in without waiting for an answer. He had been studying the pictures in the latest *Playboy*. Now he tossed the magazine in a drawer and slammed it shut.

"What goes on?" he said irritably. "Has your wastebasket caught on fire?"

Elly was a small, bright woman and she spoke with a pronounced Maine twang. "She's here," she said. "Mrs. O'Neal is outside. She says she just dropped in on the chance of seeing you. Isn't she something, though?" I never saw her but one time on TV. Gorman and Bass are never going to believe this."

"The hell with Gorman and Bass," Gately said. "Get a hold of yourself and show her in. Don't get so excited. She's just a human being like the rest of us."

Tracy came in and Elly Fisk closed the door; Gately knew she had her ear to it. Gately stood up and they nodded. "Nice to see you, Mrs. O'Neal," Gately said.

Tracy sat down, smiling. "I hope you're not too busy. I didn't mean to barge in on you, but I was in the village and took a chance."

"No trouble at all," Gately said. "I'm glad you picked this time to call. I don't keep what you'd call regular hours. I guess you're here about the Hazlitt property?"

"Yes, I am, and please call me Tracy. I don't want to pressure you, but have you talked to the heirs? I'm deathly afraid of that man and his motel."

Gately spoke carefully, sorting out his thoughts. The motel builder's offer was firm at forty thousand, though there was a small chance of pushing him up to fifty if he wanted the property badly enough. Why was this rich bitch so skinflint, with all the money she had? Still, just being able to tell people that he was a friend of hers might be more valuable than money. As a public relations dodge, it could hardly be bettered.

"I called the heirs, but they were away for the day," he lied. "They'll be back this afternoon and they'll call me back. I still think your offer of thirty-five is a bit low. Anyway, I'm afraid that's how they'll see it. Could you go to fifty?"

"Oh no, Tracy said. "My accountants would never permit it. But it will be a disaster for me if they build that motel. I wish there was something that could be done."

"I'll do my best for you," Gately said. "That I promise you." He looked at the wall clock; it was nearly noon. "By the way . . . Tracy . . . have you had lunch? I had a light breakfast and was just about to go over to the Cap'n's Shanty. That's a very good seafood place right here in town."

Tracy smiled. "I think that would be very nice. Do they have steamed clams? I haven't had steamed clams in the State of Maine."

"And they have good Canadian beer, ice cold, Molson's and O'Keefe's. They have German beer too, if you like that."

"I think I'd like to try the Canadian."

"I better warn you it's rough and ready over there, but you can't beat the food. People come from all over for the lobsters and clams."

"I like simple places," Tracy said. "Some of the best places in New York are little restaurants most people never heard of. Shall we go then?"

"You bet," Gately said. It was true that he had been planning to go to the Cap'n's Shanty, but the "light breakfast" part was a lie. In fact, he had eaten two big steaks and drunk three bottles of beer before he left the house that morning.

The black driver Ralph was standing by the Rolls in the parking space. Tracy told him to get a cup of coffee if he liked. Gately thought he looked like a snotty son of a bitch. The seafood place was closer to the beach than it was to the town; they were able to walk there in five minutes.

"It's got a very interesting history," Gately said, very much aware of the stares that followed them. "In the old days it was a boathouse, then when Cap'n Jack bought it he built onto it and has been building on ever since. But he didn't change the inside all that much. On weekends he has to turn people away, there's that much business. I'd like you to meet Cap'n, a real character."

"I'm sure he is," Tracy said.

On the way they met Colonel Mike Burns coming the other way. Instead fo his usual brisk military greeting he gave a slight nod and went on without stopping.

"That's Colonel Burns, a good friend of mine," Gately explained. "Served in World War II and Korea. Fine man."

Gately thought: Mike looks like he's got a bee up his ass. What the hell am I supposed to do? Turn down a sale because Mike doesn't like somebody? At least the old bastard could have done more than nod.

"You seem to know everybody," Tracy said.

"Well, I've been here a long time," Gately said modestly. "I know everybody and everybody knows me. That's the real estate business for you. I like this old town."

"I can tell that. My, isn't that sun hot?"

"We'll sit out on the deck where it's cool. There's sure to be a breeze off the water."

I'm looking forward to that cold Canadian beer," Tracy said.

There were a fair number of cars in the parking lot, but Gately was glad the place wasn't too crowded. Stares still followed them. It's like walking with a famous movie star, Gately thought. Better. Few movie stars got this kind of attention. He wished Darryl could see him now.

To get to the deck, built on pilings, they had to pass through the restaurant. The restaurant was low-roofed and there were rough tables and benches, fishnet and green glass floats on the walls; instead of ashtrays there were the bottom halves of old rum bottles. Against one wall stood a big tank for lobsters with a warning to tourists to keep their hands out of it. Clams in net bags steamed in big pots behind a wooden counter; the orders were called out by number as soon as they were ready.

"Clams on fifty-seven," was being announced when they went in.

Cap'n Jack Smiler, standing by the cash register, greeted them with a smile that was more for Tracy than for Gately. A rangy man dressed in faded denims, Cap'n Jack wore an old captain's hat with rusty gold trim, and he said in salty tones that were too good to be true, "Good day to you. It's a fine day all right. How are things, Lenny?"

"Couldn't be better," Gately said. "Jack, I'd like you to meet Mrs. O'Neal. Mrs. O'Neal just finished that big house down by Hard Luck Bay."

Cap'n Jack touched a forefinger to the peak of his cap. "Honored and delighted, ma'am. I know the place well. Many's the time I pulled lobster traps off there. What will you be having, Lenny?"

Gately said, "I've been telling Mrs. O'Neal about your famous steamed clams. No better in the whole state, I told her. Can you steam up two batches and we'll have them out on the deck? And two O'Keefe's beers right off the ice."

Cap'n Jack didn't like Gately. "That's where all my beer is, Lenny. Your order will be number sixty-eight. A pleasure to meet you, Mrs. O'Neal, and good luck in your new house."

"Thank you, Cap'n Jack," Tracy said.

Gately carried the two beers to the deck and

they drank them while the clams were being prepared. There was a sea breeze, as Gately had promised, and it ruffled the surface of the water. Everything smelled of salt. The tourists stared openly and the boys who worked for Cap'n Jack came out to the deck more than they had to.

"It's lovely here," Tracy said, drinking delicately from the moisture-beaded bottle. Cap'n Jack did not provide glasses. "Such a sweet place and Cap'n Jack is so friendly."

"Years ago seals used to swim right under this deck," Gately said. "They'd swim around and bark. They're all gone now, hunted out of existence."

"That's sad."

Gately had convinced himself that he cared about the vanished seals. "Yes, it is sad. This town is getting too big." The bigger the town, the more money in his pocket, but he said it anyway because he knew she'd like it. All these newcomers wanted to stop progress.

But as he drank his beer, drinking it rather than guzzling it, he thought: I'm having a kind of lunch date with the richest woman in the God damned world! The whole world is sucking up to her, but she's having lunch with me. Me, Leonard Gately, that didn't have a pot to piss in when I got out of the service! No matter what they said about her, and they said plenty, she was all right. The hell with Mike Burns. If he wanted to act like a jerk, that was his business.

The clams were ready and Gately went to get them. Tracy had most of her beer left and she said that would be enough. Gately, feeling a twinge of last night's hangover, got another cold one for himself. He went back to get a handful of paper napkins.

Tracy was picking at her first clam with a plastic fork when Gately said, "Excuse me. The best way to do it is to leave the clam in the shell and use the shell to scoop the drawn butter. Watch me do it."

Gately demonstrated the right way to eat a steamed clam. "You use the clam shell like a spoon," he said. The tourists continued to gawk. There were a few local people there, too, and Gately knew all of them. It was a wild scene all right.

Tracy tried it Gately's way and smiled. "I think I'll get the hang of it. You're right about the clams. They're so good. I must say all this is very pleasant. They have places something like this on Long Island, but they don't quite make it. What's missing, I suppose is Maine. I'm glad I decided to build here. I do hope you'll be able to talk some sense to the owners."

Tracy's eyes always grew wistful when she talked about money.

"I'll give it a try," Gately said. "I was just

thinking. Could you go as high as forty thousand? I don't say they'll take forty, but I'd feel better if I could say forty."

Gately thought: Screw the motel builder. If she agrees to forty, then I'll take it. Fifty would be more like it, but he had the feeling that she was going to tough it out. These really wealthy people sure knew how to hang onto their money. But she was right. The only thing that bothered him was why she hadn't said anything about the party. Here she was asking for favors and. . . .

"I don't think I can go higher than thirty-seven thousand, five hundred dollars," Tracy said after thinking about it. "I think my accountants would permit that. But that has to be the limit, I'm afraid."

Gately thought: She's asking me to give up the commission on twenty-five hundred dollars. On the other hand, it wasn't that much—but why hadn't she invited him to the party? If a dummy like Bruce Whipple had been invited. . . .

"Oh, Leonard," Tracy said. "We've been talking business so much I forgot to mention a little housewarming party I'm giving on the Fourth. I've been so preoccupied, it went clear out of my head. I'd like you to come if you can. People from New York are coming; some local people will be there too. I'm sorry I left it so late. Perhaps you have other plans

212

for the evening."

"Nothing that can't be changed," Gately. said. His only plan for the Fourth was the usual one: to get drunk. Every year, wearing his old dress uniform, he marched in the small parade put on by local veterans' organizations, and there were several bands—the best was from Yorkport High School—but this time he decided to give it a miss. This year he would be an onlooker; somehow he didn't think it was dignified for a friend of Tracy O'Neal's to be seen marching with a lot of kids and old men.

For years Gately had presented the most martial figure in the Fourth of July parade; with his burly body, his medals, his fierce blue eyes and slight limp, he looked every inch the warrior back from the wars. Now, for the first time, he caught a quick glimpse of himself as faintly ridiculous, so strong was her influence upon him.

"Then it's settled, you'll come to the party," Tracy said firmly. Then she told him about the catering problem that had come up and how Sandor Antonescu had helped her solve it by suggesting Lacey Putnam.

"Do you think he'll be all right?" she asked with anxious eyes.

"He knows his business," Gately said, thinking that of all the fags in town Putnam was the one he hated most. Another snotty, wiseguy

213

son of a bitch. Gately hated all quick-witted people except Darryl. Where the hell *was* Darryl? He had a mental flash of Darryl coming in to Cap'n Jack's to order maybe a lobster roll, then taking it out to the deck—and then he'd see them together, dipping clams, drinking beer straight from the bottle like old college friends. . . .

Gately was curious to know the name of the other local people who were coming to the party, but there was no tactful way to ask about it, and even to hint would be bad manners. He had no way of knowing about Sarah and Dee, Greg and Carol Delaney. Sandor Antonescu would be there; the way she spoke about him was enough to verify that. It figured that she knew him from New York. Antonescu was a weirdo, but he was a very rich weirdo, so the invitation made sense. Bruce Whipple was the one that bothered him; somehow inviting that idiot took away from his own invitation. Not only was Bruce just a kid, a not very bright kid, he had no connections of any kind. His father, who had a small one-man aluminum siding business, was just as big an idiot. Gately guessed she knew Bruce from the supermarket—how else could she know him?—and it still didn't make any sense. If Bruce tried to talk to him at the party he would give him the cold shoulder; he didn't want to be associated with an assistant supermarket manager. Afer all, he was a realtor and that was as much a profession as a doctor or a lawyer or an engineer. He had a postion in the community and Bruce Whipple did not. It would be okay to say a few words to the kid—the successful man exchanging nods with a store clerk—but that was as far as he would allow it to go. Not for a moment did he want people to regard them as social equals.

The names of some of Tracy's New York friends were well known to him through the gossip columns. During the summer season the Yorkport drugstores and the store at the beach got all the New York, Boston and Montreal newspapers. The Montreal newspapers were in French since French-Canadians were an important element in Yorkport's tourism; they came south to Maine because Canada's east coast waters were too cold to swim in even on the hottest day of summer.

So Gately read all the columns in the English language papers; he knew about Linwood Duval, Ormond Bailey; other writers, artists, dancers, politicians, dress designers, and poets. All important people in their way.

Bruce Whipple, for Christ's sake!

Gately said, "It's going to be a struggle, but maybe I can get you the house for thirty-seven, five. The reason I say that is this. The two sisters, the heirs, own some more lots and houses that won't be easy to sell because

215

they're way back in the woods, miles back on a dirt road they don't plow too hard in winter. But I can move the lots and houses for them if I put my mind to it. Let's just wait a few hours and we'll see what they have to say. I have a feeling they're going to say yes."

"That's wonderful news, Leonard. Will there be problems with your motel man?"

Gately said, "No problem. He just made an offer. There was no down payment, no binder. You're probably wondering why I'm ready to pass up his offer of eighty thousand. Well, for one thing, he's short of ready money, from what I hear, and there's talk that several construction companies had to sue him to get their money. That's none of my business, of course—I just sell the properties—but in a way it *is* my business because I'd be linked to him in people's minds. Everyone has enemies and I don't want it said that maybe I'm some kind of silent partner of this man. I intend to stay in this town for the rest of my life. Do you follow my thinking?"

Tracy smiled. "I certainly do, Leonard. I've always heard it said that a good business reputation is better than all the profits in the world. So it seems to be working out quite well for both of us. I'm really grateful to you."

"Not at all," Gately said. "If you get the house, are you going to burn it or tear it down? Naturally burning costs less, but you'll have to get a permit and have a fire truck standing by. The township will bill you, but it's still cheaper than demolition and cartage."

"Then we'll burn the old place," Tracy said. "That would be a fitting end, in a way."

"Or you could sell it and have it moved."

"Oh, really? A house as old as that?"

"You can move almost any house if it isn't too big, isn't falling apart. The old place is solid enough to be moved, all but the chimney. That stays behind. You can use the old bricks to make walks, things like that. Or if you don't want to do that, there's a man near town who'll cart them away for nothing."

"For *nothing?*" Tracy said.

"I doubt that he'll buy an old chimney from you, Gately said. "*He* uses the old bricks where people want a well-used look. When they tore down Scollay Square in Boston he had three trucks hauling bricks that dated back to the 1840's. I know I can sell the house for you—moving a house is cheaper than building one—but the cost of moving is going to bring down the price. There's no way to get away from that. It depends whether they want to move by land or by water."

"By water?"

"By sea. Along this coast they sometimes move houses that way. They put them on things that look like great big barges, then wait for a day when the sea is calm. A few years ago a house got caught in a squall and sank to the bottom of Casco Bay. That's up by Portland. It made all the papers: house lost at sea. But that was a freak thing, and I don't think it ever happened before or after. If it did happen you wouldn't suffer any loss."

"I'm glad to hear that, Leonard." Tracy put her hand on his wrist for a moment; a spontaneous gesture of appreciation. "If the heirs agree to my price I'd like to give you a certified check for the full amount this afternoon. That way they can't change their minds. Can they?"

"Not very easily. In fact, no. Once the check has been accepted—especially a certified check—they'd be open to a lawsuit. You could even sue *me*, I guess. Unless there is some legal impediment—and there isn't, the title is clear—the house is yours once you hand me that check."

"You make it sound so simple, Leonard. Most realtors are so red-tape-ish."

Gately said seriously, "Most realtors aren't me . . . Tracy. There's no need for the red tape and the mumbo-jumbo. Make sure your titles are clear, with no outstanding tax debt, be certain you have the owner's authorization in writing, and that's all you need. That's the way business used to be conducted when this country wasn't strangled by state and government regulations."

"I've heard that said," Tracy stated cautiously; her first husband, President Callaway, had been a vigorous proponent of centralized government with all its regulatory agencies.

Gately climbed down hastily from his soapbox. "Times change," he said with less passion. "I take it you want the house sold and moved as soon as possible? I can arrange everything in that line."

Tracy had finished all her clams, but not all her beer. Now she smiled at Gately and dabbed at her lips with a paper napkin. "I don't know when I've enjoyed lunch more than today. Shall we be getting back then? I know you have things to do."

"Will you be at home later in the day? Gately asked.

"All day," Tracy said. "You'll call me?"

"Soon as I have positive word."

"Let's hope it's a happy word. Now I'll go to the bank and arrange for the check. Thanks again for the lovely lunch."

"Any time," Leonard Gately said.

"The builder offered Gately forty thousand," the senator said when Tracy found him sitting on a rock down by the beach. He was wearing chinos, a Lacoste shirt, old loafers without socks. "My people didn't have much trouble finding out. The builder's in a financial hole because his last project failed. Recently he's

219

been trying to borrow the forty thousand and is having trouble. Gately lied, but that's hardly unusual in his business."

Tracy's smile was triumphant. "I think I have it for thirty-seven thousand five hundred. Yes, I'm sure I have. This afternoon Gately is going to call me back and give me the good news. He says he has to call the heirs in Florida, but I don't believe him."

The senator picked up a pebble and threw it in the sea. "I used to love to skim flat stones on the water when I was a kid," he said. "If Gately can jump around with the price, then he must have full authority. The price you named is pretty good. For this part of the coast it's very good. Gately is losing commission on twenty-five hundred dollars."

"And I'm saving twenty-five hundred dollars, Johnny. I would have paid the forty thousand, a little more than that, even.

"What would you have done if the motel guy beat you out of the house? By going way up in the price, I mean?"

"Throw every legal obstacle I could think of in his way that my lawyeres could think of."

"That could cost more than the house," the senator remarked.

"Probably not. The motel man would back off. If he's having trouble raising forty thousand, how could he afford the right kind of lawyers?"

"You're right," the senator agreed. "You went to Gately's office and talked him into it? Is that it?"

"I went to his office and then we went to lunch at a seafood place at the beach. We had steamed clams and Canadian beer. He's rather a strange man—there's some sensitivity there—but most of the time he speaks in a business jargon. He talked about the seals that used to swim under the deck at the restaurant."

The senator's interest in seals was zero. "Did you invite him to the party? Sure you did. When did that happen? After you made the second offer of before?"

"Right after the second offer," Tracy said. "And you musn't think I'm a conniving person, Johnny. I knew Gately wasn't telling the truth, so I used my own methods to combat his. But I'm not a schemer."

"Nobody's judging you, Trace," the senator said, smiling at her. "It's just that you like money a little more than most people. We all have our quirks. That one is yours. So what if you dazzled this Gately fellow? You got what you wanted and saved twenty-five hundred into the bargain. All it took was a lunch and an invitation to a big party where he won't even be noticed."

"That's true," Tracy said.

Leonard Gately sat in his office wondering what kind of broads would be at the party. Did he need to bring a date? He couldn't be sure. The girls that were available just wouldn't do; the party was too important, socially and professionally, to turn up with any old piece of tail. A realist in some things, Gately knew he could have his pick of the girls in town; the reason for that was the party and only the party. They would jump at the chance to go, no matter what they thought of him personally.

Colleen Rizzo at the bank was considered and rejected. Pretty face, nice tits, but still just a bank teller. High school only. No college. Nancy Pickett was a possibility. Mid-thirties. A tall leggy blonde. Ex-American Airlines stewardess. Divorced. Two children. Colby College in Waterville.

But she failed the Gately eligibility test: she had absolutely no brains. Anyway, she drank too much and couldn't hold it. When she had too much she threw up—*barfed*. That's all he would need at Tracy's party.

Delaney's wife Carol would be just right. Her family used to have money, she had graduated from Wellesley, she had published in the *New York Times*. What the hell was the name of that magazine of hers? *Ambush*. But what was the use of thinking about it? He had roughed her up a little and that was the end of it.

Apparently his ex-wife had left town; he didn't want her wherever she was. There was no telling what she'd do if he took her along. The woman wasn't fit to be in decent society. He knew Tracy would greet her politely, but he squirmed at the thought of what must surely come into Tracy's mind.

He glanced at the wall clock and decided to give it another hour before he called her about the house. Mustn't seem too eager. Mustn't look like an ass-kisser.

Finally he decided to give up on the local talent—none of them was right—and go to the party on his own. Bringing a date would be coals to Newcastle, etc. There would be broads there from all over, so what was he worrying about? But he had to buy new clothes; nothing he had was suitable and he'd been putting on weight. More than usual, that is. Dress was to be informal, Tracy said, and that was fine because he felt like a monkey in a monkey suit, though he did own one. He'd need a good, expensive, lightweight summer suit in a size 44. Gately grimaced. Maybe a size 46. It was better to face facts than to come apart at the seams. Never one for dancing, he wondered what kind of band she'd hired for the evening. He hoped it wouldn't be all that disco shit. But what the hell. The house was big and he could wander around and look at the broads. If they asked him what he did he wouldn't just say "realtor," which sounded kind of stuffy and tame. People always thought realtors wore rimless glasses and were Methodists. No, if they asked him what he did, he would say he bought and sold things for profit, hint that he was some kind of business pirate. Women loved money and were less hypocritical about it than men, and they would admire an outright business pirate but look down on a careful realtor. It wasn't that he was ashamed of his profession—he was proud of his success—but to score with a certain kind of broad you had to say the right thing. If not, you struck out before the game started.

God damn that Bruce Whipple, Gately thought. Then he realized that the whole thing might have been a joke on Mike Burns. Mike had little sense of humor; there was a chance that the Whipples, father and son, were putting him on. Or it could be that Bruce was hired to park cars, something like that, and had turned it into a joke on the colonel. It was the kind of dumb stunt Bruce Whipple would pull. Maybe it was time to find out for sure.

Gately looked at the clock and picked up the telephone and dialed Tracy O'Neal's number. A maid answered it and there was about a sixty-second delay before Tracy's breathless voice whispered down the line.

"Is that you, Leonard?"

"Yes . . . Tracy. It's all set. I got the house

for you."

Caleb Brown wasn't glad to see Lester Briggs and the four lobstermen who came into his office, but he had sent for them and now was as good a time as any to get this thing settled if he could. He knew every man there; the only one he didn't like was Lester Briggs, who had a bigger mouth than Joe E. Brown and wasn't half as funny.

Lester had red hair and red hands, a bent nose and a full set of artificial teeth. He was fifty-three and a very rough man for his age. The other men were in their thirties and forties, hard working lobstermen who allowed Lester to do most of their talking. Lester had been captain of the debating team in high school and knew a lot of big words. Everybody in town said all that knowledge was wasted on a lobsterman.

"You wanted to see us, Caleb?" Lester asked with his usual aggressiveness.

"Find chairs, boys." Caleb Brown said. "What I want to talk about is a number of complaints I've . . ."

"Who complained?" Lester cut in.

Caleb brown made a palms down gesture. "Let me finish what I was saying, then you can talk all you want. As to who made these complaints, George Simpson, Garrett Murphy and

Fred Steiner complained, that's who. Simpson runs his own lobster boat with a couple of college kids. Murphy and Steiner are partners in their boat. But you know all that. Simpson reports that some of his kids were roughed up on the dock after dark. It was too dark for them to see who did it, but Simpson says he has a pretty good idea."

Lester stuck out his heavy jaw. "Did the son of a bitch mention my name? If he did I'll sue the shit out of him. Where does that Canuck foreigner get off accusing me of beating up on kids?"

"You were not accused by name," Caleb Brown said patiently. "No one was, so cool down and listen to what I'm saying. Roughing up the kids is just one part of the complaint. Simpson says somebody dumped red paint all over his boat when it was moored for the night. It took him the best part of a day to get it cleaned up."

"That scow of his was badly in need of a coat of paint," Lester said, grinning all over his meaty face. The other lobstermen grinned too.

"Anyway, Simpson's complaints have to do with assault and vandalism," Caleb Brown went on. "But we'll let that go for the moment. Murphy and Steiner's complaint is much more serious. It seems that somebody dropped a concrete block on their boat from the bridge and sent it to the bottom of the harbor."

226

Lester grinned again. "Now who do you suppose did a terrible thing like that?"

"Somebody did," Caleb Brown said. "Sinking a boat is one thing, negligent homicide is another."

Lester's grin faded. "What the hell are you talking about?"

"Murphy was asleep on the boat when it sank. He'd been drinking beer and wanted to sleep it off. Steiner went ashore and left him. Murphy says he woke up when the block ripped out the bottom of the boat. But he was still groggy from the beer and nearly drowned."

Lester stared at the chief. "But he didn't."

"A good thing he didn't," Caleb Brown said. "If he did you'd have state police detectives swarming all over the place. You know how the staties are: They don't leave till they have somebody in handcuffs. I'm not sure what the courts hand out for negligent homicide. Never had a case of it here. But I would think ten years at the very least. I'd hate to spend ten years in the Thomaston jail."

Lester cracked the knuckles of his salt-reddened hands. "Well, for Christ's sake, you don't think we had anything to do with it?"

I'm not going to answer that right away," Caleb Brown said. "I want this business to stop and I'm hoping you men can help me. You're all well-known lobstermen like your fathers

before you and I know you don't like these outsiders coming in and lobstering where they
aren't wanted. On the other hand what they're
doing is legal. I'd have the fishery department
down on them in a flash if it wasn't. Face it:
they have as much right as you have to pull
traps in these waters. I know, I know. Your people have been here for three hundred years
and God knows where these outsiders came
from. But that's neither here nor there. I'm not
talking about how you feel, I'm talking about
the law."

Lester's face got redder. "Fuck the law!" he
said. "Where's the justice when these outsiders can come here and take the bread out of
our mouths? It's not like they need to do what
they're doing. I don't know what Simpson does
the rest of the year, but you know the kind of a
car he drives? A 1981 Corvette. You know how
much a car like that costs? Sure you do. And
the other two, Murphy and Steiner? They're in-
structors at some snazzy girls' college down in
Massachusetts. So why are they screwing
around with a lobster boat? They don't need
the money, that's for sure. What they're doing
may be legal, but it isn't right. I ask you: is it
fair?"

"No it isn't fair," Caleb Brown agreed. "But
the law is the law. There's no getting round
that."

"Then maybe the law should be changed,"

Lester argued.

"Fine with me," Caleb Brown said. "If the law can be changed, which I doubt, then do it by all means. Get up a petition and take it to Augusta. Talk to the governor, talk to the legislature. But this business has to stop, I mean it."

"You still think we had something to do with it?"

"Let me say I think you men could be the means of stopping it. Pass the word along to whoever is causing the trouble. Tell them they're going to be in serious trouble if it doesn't stop. The thing is, there's no way I can stop these men from going over my head right to the state police. That would make every lobsterman look bad, not to mention myself. And I might as well tell you it isn't just the state police I'm worried about. It's the FBI."

Lester frowned. "How did the FBI get into this? They have no jurisdiction in something like this. It has to be interstate for them to come in."

Caleb Brown said, "You ever hear of such a thing as violation of civil rights? If these people call the U.S. Attorney's office you'll see the FBI sooner than you think."

Lester was mad now. "Jesus Christ, this country is getting just like Russia! I thought when Reagan got in it would be different. Instead it's getting worse. All we're trying to do is make an honest living and we have to worry about the fucking FBI. Who the hell built this country anyway? Not these outsiders that are stealing what's ours. These outsiders, these summer people, these tourists come and go but we *live* here. They have nothing to do with us and we have nothing to do with them. When winter comes we'll be out on the sea in the dark while they're off somewhere rolling around in their beds. To them this whole thing is a joke, something to keep them from getting bored. Ah, what's the use! The poor man always gets the dirty end of the stick."

Caleb Brown knew what lobster was selling for. He knew that Lester owned a new ranch-style house worth at least ninety-thousand dollars, maybe more. Probably more. And he bought a new car for cash every year. His wife drove a Japanese sports car and didn't have to work. So Lester was doing better than all right. Caleb Brown said, "All we can hope is that things will get better all round. Anyway, Lester, what do you think? I'm asking for your help as an old friend. Noboby wants the FBI poking around down on the dock."

Lester stood up and so did the others. "We'll see what we can do, Caleb. But I'm telling you this thing is unfair."

"Sure it is, Caleb Brown said. "I couldn't agree with you more. Be seeing you men, and thanks for coming."

They went out and Caleb Brown smiled to himself.

CHAPTER THIRTEEN

The news of Leonard Gately's invitation was spread all over town by Gately himself. For all its many thousands of summer visitors, it was a small town at heart; in the off season its population dwindled to nine hundred permanent residents, sometimes even less than that, and Gately's name and face and figure were more familiar than most. His bulk made him the most visible of men; his loud voice and chrome-laden pick-up truck made him more so; his large boxed ad always appeared on the same page of the *Yorkport Star* and was well known to everyone who read the paper, which was nearly everyone in town.

As if the tourists weren't there, the news of

the invitation was passed around with varying degrees of amusement, disbelief, envy, rage, and indifference. The people at the bank believed it more readily than the rest; they had certified the check for Mrs. O'Neal, and now that she knew about the invitation, Colleen Rizzo developed an interest that hadn't been there before. A pretty, dark haired girl with a worried expression that had nothing to do with her mental processes, she guessed about half the wild stories about Gately must be true, and if only a quarter of the stories were true, that was quite enough. Yet what could happen at a party, she asked herself? She very much wanted to go. It wouldn't do her any good at the bank when it got out that she'd been with Gately, but she didn't care about that. The bank job was a drag as well as low-paying; all she needed was an excuse to quit. Even with Lenny the party would be fun; something to talk about for years to come. There would be problems at home as well as at the bank; her mother would have plenty to say about Gately's doubtful reputation. But he was a well-off businessman, after all, and if he did such bad stuff all the time why didn't they put him in jail? The more she thought about it, the more she found herself defending Gately. These small towns were all the same: once they got down on a person they never stopped.

Colleen Rizzo decided that she sincerely,

positively hated Yorkport. Summer was okay, but the other nine months of the year were the pits. Winter was the worst of all. Daylight came late and dark came early. The two movie houses were closed—no business—and the only places to go were three cocktail lounges with the same dreary faces night after night. In winter people stood around the magazine racks in the two drugstores and read the magazines for free. And late at night the only sound was the clank of the snowplows passing through the town or the swishing noise made by the sand spreader.

I want to go to that party, Colleen Rizzo thought, waiting for the bank to close so she could get cashed up and see if there was any way of bumping into Gately. She didn't want to go to his house except as a last resort. She watched the sweep hand of the clock circling silently and wanted to cry out and startle the rest of the staff, from the manager to the career tellers now bent over the cash drawers in reverent attitudes as the bank closed for the day.

Officer Daley got the story from Joe Gorman, one of Gately's two salesmen, and passed it on to Chief Brown. In summer the Chief worked the night shift because it was quieter, but he liked to walk around the village

233

after eight hours of sleep and a second breakfast. That was what he called the meal; never
lunch.

"Joe Gorman tells me Gately broke down
and gave Mrs. O'Neal a good price," Daley said.
"Even took a loss. That guy from Boston, down
that way, made an offer of forty thousand, but
Gately let Mrs. O'Neal have the property for
twenty-five hundred less. Gorman says not to
let it out or Gately will fire him."

"It won't get out from me," Caleb Brown
said. "I wonder what's got into Gately? He's no
miser, but he does chase the dollar like most
of us. Twenty-five hundred is a lot to pay to go
to a party—a dozen parties. They say that
O'Neal woman is a hard-nosed lady. I used to
think that was just propaganda. Now I'm ready
to believe it, provided this isn't a yarn."

"It's no yarn, Chief. Joe Gorman is a straight
guy and he can't stand Gately."

"Maybe he's a straight guy. But I wouldn't
put it past Gately to put out these rumors."

"Beg to differ with you, Chief," Daley went
on. "Mrs. O'Neal had the check certified at the
National. And listen to this—Gately and Mrs.
O'Neal had lunch at Jack Smiler's earlier today. Steamed clams and beer. They had a long
lunch on the deck, smiling and talking all the
time."

"I'll be damned," Caleb Brown said. "No
wonder the town is buzzing! A woman like that

and a fellow like Gately. Looks like she charmed him into giving her a reduced price. I guess it's worth twenty-five hundred to her, but if I had her kind of money I wouldn't give Gately the time of day."

"You think it's just the money?" Daley asked. "Some of these rich women like their men rough. Gately's pretty rough. Jack Smiler said they were acting real friendly. Said she was playing up to him all the time they were eating."

For some reason Caleb Brown found it hard to swallow Daley's second-hand account of the lunch. "Jack Smiler is a bullshit artist himself. Maybe the woman was just being pleasant, polite."

Daley begged to differ again. "That's not how Jack told it."

Caleb Brown waved his hand. "We'll see how friendly they are after the sale goes through. "Ah, who in hell cares about one more God-damn party? I can't wait for Labor Day to come so all these people will pack up and get away from here. See you later, Steve."

When Caleb Brown got home his wife Katy came into the living room from the kitchen and said there had been a telephone call from Mrs. O'Neal's secretary. "Mary Galligan, she gave her name as," Katy said, still holding the scrap of paper she had used to write the information. "That's the number and she'd like you to call her back when you get the time. Nice voice, a bit snippy."

Caleb Brown took the piece of paper and looked at it. "She say what she wanted?"

"Miss Galligan didn't confide in me, Caleb. It's probably a lost dog or cat, tourists getting too close to the house. You know how these city people are. Call her back, why don't you? That's her own private office number at the house."

"Why didn't she call the police station?"

"She did, but you weren't there so they gave her the home number."

Caleb Brown called the number and Mary Galligan answered it and said, "It's very good of you to return my call so soon . . . No, there's nothing wrong. Perhaps you've heard that Mrs. O'Neal—Tracy O'Neal, President Callaway's widow—is giving a rather large party on the Fourth of July . . . Yes, a housewarming. Why I'm calling is to ask if you can send a couple of your officers to keep an eye on things?"

"You mean to provide security, Miss Galligan?"

"Yes, generally, Chief Brown."

"Excuse me. I thought Mrs. O'Neal was under the protection of the Secret Service. A President's widow."

There was a pause. "Not now, not officially. You see she remarried, as you know, and that changes her protected status. I know it isn't

236

the function of local police to provide protection, but Mrs. O'Neal would take it as a personal favor. Mrs. O'Neal has always lived without private guards and she doesn't want to start now. There will be a lot of cars, a lot of traffic."

This snippy girl wants me to direct traffic, Caleb Brown thought sourly.

"Senator John Callaway will be attending the party," Mary Galligan continued, firing off her big gun.

"In that case I'd better come myself," Caleb Brown decided. There might be a few bucks in it. Forget the money. There was nothing to be gained by getting on the bad side of these people. The Senator probably knew most of the important politicians in the state, including the governor.

"Thank you, Chief. Mrs. O'Neal will be pleased that you're taking such a personal interest."

Caleb Brown went to the kitchen to get a cup of coffee. His wife looked up from the meatloaf she was making for supper. "You heard all that?" he asked her.

"Your end of it, I did."

"Oh sure, I forgot you couldn't hear what she said. President Callaway's brother—the senator—is going to be there. I said I'd go myself. I could send Daley, but then they'd remember him and not me."

"You old fox," his wife said fondly, putting the meatloaf in the oven.

"I don't like any of it," Caleb Brown said. "I like to keep away from these kind of people. Lots of rich people summer here, only they don't attract so much attention."

"It'll strengthen your position in the job," his wife said. "That's what you want, isn't it?"

"All I want is peace and quiet. By the way, did you know that our friend Mr. Leonard Gately has been invited?"

"That crazy man," his wife said, shaking her head. "What must she have been thinking of when she invited him?"

Caleb Brown poured another cup of coffee and sat down at the kitchen table to drink it. "Never mind all that. It's true. I'll be out there showing them empty parking spaces and that cutter will be in there kicking up his heels with the gentry."

"Never you mind," Katy Brown said. "They'll soon get tired of him."

Freddy DiSalvo heard the news from the Yankee manager of the steak house he owned one mile from the north end of the village. It had a fine reputation for steaks and chops; it was called The Red Bull and there was a stampeding bull outlined in red neon with blue smoke jetting from the animal's nostrils. The meat served in The Red Bull was excellent and it was all stolen in the meat district of Boston and trucked to Maine once a week. Ostensibly the owner, the Yankee, Ezra Fuller, was just a hired hand, but a very well paid hired hand. He was an honest man in that he didn't tap the till— he knew better than that—and he got along well with DiSalvo; could even kid him a little. He was doing that in the office of the cinder-block and stained-wood building.

"Listen, Fred," he said in his nasal voice. "How come a bigshot like you ain't been invited to the big doings at the O'Neal place?"

"You're full of shit, Ezzy," DiSalvo said, grinning with his full set of uppers and lowers. His false teeth were so perfect, so expensive, they were slightly crooked, slightly discolored.

Fuller grinned back, happy in his job, pleased that he was on such good terms with the boss. "Maybe the mails are late," he said. "Or maybe you got your invite, but decided not to go."

DiSalvo had been looking at the bank deposits for the first part of the previous week. "Fuck the party," he said. "My age, who wants to go to fucking parties? I leave that shit to rummies—young guys with a bone in their pants. Any city in the country I been to parties in. I don't think about parties these days, Ezzy. A good Italian dinner cooked by me in my own kitchen. That and a few drinks and a few hours of TV and I'm ready for bed. Now and then a piece of ass. What more could a man ask for? You tell me this asshole Gately got an invitation. What's that supposed to mean? Who the fuck cares where the yo-yo goes?"

"You mean you wouldn't go if you was invited, Fred?"

"What do you mean, if I was invited? I ain't been invited. I ain't going to be invited. Why would I be invited? I don't know these people, they don't know me. This thing I got going here, a few other things, are all I want these days. You know what the trouble with most guys is? I'll tell you if you don't know. They don't know when they're well off. They want to be what they ain't. All the time they're trying to push their nose in where people don't want them. That's why I was a success in my old business. I never pushed too hard. My people respected me for that. I made my little pile and got out with no hard feelings. Be yourself. That's how I see it—don't fuck around."

"Yeah, Fred, but would you go?"

DiSalvo, holding out his manicured hands, considered the question while he shook his head at the other man's foolishness. "I guess I'd go. It ain't going to happen, but I guess I'd go. What the fuck? I'm a retired businessman, right? Never been in jail, never been arrested. I'm a good citizen and pay my taxes."

He smiled. "Always pay your taxes, Ezzy.

People pay the federal, then fuck around with the state. Dumb. To get back to your stupid question, the answer is, yeah, I'd go. Might be interesting to see what goes on over there. Now get out there on the floor and keep an eye on the waiters instead of bullshitting in here."

Ezra Fuller paused with his hand on the doorknob. "One last question, Fred."

"Ask it and get your ass out that door."

"What do you think of Tracy O'Neal?"

"I think I could get it up for her," Freddy Di-Salvo said.

Darryl Bates, drinking a chocolate malted and nursing a hangover, heard the news by accident. No one told him because he wasn't really known in the village. A few people knew him by sight; essentially he was a weekender, someone lacking local identity, one of the thousands of people who flocked to Yorkport from the Greater Boston urban sprawl. The ice cream shop was jammed with kids and middle-aged tourists; there were no men of his own age. Darryl Bates cringed at the noise, but he needed to put something nourishing in his stomach to offset the effects of the vodka.

A pretty, dark-haired girl who looked Italian came in and asked one of the boys behind the counter if he'd seen Leonard Gately. "I know he comes in here for coffee," she said.

Bates pricked up his ears.

"Lenny the Moose wasn't in today," the boy said. He raised his voice above the noise of the blenders all going together. "Any of you guys see the Moose today?"

They hadn't.

"You don't have to call him that," the girl said. "I just asked you if you'd seen him."

The boy grinned. "You sticking up for him now, Colleen? That guy is nothing but a Moose's ass."

"So you say," Colleen Rizzo snapped. "If he's what you say, how come Tracy O'Neal invited him to her party? That's right. She drove down and invited him personally. He did her a big favor and so she invited him. She had lunch with him at Jack Smiler's. *You* got left out."

"Oh the shame of it all," the boy said. "I'm going right home, put on The Stones—and slash my wrists. The best favor the Moose could do for this town is get the hell out of it. That guy is a menace to society. What do you want me to tell him if I'm unlucky enough to see him?"

"Nothing," Colleen Rizzo snapped, and went out.

Now hardly aware of the noise, Bates sat thinking about what he had just heard. He wondered what big favor Lenny had done for Tracy O'Neal. Had to be something to do with real estate, naturally. But how often did someone like Tracy O'Neal invite small town brokers to what some newspapers called, with typical exaggeration, the party of the year, the decade, and so on? And to think they had lunch together in full view of the town. It was true that O'Neal hobnobbed with all sorts of people in New York, but they were always arty types, which Lenny was not. O'Neal's real friends were the very rich, the very powerful: investment bankers, museum directors, millionaire painters, millionaire writers like that bastard Duval. Money to money, as people said when one rich person married another. Old Lenny fitted into none of it.

He didn't think the kid named Colleen was making it up. He wondered who she was. A local kid, by the sound of her. Bates knew he had seen her before. On the street, probably. He knew he hadn't seen her with Lenny. She wasn't spectacular, not even outstanding, but he would have remembered if he'd seen her with Lenny. Lenny the Moose. That was something he hadn't heard before, and he doubted if Lenny had. It fitted him like a tight rubber.

It was very, *very* interesting. Bates, the mimic, gave the words a German accent in his head. There was no doubt that Lenny would go to the party, and for all the things he said about O'Neal and her crowd, Lenny must be crowing now. Yorkport had many parties, but Lenny was invited to none, or almost none.

And if invited, seldom invited a second time. Now, after all the snubs, the son of a bitch was in the bigtime. It was a hell of a note.

Hey, Bates thought, maybe I could get in there on Lenny's coattails. At a party like that you might be introduced to *anyone.* The head of a TV network, a movie producer looking for scripts, a famous comedian hungry for new, fresh material. That's how half the business in the world was transacted—at parties. The right kind of parites, not these little bullshit things in beach cottages where half the time you had to bring your own and hardly a person there made over twenty-five thousand a year.

Bates made $400 a week at the radio station. Chickenfeed. He doubted that any of O'Neal's friends, even those on the outer fringe, made less than twenty thousand a week. The real heavy people in her crowd made five times that much.

I'd settle for twenty thousand a week, Bates thought. Naturally his ex-wife would petition for an increase in child support. He knew the bitch would do that. So what? He could afford it. In a way it gave a man status to have to pay so much.

Bates decided that he wasn't simply daydreaming. Anything was possible. Of course a word in the right ear wasn't enough. A guy had to have talent. Well, he had plenty of that. Talent to spare. But it was all in the breaks.

Bates knew he was an ace at writing comedy stuff, yet the scripts he submitted to the TV networks had been rejected with little comment or no comment. It galled him to get a script back in the mail, a script that was infinitely better than any of the feeble shit you saw on the tube. The point was, you had to be an insider, part of the gang. Those on the inside wanted to keep everyone else *out!* Fresh new talent was a threat to their fat salaries, to their own mediocre work.

Jesus Christ, Bates thought. Imagine twenty thousand a week! At least that. And when you were established, a lot more.

Good old Lenny the Moose. The hell with Lenny and his free steaks and vodka and company car. Small potatoes. Now was the time when Lenny could do him some good in a big way. And it had to be now because Lenny wouldn't last long with that crowd.

Could Lenny bring his best friend as a guest? That wasn't usual, he knew. But the opportunity was too good to be passed up because of party etiquette. First he'd have to patch things up with the Moose. He began to wish that he hadn't called Lenny a faggot, but how was he to know that Lenny was going to become so useful? Probably the big bastard didn't remember any of it. That was how he had to proceed: as if Lenny didn't remember a thing.

Darryl Bates smiled his crooked movie star smile. The mocking, cynical one. Lenny might even beg his forgiveness. Ask him to overlook his beastly behavior. Well, it had been beastly. Of course it was. Lenny was a beast.

Darryl Bates smiled again and felt his sore knee. He would rub it in, limp a lot. If that didn't make the Moose feel guilty then nothing would. He was glad that Angela had departed for Boston. He didn't want her around. She was a nerd. No class, really. At a party like that they'd mistake her for one of the help.

That was it, Bates decided. He'd been thinking small for too long. You thought small and you stayed small. Upward and onward. Good old Lenny.

Darryl Bates went out to look for his best friend, or to call him if he didn't find him.

Dawn Brodie knew nothing about Gately's invitation, but the party remained very much on her mind. This was the third time she had brought it up in the course of an afternoon in bed with Danforth.

"Please, darling," she said, playing with the hair on his chest. "It's so important to me. Why haven't you done something about getting us invited? Or *have* you done something and want it to be a surprise?"

Danforth scowled at her. "Look, kid, I'll be

246

opening in the play in a few hours. Can't you talk about something else? Don't forget, you're in it too."

"Just one dinky line," Dawn said. Dawn was stupid, but she knew the hold she had on Danforth. At least for a week.

"One line or not," Danforth said, "it's a start."

Anything to shut her up about the frigging party.

"Not much of a start, darling," Dawn complained.

"You're in the play, you're in the play, darling. I'm a star, right? Julie is a star, right? So you're onstage with two stars. Your name is in the program—that's a credit."

"The bottom line," Dawn said. "Mr. Cameron didn't want to list me at all. I had to persuade him."

Did you now? Danforth thought. In what way did you persuade him? A blow-job?

"You think Tracy will be at the opening tonight?" Dawn asked, brightening at the thought. "That's what rich people usually do, come to play on opening night. If she does, maybe she'll want to congratulate you or something. Then *you* can congratulate her on her new house, then say. . . ."

"And then say, 'I'll crash your party if you don't invite me. I'll come in the back door if they don't let me in the front.' She'd like that, I'm sure."

"That's silly, darling," Dawn said. "That's not what I meant at all. There are ways of doing things."

"Tell me what they are."

"Oh come on, Zachary. You know how these things are done."

"I don't. This isn't Hollywood where half the guests at a party don't know the other half. By that I mean the usual Hollywood party, not the Beverly Hills stuff."

Dawn pulled away to her own side of the bed—a warning. "You know if Mr. Cameron is going?" she asked.

Another warning, Danforth thought.

"How do I know?" Danforth said irritably. "Cameron is a wheel in this town. In lots of places. I guess he knows her from past years. Maybe from New York. He spends the winters there going to shows, pinching asses. Yeah, it's possible he's going."

Dawn had another bright idea. "Why don't you get Mr. Cameron to introduce you to Tracy? What could be more natural than that?"

"I suppose it's possible," Danforth admitted. "But you know Cameron hates actors the way Arabs hate Jews. But maybe, maybe. It depends on how the show goes tonight. If it opens strong he'll be in a good mood. For *him* a good mood."

"He'll be in a good mood, darling. We'll be

wonderful tonight. We'll knock 'em dead," Dawn said, remembering a line from an old show biz movie.

"Just because Cameron introduces me, if he does, is no guarantee of an invitation. Nothing is. Cameron will do as he pleases."

"What's the harm in asking?"

"I hate to ask a favor of him, that's all. It's no big thing to ask for an introduction. From most people it wouldn't be. But you don't know Cameron the way I do. That man stores up favors, then asks for bigger favors in return. He gives you five and expects to get back six. Like a bank."

Dawn knew she was winning by points, so she snuggled up to him again. "Do it for me, darling. I've never asked you for anything before. I'll always think of this as our summer. No matter where fate—our careers—takes us, I'll always remember this wonderful summer. And I hope you'll think the same."

"I'll never forget you, darling," Danforth promised. She was stroking him now. He sighed, wanting to kick her out and wanting her to stay. No fool like an old fool, he thought. He thought of a line from some old play: "When you're getting older, the women you like should be getting older, too."

"I'll ask Cameron," he said. "But that's it. That's as far as I'll go. It's as far as I *can* go."

Dawn blew her breath in his ear. "With me

you can go as far as you like. Would you like me to do something special for you?"

Danforth couldn't think of anything special she hadn't done. The kid had talent, but not for acting. There had been a lot of other Dawns in his life; their faces had dimmed with time. He just hoped this Dawn wouldn't start following him around. Last year a Dawn had done that in Ohio. She even started with the pregnant bit, as if that meant anything nowadays. When that didn't work she tried the under-age routine, and when that fizzled she threatened to nail him for drugs. Finally, after she had tracked him all the way to Michigan, he borrowed five thousand and told her that was it.

After they finished screwing for the third time, Dawn lay with a dreamy look in her eyes. Danforth was exhausted. For a man his age, three times in one day was enough to kill him. He pretended to scratch his chest, but felt his heart instead. It was beating kind of fast, he decided.

Dawn said, "What do you think I should wear to the party, darling? I want to look my best for you. I have some nice things, but I'm not sure any of them is right. What do you think?"

Danforth was feeling his pulse with some apprehension.

"What did you say, darling?"

"You're not listening, Zachary. I was asking you what I should wear to the party?"

250

Danforth gave up. "Something simple, I think. Simple yet sophisticated. True sophistication is always simple."

What the fuck does that mean? he thought. His heart seemed to be slowing down a little.

"You know so much and I know so little," Dawn said. "Simplicity, yes. Do you think I should do something to my hair?"

Danforth knew he would have to pay for it if she did. "Leave it just as it is," he said. "It's your crowning glory. Now why don't we sleep for a little while so we'll be fresh when the curtain goes up?" He knew that Dawn liked any kind of theater talk even if she got some of it wrong. He was truly tired and he thought with faint regret of the things he might have done with his life.

"The show must go on," Dawn murmured as her eyes closed.

Must it? Danforth thought. Why must it?

CHAPTER FOURTEEN

Opening night at the Yorkport Playhouse was the social event of the week. Summer residents who owned their own houses, or people who rented houses for the season, came to see and to be seen. To some the play was the thing; the others didn't care a whole lot what was on. Sophisticated natives and "foreigners" of long residence came, too: college educated motel owners, restaurant operators, art gallery proprietors, lawyers, and accountants. The plain people of Yorkport stayed away, the tourists went to the movies.

Although the sun hadn't set, the Playhouse was ablaze with light; its beautifully landscaped grounds were lighted, too. Manicured lawns, and trees and shrubs not native to Maine, ran from the state highway to the entrance of the theater; beside it was the vast parking lot where college-boy-attendants lined up the cars with well mannered efficiency.

Freddy DiSalvo was easing his Rolls between the white lines when Tracy O'Neal's Rolls pulled in beside it.

Tracy pressed the button that rolled down the sheet of glass that segregated the driver from the passengers. "Honk, Ralph," she said. "You forgot to honk."

Ralph honked. Startled, Freddy DiSalvo honked and responded to Tracy's happy wave. Ralph honked again and Tracy reminded him that one honk was enough.

"We always honk when we see other Rolls Royce people," Tracy explained to Ormond Bailey, who wasn't as familiar with her ways as were Duval and Tatum.

"Like when VW's first came out," Duval added.

They got out of the cars at the same time. Freddy DiSalvo raised his hat.

"I see you belong to the fraternity," Tracy said to the elderly mobster.

DiSalvo didn't get it for a moment. What the fuck was she talking about, whoever she was? He hadn't gone past the sixth grade. "Oh, yeah," he said. "The car. You can't beat it." He

253

patted the hood of his beautiful Rolls.

"Lovely evening, isn't it?" Tracy said.

"Lovely is right," DiSalvo agreed before he went on. At the entrance to the theater he shook hands briefly with Cal Cameron, who had been watching for Tracy's car.

"Trace," Cameron cried, coming out to greet her with both hands in the manner of theater people. "You can't tell me how glad I am to see you!"

They touched faces, pouting dry kisses. Then, holding her hands, Cameron backed off just enough. "Let me look at you," he implored. "You won't mind if an old man tells you how lovely you look?"

Cameron was fifty-six.

"Will you listen to him," Tracy said to Duval.

"I am," Duval said.

"Hello, Linwood," Cameron said without offering to shake hands. He detested the faggot.

"Hello, Calvin," Duval said, knowing that Cameron hated to have his full, his slightly-hick-Protestant name, used. Cameron's mustache twitched with annoyance. He didn't know Bailey or Tatum, but he knew about them. Tatum was a false faggot and Bailey was a good writer and a public clown.

Tracy introduced them.

"Hiya doing, pal?" Bailey said, completely without interest.

Duval said, "Who was that gangster-looking

254

little man, Calvin? A friend of yours?"

"That's right," Cameron said, though he wouldn't have given the answer to anyone else. He'd take DiSalvo—or Hitler—over Duval any day of the week.

"He seemed quite nice," Tracy said. "Who is he, Cal?"

"One of the boys, if you know what I mean," Cameron said. "Used to be. His name is Freddy DiSalvo."

Duval said, "You mean he's a real gangster and not just a clothing manufacturer?"

"Real as real can be, Linwood," Cameron said. "He wouldn't like to hear you calling him a gangster."

"But you said he was," Tracy insisted.

"I didn't use the word, Trace," Cameron reminded her. He had millions, too, and didn't have to kiss ass too hard or too often, not even for *this* one.

"Then he isn't a killer?" Tracy asked.

Cameron said, "Not that I know of. From what I know about him he was sort of courier for The Outfit. That's what they call it in New England. He drove money from here to there, then retired and came here. Freddy's all right in his way, and the town has accepted him, more or less. Shall we go in, Trace? It's ten minutes to curtain time."

After Cameron showed them to their seats, while the playgoers were still whispering at their entrance, Duval said, "I'd like to meet that little Mafioso, Trace."

Tracy smiled indulgently. "Don't you know enough gangsters and criminals by now, Linny? I thought you knew half the gangsters in New York. You've written enough about them."

"But this is different, Trace. The Mafioso I know, when they retire, if they get to retire, go to Arizona or Florida. They don't retire to cutesy little resort towns in Maine. This little man, Cameron says he was a courier for the boys with the silver ties. I've never met a courier before. It sounds so—*respectable*. Invite him to the party, Trace. I want to get to know him better."

"That's silly," Tracy said. "Why are you so silly all the time? Sometimes you're such a baby I think I should put a bib on you."

Duval liked the baby-bib part, not the rest of it. "It's not silly, Trace. In the Twenties it was very fashionable to hang around with gangsters. How often have you read that in old novels?"

No reader, Tracy said firmly, "Never."

"It's true, Trace," Duval said. "It's so true that some smart people even went up to Harlem to hang out with *black* gangsters. The Cotton Club. Small's Paradise. The Savoy Ballroom. The Harlem of Claude McKay and Countee Cullen. *Nigger Heaven* by Carl van

Vechten. High yeller gals with high bony asses."

"Are you drunk, Linny?" Tracy asked, a little disapproving. It was all very well to be silly in private, but after all this was the theater.

"A little drunk, yes I am, Trace," Duval confessed. "Ormond is just as drunk, or drunker. Ormond's always drunker than everybody."

"Ormond's quiet at least. Behave yourself, Linny."

"I will if you invite the little gangster to the party. I sense there's a book in that little feller. I liked the way he patted his car. Pride of possession. And the fact that he drives a Rolls rather than a Lincoln proves he's different. Say you'll do it, Trace."

Tracy shushed him as the curtain was raised.

"We'll talk about it later," she said.

'23 *Skidoo* was a madcap comedy about a hard-up Long Island aristocrat named Schuyler Colfax who becomes a bigtime rum-runner in an effort to recoup the family fortune. (Colfax was played by Zachary Danforth.) His spoiled and beautiful wife Cynthia (Julie Ferguson), a terrible snob, knows nothing of this; she believes all the money is coming from the booming stock market speculations of the period. Starting in 1919, when Prohibition came in, the husband becomes a multi-millionaire by 1923, the year of the title. Now rich enough to retire, to escape from the sordid booze business, he decides to do just that. However, this decision is not to the liking of his bent-nose associates, and he runs into formidable opposition from the beer mob. With his class and his social and political connections, he is above the law. A money-making guy, Schuyler is, and they want him to continue.

So determined are they that they invade his South Shore mansion at the height of the social season and all but take over the place. The presence of these people bewilders his wife, the lovely Cynthia, as well as their society friends. In desperation, knowing that his wife will divorce him if the awful truth comes out, Colfax tells her that all these colorful, menacingly-comic characters are old soldiers who served under him in the Great War. They are down on their luck, he explains, and he feels that it is his duty to help. Placated for the moment, Cynthia agrees to let them become members of the household staff. So Dogface Brannigan serves as butler, Chopper Mike Morelli as assistant gardener, Snow Bird La-Marr as footman, and so on. The big scene—hopefully the funniest—takes place when Coast Guard officers invade a masked ball looking for a big shipment of booze. Somebody pulls the main switch and the lights go out and when they come on again everybody is wearing a mask. . . .

Tracy laughed girlishly, Duval shrilly, Tatum dryly—and Bailey not at all. America's most cantankerous author sat slumped in his seat, eyes closed, face sour.

"Oh my dears!" Duval exclaimed now and then. "It's just too laugh-making!"

Everytime he laughed he clapped his hands; those not annoyed by him were entertained.

Many rows behind, Carol Delaney whispered to her husband, "Linwood is having such a good time. Or he seems to be. Or is he just being nice?"

"I hadn't noticed," Greg Delaney said.

"You wouldn't," Carol said.

Along with being a reporter Greg was the *Star's* theater critic, and as such he got two complimentary tickets for opening night. The second ticket, for his wife, was to ensure that he gave favorable reviews, and so he did, allowing himself only an occasional quibble to save face. But he never panned the stars; to do that would have been to invoke Cameron's wrath, a phone call to the publisher and another phone call from the publisher to the editor. Therefore, Greg's mildly acid comments were reserved for unfortunate supporting

259

players selected at random. Cameron agreed to *that,* however reluctantly; to do otherwise could lay him open, in theater circles, to charges of running a "company town."

"Imagine seeing Linwood Duval and Ormond Bailey together," Carol whispered to Greg. "There they are—imagine! You always see them bickering on talk shows."

"Will you be quiet, please?" a voice said. It sounded like a woman, but it might have been a treble-voiced old man. Greg Delaney could have kissed both of them. He didn't pay much attention to '23 *Skidoo.* He didn't have to: a synopsis had been sent to his home weeks before so that his review would not in any way be rushed. Cal Cameron liked to do things right.

Well, it's a living, Greg thought, and what difference did it make what he wrote? It wasn't *Hedda,* it wasn't *Streetcar.* What was the harm in puffing the "superb acoustics, the luxurious appointments" of the Yorkport Playhouse? He smiled, a man misunderstood. In the *Star* offices his technical remarks had become something of a joke; the more irreverent members of the staff were likely to ask: "Hey, Greg, how were the superb acoustics and luxurious appointments last night?"

On stage Danforth and his "wife," Julie, were playing Parcheesi in the library. Old vol-

260

umes of *Reader's Digest* book condensations, painted dark brown for a leatherbound look, filled the bookshelves, and there were old-new geometric paintings and tall urns—the objects of the period. The furniture was dark and heavy. Man and wife were concentrating on the game with the irritable intimacy of two people married for rather a long time, and while they were thus engaged a pretty blond girl in a maid's uniform came to the door of the library, informally open, and knocked.

Her mouth worked but no sound came out. The audience laughed. They laughed again when she knocked again, and it seemed that her panic had grown worse. They knew she was so terrified by what she had to say that she was going to say something fantastically funny. But for all the spastc workings of her mouth, nothing came out.

She knocked again and the audience were in stiches.

Danforth turned his head as if he had been so absorbed in the game that he wasn't aware of her presence. He yawned and did a little bit of business before he spoke.

That made the audience laugh.

"Did I hear something about a telegram?" he asked. "Is it for me?"

Julie Ferguson looked up, smiling as if the interruption had won her game.

"Got you, Schuyler," she gloated.

The maid remained rooted to the floor.

"Speak, girl," Danforth said, and, seeing the maid's face—Dawn's face—added, "It can't be as bad as all that."

The maid ran away sobbing and Danforth looked straight at the audience and said, "Or can it?"

The audience howled.

Cringing in his seat in the last row, Cal Cameron vowed vengeance on Danforth and the dizzy cunt he'd been screwing. The cunt was no use for anything but blow-jobs and as a subject for a study of dysgenics. But Danforth . . . Cameron found no words for Danforth. The man was supposed to be a professional. Jesus Christ! Nothing had happened on stage that hadn't happened before in the tawdry, moth-eaten history of the theater. The moronic Danforth had covered for the cunt and Julie, then, had covered for Danforth. No harm had been done; it had gone over very well. But that wasn't the point, which was that great harm could have been done to his reputation and that of the playhouse. Now he had Danforth by the nuts. Let him explain.

Cameron's Mephistopheles mustache stopped twitching. The foul-up wasn't in the book, but he would keep it in. It got a laugh, a big laugh. But Danforth's dingbat was out because he was sure she wouldn't do it right the next time. Let her whine all she wanted. If she whined too hard he would kick her out of the theater school. As a mouth she was the best. That didn't matter: business was business. The theater was a world without mercy; to make a success of it you had to be merciless.

Feeling better now, Cameron lay back in his seat and put a Vick's inhaler to his nose.

The play continued and then it was time for intermission and those with a thirst thronged to the bar. In past years when Yorkport had local option regarding the sale of intoxicating beverages the playhouse was dry. Now all that was changed and you could buy a drink almost anywhere; Cameron was one of the first to apply for a liquor license. Actually he wasn't as interested in making money from liquor as he was in bringing out the quiet alcoholics who refused to attend the theater because it took too many hours away from their drinking. Now he was pleasantly surprised to learn that the playhouse bar was turning a nice profit.

One of those who never worried about two drinks or three at intermission was Sarah Bannard, who always carried two half pints of 100-proof vodka in two small silver flasks. First there were the drinks at home, then the nips before intermission, the drinks during intermission, and then the drinks after intermission.

Grinning and drunk, Sarah was one of the first to reach the bar, and it was said that she frequently broke the hundred yard dash in her eagerness to get there. This wasn't quite true, but she did walk fast. It was all in the hip action, she said.

In Maine you can't stand at a bar because it's against the law; you have to sit on a barstool or at a table. Sarah parked herself on a stool and said, "Double bullshot, Jimmy."

The young man said, "My name is Arthur."

"Hurry up with the drink, Jimmy," Sarah said.

She called all bartenders "Jimmy."

Three bartenders and four waiters had to work hard to supply the needs of the playgoers; Tom Collinses and vodka Collinses were the drinks of choice for most of them. Summer drinks.

The slower-moving Dee joined Sarah at the bar and asked for white wine with a twist of lemon. By then Sarah had finished her first bullshot and was signaling for a second.

"How are things at school, Jimmy?" she asked the bartender when he put the dreadful drink in front of her.

"I don't go to school," the young man said.

"You should," Sarah said.

Tracy and her entourage came into the bar

and found a table. Tracy saw Sarah and waved at her and Sarah waved back.

Dee sulked.

"We're just great good friends," Sarah said. "The one that isn't having a good time is Ormond Bailey. How do *you* like the show, dear?"

"It stinks," Dee said.

"Hey well, listen now, hey listen, give the kids a break, willya?" Sarah said.

"The one that played the maid forgot her lines," Dee said. "The others fake it, but I could tell."

"Good for you, Lee Strassberg," Sarah said. "Whoever she is, she ain't bad. You think if Cameron fires her we could hire her as a maid?"

"Flake off, Sarah," Dee said.

At their table, Greg and Carol were having the usual Tom Collins. One was the limit, at the prices Cameron charged. Carol felt so glamorous in the company of the rich and famous; Greg made a few notes on the play; perhaps he would add them to the review he had written more than a week before.

"There's your girlfriend," Carol said.

"What?"

"The Irish one. Who's the man with her? He looks familiar."

Greg looked. "That's Senator Callaway,"

he said.

Mary Galligan saw him looking, brought her hand up to shoulder level, smiled, and wiggled her fingers. Then she turned her attention to the senator, who was enduring the evening with stoic courage.

Carol decided not to like Mary Galligan. "That was cute how she did that. *She's* not cute, but the way she did that was cute."

"Sure," Greg said.

"Like a little kid," Carol said.

"What should she do? Fire off a cannon? What's wrong with you? You're getting what you wanted."

"It's not her party," Carol said. "She's just a secretary. An overaged preppy."

"She's younger than we are," Greg said.

"You want to bet?"

"Jesus! You're never satisfied."

"You think she's having a thing with the senator? I wouldn't put it past her. I know the type."

"What type?"

"The social climbing Irish-Catholic type."

"I'm Irish," Greg said.

"Yes, you are," Carol said.

"But I'm not a climber. I leave that to you. Just because your Presbyterian grandmother turned Episcopalian—that's social climbing right there—doesn't make you better than Mary Galligan."

" 'Mary' is a vulgar, tacky name," Carol said. "I think it suits her."

"You make me tired," Greg said.

Across the room Linwood Duval was back to the subject of Freddy DiSalvo.

"How about it, Trace?" he nagged. "There he is walking around looking lost. My heart goes out to him. Such a natty little gangster."

Ormond Bailey, unlike the others, was drinking straight Jack Daniel.

"Bushwah," he growled into his glass.

"*Por favor*, Trace," Duval said.

"You're a nuisance, Linny," Tracy said. "But if it will shut you up—all right."

Cameron came into the bar and Tracy made a polite, beckoning motion, smiling to show that she wasn't treating him as a servant.

Cameron came over. "Yes, Trace?"

"The play is so very, very funny," Trace said.

Cameron smiled. "May I quote you, Trace?"

It was just something he said, but when he thought about it, he liked it, and in his mind's eye he saw it in a box in the *Yorkport Star*:

"*I loved every minute of '23 Skidoo. Don't miss it.*"
                              —*Tracy Callaway O'Neal.*

"Of course you can quote me, Cal," Tracy

said. "Anything to help the theater."

"You're the best, Trace," Cameron said.

Tracy said, "This may sound silly—it *is* silly— but Linny here wants to meet your friend Mr. DiAngelo. Is that all right?"

"You mean DiSalvo," Cameron said. "You sure you want to? Whatever you say, Trace."

Cameron brought the mobster to the table and on the way he explained about the people he was going to meet.

"Mrs. O'Neal? You're not shitting me, are you, Cal?"

"Would I do that, Fred?"

None of the other names meant anything to DiSalvo; only the O'Neal name had moxie.

"Will you have a drink, Mr. DiSalvo?" Tracy asked.

"Don't mind if I do," DiSalvo said. "But I'd be honored if you'd let me pick up the whole check."

"Oh well," Tracy said.

What the fuck was going on here? DiSalvo wondered.

Carol Delaney said, "What do you think she's saying to Freddy DiSalve?"

Greg was looking too. "Maybe she wants to make a buy. Freddy's the man to see if you want to make a buy in this town."

Carol didn't think that was it. "I don't understand it," she said.

"Why don't you go over and ask her?"

"Your girlfriend is looking at you again."

"You're back to that, huh? Listen. I talked to her for a few minutes. We had a drink. Why do you always make something out of nothing?"

"Then why is she looking at you?"

"Because I'm so handsome, that's why. What other reason could there be?"

"You're going to get me mad in a minute, Gregory. That's all you ever do—get me mad."

"Everything I do makes you mad."

"That's right, Gregory."

"Then maybe we shouldn't go to the party. What I mean is, if the party is going to make you mad, why go?"

"Stop it, Gregory," Carol said. "Why do you think your girlfriend and the senator aren't sitting with the others? Tracy and the others. They didn't even come in Tracy's car. I saw them. They came in your girlfriend's MG."

"It's a Morgan," Greg said, thinking of Mary Galligan's invitation. It would be fun to take a run with Mary in the spiffy little car. They could drive over to New Hampshire and they could have lunch or dinner at an interesting Greek place he knew in Rochester. He had gone to Dartmouth with Mr. Pappas' son, George, and so the welcome mat was always out. If she hadn't tasted *retsina* before he would introduce her to it. He himself didn't much like the resiny Greek wine, but it was sort of off-beat, and it would be fun to see how she liked it. Mr. Pappas always picked up the tab and wouldn't take no for an answer, so he would do what he never did, order the best in the house. When he took Mary there—*if* he took her there—he would order the best, which might raise Mr. Pappas' eyebrows, but he would leave a really big tip, and that would get him in solid with the waiter, probably Gus, and the next time, when he had more money than he had now, he would insist on paying his way, except if George happened to be there, and then his money would be no good. George was a great guy, a real friend. He was married but he didn't let that stop him. He was in the condo business now and owned more apartments than he knew what to do with. That was living, Greg thought with a faint coloring of envy. How did a vengeful or suspicious wife track down a guy with so many places to take somebody? George had hideouts in Rochester, Dover, Hampton, Exeter, Portsmouth—and that was just New Hampshire. . . .

"What are you saying?" he asked his wife when he felt her tugging at his sleeve.

"Are you deaf?" she said. "It's time to go in."

CHAPTER FIFTEEN

Leonard Gately would have gone to the playhouse if it hadn't been for the telephone call from Darryl Bates. In fact the call came while he was dressing for the theater in one of the three new summer suits he had purchased earlier in the day at Key West North, an establishment run by a bronzed fellow of indeterminate age and sex who liked to refer to himself as a "Florida conk" but who was in actuality a native of Philadelphia. His name was Robert McBride and he explained to Gately, who didn't know or care about such things, that the ties were narrower now, and so were the lapels.

"Just fix me up with what looks right," Gately said.

The clothing sold at Key West North leaned more to Paul Stuart than to Brooks or to Chipps, meaning that it was traditional yet not too traditional—some of it. Madras jackets had not disappeared, but were on the wane; most were sold to men in the third stage of their lives, men with money and red faces and wives who looked much older; men who preferred to buy and to wear what they knew.

Old farts. McBride's word for them.

Resplendent in a Palm Beach suit, Gately went to take the call from Darryl. Of course he didn't know the call was from Darryl, so his heart didn't leap. But it leapt when he heard Darryl's voice on the line.

"You all right, Lenny?" Darryl said with studied caution; someone asking after the well-being of a good friend who has done something outside the bounds of accepted behavior.

All late afternoon and evening, Bates had searched for Lenny the Moose, in offices and shops, in the village and at the beach. Not finding him, he was forced to call.

"Darryl, you old dog!" Gately said. "Am I glad to hear from you! Hear your voice. I been looking all over for you. Gee willikers, fella—where you been?"

Bates knew he was safe. "Around and about," he said. "You were pretty heavy the

272

other night, old buddy. Look. Look. Never mind about what you did. I'm calling to see how you are."

"I'm good, Darryl," Gately said. "What you're not saying but I'm saying is I was an asshole, right?"

"I won't lie to you," Bates said. "You were an asshole. Listen to me, you old prick. What got into you anyway?"

"Ah God, Darryl," Gately said, not knowing what he had done.

Bates knew he had the fat son of a bitch. "Simmer down, pardner," he said. "You didn't piss on the flag if that's what you're thinking. Not you." Bates laughed, making it almost all right. "But I will tell you this. Where do you get your strength, Godzilla? You practically threw me through the wall. Lenny, I could murder you, my knee hurts that bad. But how are you? You didn't go out that night I hope?"

Gately didn't know. "Stayed home and felt bad in the morning. I'm sorry I hurt your knee, guy. Honest to God I am. Suzie must have been bugging me, for me to do a thing like that. You know I'm your friend."

Bates laughed. "Didn't look like it the other night, but let's not go into that. Only one thing, Lenny, you got to put a curb on that temper of yours. It's going to get you in trouble if you don't."

Bates enjoyed Gately's long silence. Then

273

Gately said, "I'd like to make it up to you, buddy. I wouldn't feel right if I didn't do that."

"Forget about it, Lenny."

"Can't do that, buddy. Where are you?"

"Public phone," Bates said. "By the drugstore."

Gately felt a gush of love for this great-hearted guy; the theater was forgotten. It was going to be okay now. Everything was going to be okay. Darryl was back with him, friends again, and there was so much he had to tell the guy. Darryl would want to hear all about Tracy and what was said about this and that.

"Get over here and don't spare the horses," Gately said. "From now on nothing but the best for you. I'll throw some steaks on the fire and we'll have a couple of drinks when you get here. That sound good to you?"

"Sounds great, Lenny," Bates said. "Anything I can get you in the village?"

"Just bring yourself," Gately said. "I got everything we need. You got Angela with you?" He hoped he didn't.

"Angie took off for Boston," Bates said. "I called in sick."

"See you in a few minutes," Gately said, glad that he didn't have to look at Angela, didn't have to listen to her. He remembered vaguely having given Angela a few licks with his belt, but that was all. The two bitches must have started the trouble. It had to be that. Why else

274

would he get into a hassle with Darryl, his best friend and an all round great guy, an ace? He wondered what Darryl would say when he saw him in the new suit. God damn it to hell, he ought to do something about his waistline. He was like a frigging barrel. As a guy got older he had to watch the pot, and he hadn't been watching it. But after he filled his tankard with two bottles of Beck's he decided that he wasn't fat, just big and solid like a lot of guys. It hadn't hurt Orson Welles to be like that.

He heard Darryl's car pulling up to the house and went outside to meet him. Mosquitoes buzzed in the evening air and a catbird was still fooling around in a tree. Gately liked the catbird and even had a name for it—Silas.

Bates got out of the car and came limping toward the house. Seeing Gately's face, he held up his hand and said, "Okay. Okay. Don't look so guilty. This isn't going to kill me."

"Shit, buddy, let me help you," Gately said. "I'd give my own leg not to have this happen."

"Cut it out, Lenny," Bates said. "I told you on the phone, cut it out." He laughed. "You got something to drink around this place?"

Gately hugged his friend and said, "You bet your ass I do! And what I ain't got I can get. God damn, it's good to have you back in the fold!"

"Good to be back," Bates said.

They went into the house and Gately told

Bates not to do a thing—just sit. Bates said he'd have a vodka and grapefruit juice and Gately went to get it like a well-tipped waiter serving an old customer.

"Steaks'll be ready in a minute," he said, handing Bates the drink. "Drink 'er down, old buddy. Christ, it's good to see you! I was going to call you, but, you know, I was kind of embarrassed."

"Stop beating your breast," Bates said, grinning. "And tell me what you're all dressed up for?"

"I thought maybe I'd go to the playhouse," Gately said. "The hell with that. I got something to tell you that'll knock you over. Fasten your seat belt, buddy. I've been invited to Tracy O'Neal's big party. The one everybody is talking about. Now don't start laughing. It's true. She invited me herself."

Bates pretended to be astonished. "You're putting me on!"

"Honest Injun," Gately said. "I know—I know. It was the last thing in the world I thought about, but you know how things happen. I got her a deal on a house—I'll explain later—and lo and behold she says to me, 'Lenny baby, if you don't come to my party I'm going to walk out to sea till I drown.' Kidding aside, she asked me to come. And listen to this. Yours truly even had lunch with Tracy O'Neal. The lobster shack down by the beach.

We had beer and clams. It's the truth, good buddy. I know what you're thinking—all the things I said about her and the Callaways. But when you get to know her she's okay. Not a bit like the things people say about her. You'd think with her kind of money she'd be a terrible snob. No such thing."

"Now I see the reason for the new clothes," Bates said. "God damn it, boy, I'm proud of you! Your friend the colonel know about all this?"

"Mike saw us together on the way to lunch. You know what a red face he has." Gately laughed. "I guess it got redder. Nodded like he hardly knew me. I don't know what he expected me to do—knock the woman down and kick her in the ribs."

Bates mimicked the colonel's military bark. "That's exactly what you should have done, Leonard my boy!"

They laughed and it seemed that their friendship had been restored. Gately got the steaks and they ate at the long table in the Great Hall. As usual, the steaks were excellent. As usual, Gately covered his steak with ketchup, garlic salt, onion powder and red pepper. He filled his tankard and got a drink for Bates before they sat down.

Bates raised his glass. "Here's to friendship and good times."

"Amen to that," Gately said fervently.

They clinked glasses.

"To the future," Gately said.

"To the future," Bates said.

They pushed their plates away and sat in the big paneled room with its SS battle flags, rifles, swords, spears. With six Beck's under his belt, Gately couldn't have felt better. Life was good; there was no disputing that. His father had been a club steward, a poor old deferential limey who took pride in his job. There were a lot worse jobs in the world, he always said. Gately, thinking back, found it hard to think of one. The old man never understood that in America a man had to have push, drive, ambition. Gately felt that he owed nothing to anyone but himself, but even the most successful man had to have friends—and Darryl was the best friend a man could have.

"How are you fixed for dough, old buddy?" he asked Bates. "You've been renting rooms and renting cars when by rights you should have been here. Yeah, yeah. I know. You would've been here if I hadn't acted like a turd."

Bates protested. "I'm all right, Lenny. I owe you money already."

"Like hell you do. As of now you don't owe me a thing. Forget about it. It's forgotten, okay? When you're going good in Hollywood you can fly me out there and get me laid. Would a couple of hundred tide you over for a while?"

"I won't say I can't use it," Bates said. "That child support thing keeps me on the ropes all the time."

"No explanations, please. I *know* how women are. I'll be paying alimony to that bitch for the rest of my life. Like they say, it's the fucking you get for the fucking you got. Here's a couple of bills and there's more where that came from."

Bates pocketed the money. "You're a pisser, Lenny," he said. "But a nice pisser."

"I hope so, old buddy."

"You're aces with me."

"And you with me, soldier."

Gately got up to make Bates another drink and when he came back he saw Bates massaging his injured knee. Bates took his hand away quickly, but Gately wasn't fooled for a minute.

"Hurts that bad, huh?"

"Don't make a big thing out of it, Lenny. Call it the fortunes of war."

Gately drank off the two Beck's in his tankard and studied his friend. "What happened here, buddy?" he said quietly. "Don't pull any punches, give it to me straight."

"If you insist," Bates said, and like all good liars he didn't lie more than he had to. Anyway, why should he lie? The facts could not have been much worse than they were. Gately began to sweat when he mentioned the law.

"Angie wanted to go to the cops," Bates went on. "I don't know how long it took to talk her out of that. First she said okay she wouldn't and then she got mad again and said she was going to send you to the can. You beat her pretty bad, Lenny. I have to tell you that."

"How about Suzie?"

"Suzie just took off I don't know where. Suzie wasn't a problem. Angie was the problem. Jesus Christ, if you knew what I had to do to calm her down! Okay, I said to her, getting mad myself, you want to go the cops, I can't stop you. Just remember this. You won't have me to back up your story. I'm not going to turn on a guy who is my friend no matter what he did and you're going to look stupid sitting there in the police station telling a wild story like that. And how's it going to look when this shit gets in the papers and not just here, in Boston too? You know the Boston papers'll pick it up if it's dirty enough. Then where are we? What happens to our jobs? We'll be shit out of luck, that's where we'll be."

"Christ," Gately said.

"Don't sweat it," Bates said. "Finally I straightened her out and sent her back to Boston and got a promise that she wouldn't say a word. It's in the past, Lenny. Forget it. Go thou and sin no more."

"I'll never forget you for this," Gately said. "On my word of honor I'll never forget what you've done for me. Even if I didn't go to jail I'd be ruined in this town. Who would want to deal with a guy convicted of that kind of stuff? That would be a bitch of a thing, now that I'm moving up a bit."

"I hate to say it, but you're right. Tracy O'Neal would think twice about having you over no matter how many deals you made for her. But she doesn't know about it and she isn't going to. You're out of it, Lenny."

"Thanks to you," Gately said. "Nobody but you."

Jesus Christ, Bates thought, if this keeps up the son of a bitch is going to kiss me. He wanted to spit in the fatso's face. All in good time. Spitting time might not be too far off.

"You're getting to be a bore about this, good buddy," Bates said. "Let's close the case and say no more about it. Is that a deal?"

"A deal," Gately said. "Let me freshen your drink for you."

While Gately was rattling ice cubes in the kitchen, Bates thought, It's too early to start about going to the party. I'll work up to it in easy stages. If he hesitates, my knee will get worse and I'll be brave as hell about the pain. I could sue the bastard if I wanted to, but if I do that all the gory details will come out. No, what I have going here is better than a lawsuit. I might not even win a lawsuit; in front of a Maine jury we'd be tarred with the same brush.

Bates found himself thinking of what he would wear to the party. Hey, maybe Lenny the Moose will spring for some new clothes at Key West North. Why shouldn't he? I have it coming, and more.

"First thing tomorrow you're taking back that car," Gately said, putting the drink on the table. "Use my car like always. And no more motels. A guy could go crazy in a motel room, staring at the four walls. Half the time the TV doesn't work and you have cars coming and going all night long. This is your home."

"Thanks, Lenny," Bates said. "I'd hate to think that one lousy incident would come between us—sorry. I'm the one said not to talk about it. Sit down and tell me what Tracy O'Neal is like. You got any plans in that direction, heh, heh?"

Gately liked that. "You know me, buddy. I always start making plans when I meet a good-looking woman. Be a fool if I didn't."

"I've seen her on TV a few times."

"Me too. She's a lot different in person. On TV she comes across as kind of wishy-washy like she isn't sure of herself. That was the impression I got and it's wrong. She's got plenty of confidence and she's smart. Knows how to handle her money."

"She's got plenty to handle."

"They say at least a billion. Christ, I wonder what it's like to have that much money! I guess after a million it all gets to be the same."

"Not to me it wouldn't," Bates said, and once again he had visions of himself taping or typing TV and movie scripts beside a swimming pool in Beverly Hills. Good-looking heads in bikinis bringing him tall drinks, giving him back rubs. Like the "gracious living" section in *Playboy.* He would drive a Maserati.

"Yeah, I have plans," Gately went on. "The thing to do is to start with basics—that's bed. That's where everything starts. All the rest is just talk, talk, talk. No matter what they say, women just want one thing. The only thing wrong with these Women's Libbers is they aren't getting enough or they aren't getting it right. I don't doubt that Tracy has been getting enough—how could she not?—but no matter how good a cocksman a guy is, there's always somebody better."

"Like a gunfighter in the Old West."

Gately laughed. "It comes to the same thing, old buddy. I've had my share of women, you know that, and they never had any complaints about not getting enough. No complaints about what I'm like in bed."

Maybe not in bed, Bates thought, but everywhere else.

"I don't expect to score that easy," Gately said. "If I do, then good luck to me. But I see it as a fairly gradual thing. I won't come on too strong at first. That stuff works with a lot of women, but I don't think with Tracy. I may be wrong about that. I just don't want to screw up and make the wrong approach. There won't be any second chance with her. I know that."

Bates said, "If you can knock that off you should go into the *Guinness Book of Records.* There's no score higher than that. Looks to me like you're off to a good start."

"Well, I won't lie to you, buddy. I think she likes me. The first time I met her she told me to call her 'Tracy.' It took a little time to get used to that. Now I don't even think about it. That's what I like about her. She doesn't put on the dog like most of these rich bitches. She could but she doesn't and you better believe she could buy this whole town if it came to that. I was thinking about that only today. Jesus, you ought to have seen their faces when I walked with her down to the beach. Mike Burns nearly pissed in his pants."

"I can see how he would," Bates said. "From what you've told me, Mike isn't one of her devoted admirers."

"Mike gets carried away sometimes," Gately said. "A good guy but all his ideas are set in concrete. I don't say he isn't right about a lot of things. That doesn't mean he's right about everything. How can he be?"

"Don't tell that to Mike or he'll call you a traitor."

"I'm not worried about Mike. I'd hate to lose

his friendship after all this time. On the other hand, Mike is an old guy with his life behind him. If he wants to think of me as a traitor, then too bad. Anyway, what Mike doesn't seem to understand is that Tracy is basically a conservative person. No matter what very rich people say, they're all conservatives."

"You've really given some thought to this, buddy."

"It's worth thinking about, soldier. The way I see it, you have to seize an opportunity when it comes along. If you don't, some other guy will take it away from you."

You dumb, dull, boring clown, Bates thought, with your lead-footed clichés and half-baked theories! You have as much chance with Tracy O'Neal as I have of becoming President. What was it some writer said about another writer—"He was invited to all the great houses—once." That's you, old buddy.

Bates swallowed his drink in an effort to fight the awful boredom he felt. When the broads were around it wasn't too bad, but Lenny by himself was too fucking much. But it was a price he'd have to pay if he wanted to get to that party.

"I was saying to Tracy. . ." Gately droned on.

While Gately continued his story, the playhouse let out. Danforth was in his dressing room removing his make-up with a cotton swab when Cameron knocked and came in.

"Hold it, Cal," Danforth said. "I'm tired and in no mood for a lecture. Okay, the kid screwed up, but it went over all right. You know it got a laugh."

"I didn't laugh," Cameron said. These fucking actors. How he hated them. Grown-ups with the minds of children. Hitchcock used to refer to actors as "cattle." Hitch was right. No one could have said it better.

"I didn't laugh and I'm not laughing now," Cameron said. "Where's your sense of responsibility? If not to me, then to the theater. You pushed me to give this idiot a walk-on. I know she's a moron, you know she's a moron, but you pushed her just the same. One line, you said. A zombie could do it, you said. But your zombie couldn't do it, could she? I blame you more than I blame her, Danforth. There's nothing there to blame. She isn't a person, she's a *thing!*"

Dawn came in at that moment and Cameron, dark with fury, roared at her to get out. "OUT, I said."

Dawn ran away in tears.

"Come on, Cal," Danforth said. "Why all the dramatics? The show was a smash. The kid got a laugh, I'm telling you."

"You're not telling me anything, Danforth. I'm telling *you*. Your zombie is out of the show.

Don't argue about it. We'll keep in the bit, but another girl is going to play it. Is that clear?"

Danforth sighed. "It's clear," he said. "How could it not be clear, the way you're shouting?"

There goes the party, he thought. Who the hell cared?

"All right then," Cameron said, no longer shouting. "Hurry up and get finished here. Tracy O'Neal wants to meet you. She's in the bar with her friends."

"She wants to meet me?"

"That's what she said. It seems her favorite niece is just mad about *Uncle Zack and The Kids.*"

"That fucking thing is going to follow me to the grave," Danforth said. "Even a murderer can be paroled after seven years, and if he behaves himself the past is forgotten. But not me."

"Stop whining," Cameron said. "Come on, my boy, let's go and see the great lady."

Tracy rose to greet Danforth. "This is the star of our show," Cameron said, clapping Danforth on the shoulder.

"It's a wonderful show, Mr. Danforth," Tracy said as they shook hands. "Will you have a drink with us? There's still a man on duty."

"I'd like that," Danforth said.

Hands were shaken all around and he sat down and asked for a Scotch on the rocks.

Cameron went away.

"I was telling Cal how much my niece Sally enjoys your television series *Uncle Zack and The Kids*. Even when she's away at school she tunes in promptly at four o'clock."

"It wasn't a bad show," Danforth said modestly.

Tracy laughed. "Don't say that to Sally. She thinks it's so funny. She thinks it's better than *The Brady Bunch* or that other show, the one with all those children."

"*Eight is Enough*," Danforth said.

"Yes, of course," Tracy said. "Sally is coming up from New York later in the week and I know she'd love to meet you. Would you mind terribly if I brought her to the theater some evening before you leave?"

"Sure," Danforth said. "No trouble at all." He laughed too. "The more kids like *Uncle Zack* the longer it will stay on re-runs. More re-runs, more residuals."

"I'm having a party on the Fourth," Tracy said. "Perhaps you'd like to come after the theater. Sally won't be here for the party, but I'd like you to come. I have a house a few miles from here. Do you have a car, Mr. Danforth? If not, I can send somebody to get you."

"Cal lets me use one of the cars here," Danforth said.

"Cal's a wonderful person," Tracy said.

"None better," Danforth agreed.

"Then you'll come?"

"I'd be delighted."

"It will be a late party so you won't miss anything. Cal is coming too. It's going to be fun."

"I'm sure it will."

"Well, I suppose we'd better be going," Tracy said. "That poor barman looks as if he wants to go home. Cal will tell you how to find my house. Good night, Mr. Danforth. I know Sally will be thrilled."

Cameron came back in time to see Tracy to her car. Danforth was having another drink when he returned. Cameron got a glass of water with ice in it. They stood together at the bar in violation of the law.

"What do you think of her?" Cameron asked, smiling sardonically.

"Very pleasant," Danforth said.

"She's a 14-carat bitch."

"*You* said that, not me. As far as I'm concerned Mrs. O'Neal is one gracious lady. She said you were coming to her party. So am I."

"Will you be bringing the idiot?"

"I'll be bringing the idiot. I hope you don't mind."

"You'll never learn, will you?"

"Probably not, Cal."

"What you do is your business, my boy," Cameron said heartily. "Just keep your idiot off my stage."

Still crying, Dawn was waiting in Danforth's car. As soon as he opened the door she threw herself into his arms and sobbed uncontrollably. "Oh Zachary, I'm so ashamed, so embarrassed! I made a fool of myself in front of everybody."

She cried so hard that Danforth's shirtfront was wet with tears. "Hey, take it easy," he said. "The world isn't going to end just because Cameron is mad. Lots of beginners get stage-fright."

"I'm sure I'll get it right tomorrow night. I've been thinking and thinking about it."

"You can stop thinking about it," Danforth said, stroking her hair. "There isn't going to be any tomorrow night."

"You mean Cameron is closing the show?" Dawn said.

"No, darling," Danforth said patiently. "The show will go on, but you won't be in it. I'm sorry but there's nothing I can do about it. Cameron is the boss and I can't fight him on this."

"I'm a has-been before I got started," Dawn said, crying again. "It isn't fair, Zachary!"

He chucked her under the chin. "Cheer up kid. That was the bad news. Now comes the good."

"You mean you'll get me a part in another show?"

"No, darling, not that. The good news is we've been invited to Tracy O'Neal's party. She invited me herself just now."

Dawn's downfall was immediately forgotton, so excited was she by Danforth's words. She threw her arms around him and covered his face with wet kisses. "You're wonderful, darling! You're the most wonderful man in the whole world! And all the time I thought you were just humoring me. What did she say? Tell me what she said! I hope she didn't say anything about me. Oh, Zachary, I'm going to be so embarrassed when I meet her! But they did laugh, didn't they?"

"You got one of the biggest laughs in the show, darling. There's no way she can tell it wasn't in the book. So forget about being embarrassed."

"Will Mr. Cameron be at the party?" Dawn asked. "That smile of his, I hate it."

Danforth didn't think Cameron would do any smiling in Dawn's direction. Once you were written up in Cameron's black book your name remained there indelibly.

"Don't even look at Cameron," Danforth advised.

Dawn kissed him again. "I love you so much, Zachary. How can I ever repay you?"

"Let's go to bed," Danforth said. "Maybe something will come to you."

Home from the theater, Carol Delaney didn't feel like going to bed. She opened the door of her clothes closet and stared into it. What she saw there depressed her.

"Damn it, Gregory," she said. "I wish I had a charge plate at Bonwit's. If I did, I'd drive to Boston in the morning and buy something really nice."

Greg was looking over his notes. "You mean charge something nice?"

"Don't be smart," Carol snapped. "Everybody at the party is going to be so well dressed and I'm going to feel like a drab—you know, I wish you'd get rid of those pajamas. I hate them. What are all those horses' heads supposed to mean?"

Greg looked at his sporty pajamas. "I don't think they're supposed to *mean* anything. Or if they have a meaning it escapes me. What do you think they're supposed to mean?"

"They mean you have bad taste, that's what they mean. It's bad enough that you wear them to bed, but do you have to sit around in them? At least you could put on your bathrobe."

"It's a warm night, I don't want to wear a bathrobe," Greg said. "Why don't you wear your green dress? That's one of your best things. I like you in the green dress."

Carol slammed the door of the closet. "I hate

the green dress, Gregory. It's cheap and tacky and I must have been out of my mind when I bought it. What are you going to wear?"

"My dark grey suit. How many suits do you think I have."

"Well, the next issue of *Ambush* is going to have to wait. I don't know why I have to bear all the expense of keeping that magazine going. You'd think some of the people I publish would contribute a little money."

"They don't have any money," Greg said, and wished he hadn't. When Carol was in one of her jittery moods it was best to say as little as possible.

"I'm going to take the money for the magazine and drive to Boston in the morning," Carol said. "I'll get you a shirt and tie because that's all I'll be able to afford. The collars on your shirts are completely out of style. So are your ties. What kind of tie would you like?"

"You decide," Greg said. If he let her choose the tie she couldn't start hating it in a week.

"Nothing with stripes," Carol insisted. "I know you like striped ties. I hate them."

Discarding good sense, Greg said, "Is it that important? People all over the world are dying of hunger. The Russians may launch a nuclear attack five minutes from now. I can't get too excited about a necktie."

"You can't get excited about anything except maybe your Irish girlfriend. I'll bet she's got plenty of dresses."

"I'm sure she does. Why are you so down on her?"

"Because I don't like her, that's why. She thinks she looks like something in an ad in that silly old sports car. The wind in her hair, her scarf blowing, smiling at the state troopers so they won't give her a ticket."

Carol had been given a speeding ticket two days before. No amount of smiling was enough to prevent it. The trooper had a face like a deacon.

"I don't know a thing about her," Greg said. He had just about made up his mind to call Mary Galligan. If Carol wanted to bitch about the girl, he might as well do what she suspected him of wanting to do. Their marriage was headed for the rocks; a change of job, a change of place wasn't going to make any difference.

"I don't know why we have to talk about her," Carol complained. "I'll bet her father runs an Irish saloon in Lawrence or Lowell, one of those mill towns in Massachusetts."

"Irish saloons serve good big sandwiches," Greg said.

"Maybe you can get her to make you corned beef and cabbage," Carol sneered.

"I don't think she's the corned beef type."

"If you haven't been thinking about her, how do you know what type she is?"

"I read about her in *Time* magazine."

Carol was furious. "You're lying, Gregory. They wouldn't write her up in *Time*. Why would they write about a secretary?"

"The piece wasn't strictly about her," Greg said. "It was about the important role a super-efficient secretary plays in the life of a celebrity. They quoted her on this and that."

"And you loved every word of it."

"I didn't know her then, Carol. I didn't clip it out and paste it in my scrapbook."

"But you'd do it now, is that what you mean? Was there a picture of her?"

"There was a picture. Her picture among others."

"They have back issues of *Time* at the library. Next time you're there you can tear out the page when the librarian isn't looking. Then when you get excited you can take her picture into the bathroom."

"Yes, Carol," Greg said. "Anything you say, Carol. It would be great if you'd shut up for a minute. I'd like to read my notes without all this verbal handball going on."

"I don't have to talk to you," Carol said, opening the closet again. "I don't have to talk to you at all!"

While Carol rummaged through the closet, Greg decided to call Mary Galligan in the morning. The great thing about being a reporter was that you could be all over the place.

You could call in and say you were going just about anywhere. You could say you had a hot tip about a surprise demonstration at the nuclear plant in Seabrook, not so many miles away. You could say you were going to interview some old codger who had passed the hundred mark. And just because you mentioned the stories didn't mean you had to write them. You could get away with all kinds of stuff provided you stayed ahead of your work.

Carol had emptied the closet; her clothes lay all over the bed. "That does it," she said. "I'm going to Boston in the morning. You better take your grey suit to the dry cleaner's and have it pressed. I should be back by early afternoon. Where will you be?"

"Well," Greg said. "There's been talk of a surprise demonstration at the nuke plant in Seabrook."

CHAPTER SIXTEEN

Other guests were arriving from New York.

Paco Melendez, the criminal poet and play-wright, got off the Greyhound and was picked up by Ralph, who disliked Puerto Ricans, especially this one recently released on parole from Attica after serving a year for loft burglary. Unable to attend the opening of his smashhit play, *Sucker,* because of his incarceration, Melendez was rich for the first time in his life but chose to travel by Greyhound as a gesture. Before leaving New York he bought five pints of Night Train and drank the awful wine in the back seat of the bus, daring the driver to do anything about it. The driver knew a badass when he saw one, so he kept his eyes on the road and did nothing.

Other guests were Jules Bernier-Salamons of Salamons Freres, the international bankers; Larry Lindberg, the frozen meat sculptor whose studio on West Broadway was known as The Igloo because of the extremely low temperatures prevailing there; Peggy Lawton, the bisexual tennis champ; Goneril Shawnessy, the Dublin designer; and many, many others famous in their fields, though perhaps less known to the readers of gossip columns.

Tracy greeted them, some with the two-hands clasp, some with hygienic kisses. Larry Lindberg, the meat sculptor, was one of her favorites because he was always sending over roasts and steaks packed in dry ice. As a consequence of his work, Lindberg was a vegetarian, but he hated to see the meat go to waste.

But she loved them one and all; they were her friends, even Melendez, street fighter and heir to the mantle of Williams and O'Neill, dressed for the party as he dressed for everything: dirty denims and motorcycle boots, black beret, a necklace he claimed was made from the teeth of cops he had tangled with in the South Bronx.

Introduced to M. Bernier-Salamons, he said, "What's happenin', sucker?" Later, however, he asked the famous Frenchman if he thought the price of gold would go to one thousand dollars an ounce.

More than twenty-four hours remained until party time, yet for all the planning, so many things still had to be done. Guests telephoned and said they were lost or their cars were out of order; the really difficult ones who called wanted to be assured that their "worst enemies" were not going to be at the party.

Manning the telephone, Mary Galligan gave directions and offered soothing assurances. Lacey Putnam and Jerry Rodriguez were there with some of their crew. Jerry was less thrilled than Lacey, but then Lacey was thrilled enough for two. With all the quiet authority of a four-star general—no, a field marshal—Lacey told his subordinates what must and must not be done at the party, and if the waiters didn't do it just right they would be drummed out of the catering business.

The house was so busy that most of the guests had repaired to the terrace, where drinks were served. Senator Callaway was in his room reading; a little of Tracy's menagerie, as he thought of the assembled guests, was too much. He had come only because she had urged him to, but, being a politician and long inured to boredom, he didn't mind very much. It was, after all, no worse than attending an Italian festival in the North End.

Paco Melendez, menacing behind mirrored sunglasses, demanded, and got, a ten ounce can of Bud in a brown paper bag, and while he drank it, he regarded the other guests with the wariness of a welfare case expecting a call from a social services investigator. The only one who attempted to make conversation with him was Ormond Bailey, who prided himself on his street smarts, but even he gave up when Melendez bared his teeth and snarled, "Cut the shit, sucker."

Linwood Duval was talking to Bernier-Salamons in Cajun French, of which the Frenchman understood not a word. Not wanting to appear impolite, he nodded now and then, but there was no need even for that—Duval did all the talking.

Giving up on Melendez, Bailey tried to engage Goneril Shawnessy in a discussion of a long forgotten Irish prizefighter named Jack Doyle who had come to America in the late 1930's only to have the stuffing knocked out of him. Later he had tried to punch his way into show business as a singer, The Irish Thrush, but he was knocked out by popular demand.

"Oh yes, it seems to me I've heard of him," Miss Shawnessy said in her polite Dublin accent. "He sounds terribly interesting, Mr. Bailey. What do you think happened to him, do you suppose?"

"I hear he got in trouble with the cops after he went back to Dublin," Bailey said. "Receiving stolen goods, something like that."

"Oh dear," Miss Shawnessy said. "How distressing."

"Those are the breaks, kid," Ormond Bailey said.

Carol had left for Boston to spend the money she had saved for the next issue of her poetry magazine. Now it was eleven o'clock and Greg had been staring at the telephone ever since breakfast. That morning he had shaved with extra care but now, feeling his face, he detected a slight rasp of stubble under his sagging jawline, so there was nothing to be done but go back into the bathroom and get rid of it. Only then did he pick up the telephone and call Mary Galligan's number. It took her a while to answer.

"Well, hello there," she said, a little breathless. "I was on the other line. So many things left to be done."

"Guess I caught you at a bad time," Greg said.

There was a pause. "I'm not that busy," she said. "I do get time off for lunch."

"Why don't you have it with me?" Greg said. "There's a little place in Portsmouth, right by the old bridge. You can be there in less than fifteen minutes if you're interested."

"I'm interested. What's it called?"

"The Cat's Cradle, and don't ask me why because I don't know. It's on the left side of the bridge as you come in from Maine . . . Oh, you know it. Okay, I'll see you in less than thirty minutes. And listen, don't forget to bring that sports car."

Mary Galligan laughed. "I knew that was the real reason you called. See you in a jiffy."

Humming, Greg hung up and gave himself a quick once-over before he hurried to his car. He thought he looked pretty good. Not tall but not short either. Straight-leg chinos from Bean's, blue oxford shirt with button-downs, black socks, Bass loafers, Haspell cord jacket. No tie, naturally. Get a move on, old sport, he told himself. You don't want to get there sweating.

Things were looking good, he decided as he bypassed the town and took a short cut to the state highway. Before the highway there was a stop sign and he drummed his fingers on the steering wheel, waiting for an old guy in an early Fifties Ford pick-up to pull out ahead of him. There was at least a quarter of a mile of clear highway on both sides of the stop sign; still the old guy waited. Greg tapped his horn. Finally, the old guy pulled out just as a trailer truck came barreling along. The big rig missed the pick-up by inches, and Greg was free to go.

Good humor restored, he hummed "*Siboney,*" an old Latin number still played on the

FM schmaltz stations. "Siboney," he sang, but that was as far as he got; as far as he ever got. Maybe the thing didn't have any more words, or if it had, he'd never heard them. But it was a romantic old wheeze and it suited his mood perfectly. "Mary Galligan," he sang to the frozen daiquiri music of "Siboney." That didn't work out so well, but he knew what he meant. "In spring a young man's fancy," he yelled, and a woman in a house dress, watering her garden, stared after his car. He slowed down when a state police cruiser whipped past him in pursuit of the trailer.

"De fuzz," he murmured, feeling young again at twenty-nine.

Ah, it was all so lovely.

Dawn woke up and whispered to Danforth, "Happy Fourth of July, darling."

Danforth covered his head with a pillow. What the hell was she talking about? Nobody said "Happy Fourth of July." It wasn't like Christmas, or Easter, or New Year's.

After many years in show business, Danforth was a night person; daylight depressed him. So did Dawn when he wasn't banging her. Right now he didn't feel like banging anyone, not even the girl of his dreams, the French actress Isabel Adjani. If Isabel walked in right now and said, "How's about eet, beeg boy?" he would just have to tell her, "Later for that, keed."

Groggy, mildly hungover, Danforth laughed at his own silliness. There was some hysteria in his laughter, and not knowing the reason for it, Dawn was prepared to be offended.

"It's not nice to laugh at a person," Dawn complained, doing her best to flounce while lying down. But when she thought about the party, now shining just over the horizon, her heart went out to the unshaven thespian. He wasn't as young or as virile as she would have liked him to be. Just the same, they were going to the party, and that was all that mattered.

"I was in a school play about George Washington," she whispered to Danforth. "They gave the same play every year when I was a little girl. I was in it twice, then I got too tall for the part. But that little play made me realize I wanted to be an actress. When you were a little boy in Canada, what did you do on the Fourth?"

"Nothing," Danforth mumbled.

"That's not very patriotic, Zachary."

Danforth turned over and looked at her with bleary eyes. "They don't celebrate the Fourth in Ontario, darling. It's a different country up there, dig?"

"Well, you don't look a bit foreign to me," Dawn said fondly. "Neither does Donald

304

Sutherland."

"Donald will be pleased to hear that." Knowing he wasn't going to get any more sleep, Danforth reached for the first cigarette of the day. He hated cigarettes but couldn't give them up any more than he could give up young girls. The thought of the party brought no joy to his heart. The only reason the O'Neal woman had invited him was to insure that he'd do his Uncle Zack number for her niece later in the week. Court jester. And he wasn't even playing to real royalty.

Danforth's father was a Scots-Presbyterian minister in suburban Toronto. The old boy hadn't spoken to him since he'd hitchhiked to Hollywood at seventeen. "Tis no work for a man," the old boy had said at the time. How right he was, Danforth thought. And he thought, too, of Doctors Schweitzer, Salk, Barnard—the useful people of the world. Though far removed from the faith of his fathers, Calvinist guilt persisted. He had sinned and must be punished. Come to think of it, '23 *Skidoo* was punishment enough, and in the years to come there would be other plays just like it. Damnation was eternal; for him there would be no redemption.

"Get thee behind me, Satan," he said when Dawn began to play with him.

Dawn was startled. "What did you say, darling? That sounded like a line from a play. Was it?"

"Yeah," Danforth said wearily. "But it needs a little work before it opens in New York."

Breakfasting with Bates, Leonard Gately knew the guy was fishing for a way to get to the party. Fully sober for the first time in years, he drank black coffee instead of beer, vowing to stay off the sauce until he took his first drink at Tracy's party. This was one day when he was going to take it easy. He knew how it was. If he took one drink, then he'd take another, and before noon he'd have a buzz on. That was okay the rest of the time, not today. Too many Beck's made him sweat, made his belly bulge; what was the good of laying out money for new clothes if he arrived at the party bulging and sweating?

Realizing that a sober Gately wasn't as manageable as a drunken Gately, Bates urged him to have an eye-opener.

"You make me feel like I'm having breakfast with a stranger," Bates said, starting to get up. "This time let me do the honors. You want one Beck's or two?"

"Nothing for me, buddy," Gately said, hating to be tempted. "I'm fine for now."

Bates laughed. "I'll be fine when I get this inside me." He clinked his glass of vodka and orange juice against Gately's coffee cup.

Gately reacted to the clinking sound by saying, "Cheers." Then he drank his third cup of black coffee in a single draught.

Bates set down his glass and pulled the platter of steaks toward him. There were fried eggs to go with the steak. "I hope you don't make sobriety a habit," he said.

"I might just do that," Gately said, vaguely irritated by the remark. Darryl was a good guy, but there were times when he kind of said the wrong thing. Like, for instance, hinting that he couldn't do without booze. That was where Darryl was wrong. He hadn't built up a good business by being a boozer. He wasn't mad at Darryl—mad was too strong a word—but he wished the guy would lay off the cracks.

"You don't mean that seriously, do you?" Bates asked, grinning in disbelief.

"I get tired of it sometimes," Gately lied. "I'm not saying I'm going to go on the wagon, nothing as drastic as that. Maybe I'll just cut down for a while and see what happens. I like to think I can take it or leave it. A guy that can't do that is in deep trouble, a slave to his habits."

Bates started on his second steak. "You mean you won't drink at the party? How can you go to a party and not drink?"

"I'll have a few drinks at the party," Gately said casually while visions of frosted beer bottles danced in his head. "What I mean by ta-

307

pering off is to cut out this all-day boozing."
Having said that, Gately felt the glow of virtue.
He was the master of his fate, he was the captain of his soul. Or was it the other way
around? Virtuous now, he was ready to be
wise.

He said, "There comes a time when a guy
has to live up to his responsibility to the community he lives in. Don't look so surprised, old
buddy. I'm not about to enter a monastery, if
that's what you're thinking."

Bates mimicked a man wiping sweat from
his brow. "Whee! You had me worried for a minute."

"Seriously though," Gately continued. "A
guy reaches a point where he has to shit or get
off the pot, community-wise. Which is not to
say that a guy and his friends can't go on having a good time. What I mean is, a guy has to
decide whether he wants to fit in or not. You
understand what I'm saying?"

"Sure," Bates said. Jesus! What a fucking
bore! They couldn't fit Lenny the Moose in with
a pile-driver.

"I see this invitation to Tracy's party as a
step in the right direction," Gately went on.
"But don't get me wrong. I'm no social climber
and never was. On the other hand, I do come
from good English stock and, as you know, my
father was associated with Yale for many
years."

A fucking club steward, Bates thought. Probably dropped his aitches.

Gately didn't know that Bates knew his father had been an executive servant, so he proceeded fearlessly. "The way I see it, buddy, a guy has to stand still, fall back, or move ahead. I think I've reached the stage when I'm ready to move ahead, personally and business-wise. Actually they're one and the same."

Bates nodded. "It takes two to tango."

"Exactly," Gately agreed, experiencing another twinge of displeasure at his friend's levity. Darryl listened but did he understand? It was possible that he did not. It was possible, too, that Darryl's flip attitude had held him back in his career. The guy was a wit, a hoot at parties, yet how many top executives, how many millionaires were known for their ability to make people laugh? Was David Rockefeller witty? Did Henry Grunwald crack jokes? Not very likely.

For the first time Leonard Gately realized that his own lack of humor might be an asset.

"I won't lie to you, buddy," he said. "I know they won't ever vote me most-popular in this town."

Bates felt he had to protest. "Hey, wait a minute, old hoss."

Gately held up his hand like a traffic cop. "It's the truth," he said. "But that's all right.

They've been standoffish with me, I've been standoffish with them. Even Steven. They may not love me—no successful man can ever hope to be loved—but by God they're going to respect me. Probably they see me as a good guy, a little on the wild side maybe."

"You've always been an individualist, Len," Bates said.

"I pride myself on that," Gately said. "In a nation of sheep I like to think of myself as one of the rams."

Bates thought: In a nation of donkeys you'd be the dumbest donkey of all.

Gately thought about Bates while Bates thought about him. It was funny to think about Darryl that way, he realized. Naturally they would be friends forever, but maybe not in the same way as before. Last night he had been ready to take Darryl to the party and hang the consequences. But now, this morning, stone sober, in the clear, cold light of day, he wasn't at all sure that a guy like Darryl would fit in with Tracy's crowd. Except for that asshole Bruce Whipple, and *he* had to be a fluke, all the guests would be people of—what was the word? *Substance.* That was it. Whoever they were, whatever they were, they had made their mark.

In all truth, that could not be said of Darryl, great guy though he was. Darryl was thirty-seven so he couldn't very well pass him off as a struggling young writer. He made four bills a week writing patter for the DJ's, but any good carpenter made as much as that, even in Maine. Anyway, it wasn't how much he made, it was the kind of writing he did: "Better put on your gas masks, boys and girls, 'cause heah comes Johnny Rotten direct from the Ritz Ballroom in the East Village." Stuff like that. It just wouldn't work with Tracy's crowd. Another problem: when Darryl got into the vodka he had a way of breaking into nigger jive talk. Funny as hell in the right company. N.G. at a party like that. Suppose some distinguished nigger heard Darryl doing his Redd Foxx routine? There would be no more invitations after that.

"I'll bet that's going to be some party," Bates said, pushing it now because he knew he had to. "You know, if you weren't such a good friend I'd be jealous of you. I'd give a lot to be going myself."

Gately faked a laugh. Why did the guy have to keep hinting? "You'd be bored stiff. I'm going because Tracy asked me herself and it's good for business. The rest of the people there I don't care about. They can't do a thing for me nor me for them, so they can go diddlyshit for all I care."

"Still, it might be interesting to see how the other half lives."

"The only difference between them and us is

311

they have more money. Look at it this way, buddy. How much booze can you drink? How much steak can you eat? How many times can you get laid? We got all that here, don't we? You know something else? For two cents I'd say the hell with it."

Bates restrained the urge to throw two pennies on the floor. "That's crazy talk, buddy. Of course you'll go. I was just thinking it might be fun if I snuck in on your coattails. What I mean is, we've always done things together."

Gately cringed with embarrassment, but tried not to show it. Why couldn't the guy have some pride? He'd been doing his best not to hurt his feelings and here he was, practically begging.

"Hey, I'd love to take you along, good buddy, but no can do. Not this time. It's a very formal thing. Guest lists, printed cards, all that shit. You'd think it was fucking Buckingham Palace. A country boy like me, they'll probably check my shoes for cowshit before they let me in the door. Forget it, soldier. Make yourself to home right here. My house is yours, as the Spanish say, and as I hardly need remind you. Call up some people and have yourself a time. I'll be back before you know it. What do you say?"

Bates smiled and forced himself to say, "Oh hell! You're right, old buddy. Come to think of it, there's a delightful little creature I've had my eye on for some time, but I never got around to giving her a call." Bates winked. "I can't promise that we'll be up when you get home."

Gately punched his friend lightly in the arm. "Don't do anything I wouldn't do."

"That gives me a lot of leeway," Bates said, and the Great Hall echoed with their laughter.

At the Cat's Cradle, Greg and Mary were finishing lunch. "This Indian pudding is delicious," Mary said. "Nothing at all like you'd get in a can."

"S.S. Pierce was the best in the canned line," Greg said. "But they've gone out of business. Their canned boiled dinners were good too."

Mary Galligan laughed. "This is a fascinating conversaton."

Greg laughed too, feeling good. "You want me to explain about Habitant pea soup? Real Canuck pea soup they can in Quebec?"

"Oh, look at that ship. What flag is she flying?"

"Norwegian, I think. You can tell she's old because the funnels are so tall."

The outbound freighter seemed to glide right past the windows of the dockside restaurant. A blond woman with a headscarf, and dressed in denims, came to the aft rail and

313

dumped a bucket of slops into the oily waters of the harbor. The great hooter sounded and the bridge at the end of the harbor started to go up. Gulls swooped down to eat the slops thrown from the ship.

Mary stirred her coffee and said, "I didn't know they allowed women on freighters. I wonder who she is?"

"The captain's wife? Maybe she's one of the crew. The Scandinavians have always been ahead of us in Women's Lib. I've seen that boat before. Next time I'll ask who she is."

"I think I'd like to be on that boat."

"No you wouldn't. It's probably clean because it's Norwegian, but you'd be bored out of your mind. I've seen that boat so often it must be on a regular run between Norway and Portsmouth. Over and back. Back and over. Like the shuttle at Grand Central. No exotic ports of call. If you want that you'd better ship out on a luxury liner or a tramp steamer."

She smiled across the top of her cup. "You decide for me, Greg."

"The luxury liner," he said. "As a passenger. They tell me working on a liner is like working in a hotel."

"You're not very romantic."

"Yes I am."

"Are you?

"Very much so."

"I think you are."

"What do you think?"

"I think I'd like to," Mary Galligan. "I'd like it to be today. Right now. But it can't be today. And it can't be after the party for . . . obvious reasons."

"For obvious reasons," Greg repeated. "What about tomorrow?"

Mary reached across the table and touched his hand. "Tomorrow or any day except today. They'll start to leave tomorrow. Some of the . . . bastards . . . will stay, but that doesn't concern me very much. We can be together every day. Every night, some nights anyway, if you can get away."

"I'll get away," Greg said, thinking it was like a movie. "I'll get away any time I like. We don't have to talk about that."

"Then we won't."

"You still want to be on that ship?"

"Not now." She looked at her watch. "We've been here for almost an hour and a half."

Greg walked her to her car after he paid the bill and they stood for a moment looking out over the harbor. "Dear Diary," she said. "Today I had lunch with a very nice man I hope to see a lot of."

She kissed him lightly on the lips and zoomed away in the little red car. Wow! Greg exulted silently. Wow!

After she left Bonwit's with the dress, Carol decided not to go shopping for earrings. The thin gold hoops she had would do fine. She fumed with impatience in the line of cars feeding into the Callahan Tunnel, which would take her to East Boston and eventually to Maine. "Idiots!" she said, grinding her perfect little teeth. The top of her elderly VW convertible was down and she looked cute and angry. A sallow fellow in a yellow Camaro with air scoops kept looking over at her from the other lane. Greaser, Carol thought, reverting to the high school slang of some years before. The idiot kept revving his engine, no doubt an indication of his momentary lust, then the clown boomed into the tunnel at a greater speed than was called for, only to be stopped again as the cars at the other end piled up a second time.

Carol tried meditation but it didn't work; it seldom worked anywhere. Maybe it only worked in Northern California. Why not? Those Marin County morons were stoned most of the time; they mistook stupor for mysticism. Gregory was up to something, she was certain. It wasn't like him to shower the night before and then shower again in the morning. And that nuke plant demonstration thing had a fishy smell to it. After all, the Seabrook plant was in another state; any demonstration there would be covered by the daily papers, so why would the *Star,* a weekly, want to get involved with stale news?

She wondered if he would have the nerve to start up with the Galligan woman. He might, the tricky little rat. He might if he thought he could get away with it. Of course the woman would have to be the aggressor; the Galligan woman looked aggressive enough to tell him what he wanted to feel. It depressed her to be married to a man so gullible. He was like Jack Lemmon in those old movies, always twittering around enormous blondes but scared to death of them. The Galligan woman would eat him alive. What did he think he was doing, anyway? Would he read to her from his unpublished works when they were alone? Did he think she could help to get him a publisher? It was just like Greg to go chasing after a secretary; he had no sense of the fitness of things.

Once she got through the seemingly endless sprawl of shopping centers north of Boston, she felt better, almost calm. Traffic was heavy but was moving steadily and though it was hot it wasn't so bad with the top down. Maybe she would meet someone special at the party, Carol thought. Someone who was going to be in the Yorkport area for the entire summer. A writer, preferably. A real writer, someone who didn't just talk about writing, but wrote and got it published. Naturally she would refer to herself as a poet. It was all right

317

to be a poor poet; no one expected poets, real poets, to be rich. Poetry and money didn't go together; a rich poet was like a rich monk—a contradiction.

If she found someone interesting, then Greg's foolishness with the Galligan woman might prove to be a blessing. So let him have his romantic little fling, if indeed it actually came to that. By the end of the summer the Galligan woman would fly away, leaving poor Gregory bereft and long-faced, an ache in his fat little heart. Gregory was such a sticky-fingered romantic; it was a wonder he didn't smoke a straight-stemmed briar pipe like the heroes in women's magazine stories. Maybe the Galligan woman would buy him a pipe to go with her dinky English sports car; there was nothing she could do to firm up his double chin.

After she passed the big sign that read BIEN-VENU CANADIENS, Carol paid the toll at Hampton, New Hampshire, and Greg and the Galligan woman were forgotten in a sudden rush of poetic inspiration. Her poem *Fried Clams* remained unfinished; it was time to get cracking.

By the time she got home it was all together in her head and she rushed to type it up.

CHAPTER SEVENTEEN

Another Fourth of July, Caleb Brown thought when he opened his eyes. In the kitchen Katy was moving about, but he didn't get up. Time enough for that, time enough for everything. The sun was bright in the yard of his small house. He hadn't slept well because it was the morning of the Fourth, a day that always bought problems of one kind or another. It was nine-thirty now; he had slept for less than four hours. In his youth, fifty years before, the Fourth had been a day of natural celebration, a spontaneous expression of patriotism that was nothing like the plastic-flag waving of today. In more recent times the Fourth had become more and more of a joke, like Mother's day and Father's Day, as if it existed for no other purpose than put money in the pockets of the hucksters. It was like the Bicentennial business a few years back; they screwed that up too with all that cheapjack shit—plates, coloring books, pennants, statuettes, soft drinks—that came pouring out of the cities, especially New York City, the source of the great river of garbage. No bigot, Caleb Brown was well aware that not all the hucksters lived in New York; Maine had plenty of the home-grown variety.

Traffic was heavier on the Fourth than any other day of the year, but that was the least of his worries. There were few collisions in town because the pace was so slow; anything that happened on the highway was none of his business; let the staties handle it. Caleb Brown didn't like the state police in their western hats and gung-ho uniforms. They were always trying to stick their noses in where they weren't wanted, especially the state police detectives. Detectives, my ass! They couldn't find a cow in a barn.

The parade, scheduled to start at one o'clock, was the main event of the day. After assembling in the high school football field north of the town, the marchers would parade through the town, then reassemble and disperse in a field owned by Jackman the farmer. The reassembly was Caleb Brown's idea; the year before some small children were lost because the parade didn't break up in an orderly fashion.

This year the parade was going to be tightly policed by regular officers and marshals wearing American Legion uniforms. The marshals, never needed in the old days, were to keep the hippies from joining the parade, as they had done the previous year. That was a real mess; a disgrace, in fact. Right in the center of town a bunch of the doped-up shitheads forced their way into the ranks, scaring the little kids and making everybody else mad or silly. Ira Molson, the big ape, jumped on a bunch of them and rolled all over the street with them. Finally the long-haired bastards were forced out of the parade, yelling and giving the peace sign or the finger, and the parade went on, more or less. But the spirit of the thing was spoiled. This year, by God, there would be none of that. Of course, as usual Mike Burns wanted to call out the state guard to protect the parade from the nuts. They sure knew how to handle the bastards at Kent State, the red-faced maniac liked to say. That was the trouble with America nowadays: a once fine country was full of nuts, right and left and up in the air. Caleb Brown was an old-fashioned and sensible Republican as his family had been for generations. This wanting to call out the guard for every little dogfight was old-womanish and hysterical, which Mike Burns was for all his military service.

Caleb Brown knew he ought to get up; he gave it another few minutes. By late afternoon there would be a lot of parties going full blast; in their cabins and tents, in the hotel dorms, the kids would be filling clean garbage cans with cans of beer and bags of ice. Cheap, sugary wine would flow and the air would be bluegray with marijuana smoke. The potheads didn't worry him too much; it was the pillheads who made the most trouble. According to the State Drug Control people, LSD was much less popular than it had been ten years before. It seemed that the little bastards, spoiled brats really, were afraid of it. The hard stuff, heroin, never had been a problem in Yorkport or in any other part of Maine.

He wished he didn't have to police the O'Neal woman's party. It wasn't that he expected any trouble there, but he hated to be tied down to one place. His usual Fourth of July routine was to cruise around, paying special attention to the trouble spots, meaning the ramshackle houses where any number of teenagers lived and you could do anything short of burning the place. The bastards who owned these places fixed nothing, replaced nothing from one year to the next. If you wrecked the furniture, such as it was, well then you had to live with broken furniture.

And the not so funny thing was, they got some of the best summer rents in town because no one else would rent to the delinquents who lived there. These were the places trouble would be, not at Mrs. O'Neal's party, but he didn't seee how he could get out of it. Obviously Mrs. O'Neal was planning to become a permanent fixture in Yorkport, and more than likely she'd start giving money to the town. They already had a new community center courtesy of Sandor Antonescu who believed in clean-living young people (haw-haw); the library had been repaired and enlarged thanks to old lady Stein. What could Mrs. O'Neal give? No sweat: the town fathers would think of something they didn't want to pay for. But whatever she gave, and it was sure to be big, it would make her a power in the town, and a smart police chief stayed on the good side of those with the power. Therefore he would guard her party like it was some big doings in Washington, D.C. There might even be a little money in it; a discreet gratuity was okay as long as it wasn't in the form of a check. But money or no money, he'd have to be there. It was as plain as the nose on his wife's face.

This time tomorrow it'll be all over for another year, he thought, looking at the clock. Then one more big holiday, Labor Day, and he could look forward to nine months of peace. Long, dark, rainy or snowy days on which nothing happened.

Caleb Brown longed for inaction as a Muslim longs for paradise. In better humor now, he called out, "What's for breakfast, Katy old girl?"

"That's for me to know and you to find out," Katy called back.

It was a joke they had.

While the chief of police was having breakfast, Gately was talking to Colonel Burns on the phone. Darryl was out on the deck getting the early sun when the call came.

"Good morning, Leonard," the colonel said briskly. "Beautiful day for the Fourth, isn't it?"

"Couldn't be better, sir," Gately answered, wondering what Mike wanted. Holding the phone to his ear, he stretched out his free hand and looked at it. Only a slight tremor remained; his no-drinking policy was paying off.

"The parade steps off promptly at one," the colonel reminded him. "It's going to be a lot more orderly this year, I can promise you."

"I'll be there, sir," Gately said.

There was a sharp intake of breath at the other end. "What do you mean you'll be there, Leonard? Aren't you going to march with us, as always?"

Gately didn't miss the iron in the other man's voice. "Well, sir, I'd very much like to, but my knee has been acting up. These old war wounds stay with us all our lives." Gately had decided there was no way he was going to march in the parade, not with Ira Molson and his beer belly. His life was changing and he had to change with it. Hell! He'd done his bit for his country. He'd gone willingly to Nam while the rest of the cowardly bastards were running off to Canada or Sweden. He didn't have to march in any parade to prove his patriotism.

"Your leg hurts that much?" the colonel asked without much sympathy. He sounded like an officer trying to shame a malingerer out of a hospital bed and back into the front lines. That was Mike's style and it irritated Gately because now it was directed at him.

"Pretty bad, sir," Gately said. "It's red and swollen. It's been like that before . I'm not complaining. There's nothing much can be done for it. I'll just have to take it easy for a few days."

The colonel had a suggestion. "You could ride on the float with the other disabled veterans."

Jesus Christ! Mike wanted him to ride with basket cases, paraplegics, doddering geezers from World War One! The guy must be out of his fucking mind. Maybe he was, a little. Suppose Tracy turned up out of curiosity? There he'd be, part of the freak show. She'd think it peculiar, to say the least.

"Did you hear what I said, Leonard?" the colonel barked.

"I don't think I'm up to it, sir," Gately said, wanting to tell Mike to go to hell. But Mike was a friend, after all, and there was no sense burning his bridges until he knew what was on the other side. "The sun will be hot and the pain's made me kind of woozy. But I'll be there on the sidelines, you can depend on that."

Again there was the sharp intake of breath, always a sign that the colonel was annoyed. Then he said stiffly, "If that's your decision, Leonard, I wouldn't think of trying to change your mind. Sorry I didn't stop to talk to you the other day, but you seemed so . . . preoccupied with Mrs. O'Neal."

"A business thing," Gately said casually. "She wanted to buy a house that abuts on her property. I gave her a price and she agreed to it. Now the house is hers. Like I said, a business thing. You should have stopped. I'd have introduced you."

The colonel gave out with a creaky, unpleasant laugh. "Yes, I'm sure you would. However, that's one pleasure I'm willing to forego."

Fuck you, Mike, Gately thought. "I guess she's nice enough in her way. I thought she'd quibble about the price, which I might add was kind of steep, but she didn't bat an eye. I made a nice piece of change on that and all I had to lay out was the price of a lunch."

The colonel's tone grew sharper, more unpleasant. "You seem quite taken with the lady."

Gately tried to turn the thrust aside without losing his temper, which was close to the surface now that he had condemned himself to temporary sobriety. "I'd hardly say that, sir. Mrs. O'Neal is a client like all the others I have dealings with."

The colonel laughed again. "Don't be so modest, Leonard. I've been told that the lady has invited you to her quote-unquote fabulous party. You're the talk of the village, my boy. Wherein lies the secret of your fatal charm?"

Mike was going too far; who the fuck did he think he was talking to? Some redneck recruit? But Gately made one last try for old times sake. "She invited me all right and you can imagine how surprised I was. I guess I'll go if only out of curiosity. See how the other half lives."

"Don't you know, Leonard? Don't you know how these people live?"

"These people didn't invite me, sir. Mrs. O'Neal did."

"Is there a difference?"

"I think there is, sir, and I'd like to remind you . . ."

The colonel cut in. "No, let *me* remind *you*. You may be ready to make distinctions, but

I'm not. As far as I'm concerned they're all cut from the same cloth. Mrs. O'Neal, all of them. How many times have you said so yourself? Were you just talking or did you mean what you said? As a member of Sentinel you must know the danger these people pose to our country." The colonel was close to shouting. "Well, don't you have anything to say?"

"Sure I have, Colonel."

"Then say it."

"Fuck you and Sentinel, sir," Gately roared, and slammed down the phone.

Darryl came in from the deck with a puzzled grin on his face. "What was that all about, old buddy? I couldn't help overhearing the last part. Did I just hear you telling Mike Burns to go fuck himself?"

"You heard right," Gately said, socking one fist into the other palm. "I don't have to explain my actions to that old fart. Where does he think he is? Russia? If there's one thing I hate it's people telling me what to do. 'Wherein lies the secret of my fatal charm?' I don't need that kind of sarcastic shit, not from Mike. I don't even know why I'm going on about it. Life is too short, right?"

"You look a little shook up, buddy. Sit down and I'll fix you a drink. Just one. I'm not trying to get you started on the demon rum. I'll have one with you."

"No thanks," Gately said. "But you help

yourself."

Bates held up his vodka and tonic. "I have one, buddy. You sure you want to break with Mike and Sentinel? Both have meant a lot to you. Why don't you call Mike back and say you got out of the wrong side of the bed? Two old warhorses like you guys shouldn't be fighting."

"Not a chance," Gately said. "Let Mike talk to Ira Molson any way he likes. He won't talk that way to me. Shit! I was about the first to join when he started Sentinel here. So who is he to question what I do?"

Bates sipped his drink. "You got a point there," he said thoughtfully. "Mike would be one up on you if you called."

"That's why I'm not calling. If there's any calling to be done, let him do it. He won't"

Bates raised his glass. "Then here's to life without Sentinel."

"Cheers," Gately said, cupping his fingers around nothing and raising his hand in salutation.

"Will you go to the parade?" Bates asked.

"Mike doesn't own the parade," Gately said. "I guess I'll put in an appearance. It's expected. Anyway I'll go for a minute and won't wear my uniform. Everybody knows I was in Nam. A lot of guys in that parade never got out of the States or were in supply."

"Don't I know it." Bates had used his rheu-

329

matic heart to dodge the draft. "Maybe you did the right thing telling Mike off. Power means making other people do what you want them to do. Some people try bribery and flattery, but when you come right down to it power is based in fear of some kind. Mike thinks you can't do without him."

"That's where he's wrong."

"He thinks you'll miss the comradeship of the organization."

"Wrong again. I can stand on my own two feet."

So can a blue-assed baboon, Bates thought, hating the man he was smiling at. If I work it right, I can destroy the son of a bitch, make him an object of ridicule, leave him with nothing. How sweet that would be!

I'll do it after the parade, Bates decided. That should give them enough time to check him out.

Gately said, "You want to see the parade?"

"Yeah, I'd like that," Bates said. "It's getting to be about that time. Let me have another blast and I'll go and get dressed."

At 2:15 Mary Galligan answered the telephone and a man with a foreign accent asked to speak to Mrs. O'Neal. The accent was heavy, and Middle European, but the English was good. "Would this be Mrs.

330

O'Neal?" he enquired.

"No, it isn't," Mary Galligan said. "How did you get this number?"

"That is of no importance, young lady. I must speak to Mrs. O'Neal. You will be so good as to bring her to the phone immediately. I will wait."

"I'm afraid I can't do that. Mrs. O'Neal isn't here. I'm her secretary, Miss Galligan. Please tell me your name and what this is about."

"My name? My name is Hauser. All right? I am with an organization dedicated to resisting the forces of fascist repression. We have done much good work in this country and in Europe. They must be stopped, Miss Galligan. Please do not be impatient. It is vital that you listen to me. It has come to our attention that Mrs. O'Neal will have a guest at her party, a certain Mr. Leonard Grimes Gately. Is that not so?"

He sounded quite old, definitely Jewish. "I'm listening, Mr. Hauser," Mary Galligan said. "Please be brief. I'm expecting other calls."

There was a dry laugh. "Let them wait, Miss Galligan. My organization, I too, believe this Gately to be an extremely dangerous man. He has that potential as I will explain to you. He is a member of an extreme right wing group known as Sentinel. Some of its members are harmless cranks. Gately is not. He is violent, unstable, alcoholic, and has many weapons in his possession. No, I am not talking about his gun collecting. Military weapons, Miss Galligan. Semi-automatic weapons. It is rumored that he has submachine-guns and he has boasted that some day he will use them."

"I think you're exaggerating, Mr. Hauser. I've met Mr. Gately and he seemed all right to me. But go on."

"I was about to, Miss Galligan. I do not doubt that Gately can be personable enough at times, yet not more than a few evenings ago he brutally beat two young women during a party at his house. He also inflicted severe injuries on a young man named Darryl Bates who attempted to come to their aid. This is true, Miss Galligan, every word of it, and I can prove it."

"Why didn't they go to the police, Mr. Hauser?"

"Because they were afraid, because Gately threatened them with further harm if they did. That is the kind of man he is. Hearing of this incident, the leader of the Sentinel group, a Colonel Burns, has expelled him from membership. Even they are afraid of him, you see. These brutal beatings may yet be investigated by the police."

"I see," Mary Galligan said, making notes on a pad.

"You will see when I have finished. It is a well known fact that all the members of Sentinel hated President Callaway. It was even believed that Sentinel was somehow connected with President Callaway's assassination. This connection has yet to be established. Perhaps we will do it some day. And now you have invited this Gately to be a guest at a party where Senator John Morrison Callaway will be present. You think this is not a cause for concern?"

"You seem to know an awful lot about the guests, Mr. Hauser."

"It is our business to know, young lady. Now I will give you the names of the women assaulted by Gately. Write this down. They are Susan Patricia Gately—yes, his ex-wife—also known as Suzie; and Miss Angela Frances Beal. Both are residents of Boston and I will give you now their addresses and telephone numbers. The man is Darryl William Bates, also of Boston. You have that? Good. Miss Beal and Mr. Bates work together at a radio station. Here is the telephone number. I beg you, do not take this lightly, Miss Galligan. Goodbye."

"Wait, Mr. Hauser," Mary Galligan said quickly. "I think you should come here and tell your story to Senator Callaway. Where are you? Are you in Maine?"

"I have given you the facts, Miss Galligan. Do you need to have them repeated? No? Very well. Then the rest is up to you. Once again I will say goodbye."

The line went dead.

It was 2:30 when Bates joined Gately at the lunch counter in the drugstore. The place was filled with people from the parade. Gately had a glum look on his face, but he brightened up when he saw his friend.

Bates climbed onto the next stool and ordered a vanilla milk shake. "I called the cottage and her roommate told me she'd gone back to Boston. So I had to call Boston and finally got her."

"What's she doing in Boston?"

Bates grinned. "She had a fight with her roommate and left in a huff. And I was counting on having her over tonight while you were at the party. She's something all right. I got horny just hearing her voice on the phone."

"The town's full of broads, old buddy. Don't sweat it. You'll find something else."

Bates made a lewd noise and rolled his eyes. "Not something like this. It's me for Boston, old boy. That's right, I'm invited. Much as I hate to leave you, duty calls and I must obey. For yours truly this will be a glorious Fourth. With her I know I'll be able to go at least four times."

"You dog," Gately said in a dull voice.

"Hey, what's eating you? This is your big day, the party and all."

"Ah, it just pisses me the way Mike looked right through me at the parade. I was standing there on the sidewalk and I know he saw me. Well, you know, I snapped a salute out of respect for the uniform, but he pretended not to see me."

Bates said, grinning, "Well, as you put it so succinctly, 'Fuck him.' "

Gately grinned back. "I did say that, didn't I?"

"If you need a witness I'm available. And now I'm off to Beantown by the fastest possible accommodation."

"Take the office car, buddy. I'll drive the other one to the party. You can bring it back on the weekend."

"You're tops with me," Bates said. "Have yourself a high old time, buddy. I'll be looking foward to hearing about it."

"That you will," Gately said. "Don't forget to give her one for me."

The senator was listening to Mary Galligan with complete seriousness. Tracy was there too. The door of the library was closed and Shaw, the butler, had been told to allow no interruptions for any reason.

Prompted by her notebook, Mary Galligan repeated the conversation almost word for word. "I don't think Hauser is his real name," she said.

"Probably not," the senator agreed. "But you have no doubt that he was serious?"

"None at all. I've had some experience with crank callers and you get to know after a while. I'd say he was very serious. No hysteria, no wild talk, no mention of money. He sounded old and Jewish. German-Jewish, I would say. Peremptory. You know how they sound."

Tracy said, "It's all so hard to believe. I had lunch with Mr. Gately just the other day."

"Yes, I know," the senator said sharply. "I don't like it, Trace. It will have to be checked out. I still remember how Dan got shot. A meek little Arab with thick glasses and a smile on his face. A dirty little raghead, but he killed the President of the United States. All right then, it's time to go to work. Mary, you stick with me. We've got a lot of telephoning to do. Of all the days for this to happen. Let's start with the director of the FBI."

Driving home, Gately thought it was just as well that Darryl had gone. There had been too much talk about the party and he didn't want to hear any more of it. Darryl was better off with the broad; that was where he belonged, with the bullshit talk, the drinks, the radio tuned in to what Darryl called "music for fucking." He'd be back on the weekend because Darryl loved Yorkport.

Gately looked at his watch. Three o'clock. Opening the refrigerator, he stared longingly at the rows of cold Beck's standing like good soldiers; there were three quarts of vodka in the bin that was meant for vegetables. No, he decided with grim resolution, no drinks till the party. He smacked his lips, thinking of the first tall cold drink. What would he have? Scotch and soda with plenty of ice? A vodka Collins? Definitely not a beer.

He cursed while he tried to open a container of grapefruit juice. Damn these fucking paper things; it said "Open here," so why the fuck didn't it open? Furious now, he took a knife with a serrated edge and sawed off the top of the container. Then, trying to avoid the drips, he drank a quart of juice without moving away from the refrigerator. He belched windily and threw the empty container away.

Time hung heavy on his hands.

He had showered that morning; now he showered again. For a while he sat in the Great Hall with a bath towel wrapped around him. The bald eagle in the Uncle Sam suit stared down at him with beady eyes. Ranked along the walls were his weapons, ancient and modern. On this day, for some reason, they brought him no comfort. Fuck it.

In his bedroom Gately set the alarm for six-thirty; that would give him three hours sleep before he dressed for the party. Then he would broil part of a steak to set him up for the evening ahead. It was a strange way to be spending the Fourth, always his day more than any

337

other. Since he first came to Yorkport the Fourth had been a blast that lasted all day and all night. But he was doing the right thing. He knew that. Still, he felt some nostalgia for a simpler past.

Leonard Gately drifted off to sleep.

The last of the calls had been returned; now the senator sat with Tracy and Mary Galligan. It was fifteen minutes before six and the senator had all he needed to know about Leonard Gately. The last call had come from the FBI office in Boston.

"Your Mr. Hauser knows his stuff," he said to Mary Galligan. "The only thing that remains a mystery is Mr. Hauser himself. Gately beat the women, all right. The ex-wife didn't want to talk about it and my people had to use national security before she'd say what happened. Angela Beal was much less reluctant, but her story fits. There was some kind of wild party and Gately tried to force the women to commit unnatural acts. I'm not sure they were so unwilling. That's beside the point. Gately beat them savagely with a leather belt. Bates tried to stop him and was injured himself. The Beal girl thinks Gately used some kind of judo. Bates told the same story but my people had to push him hard to get him to talk. My people had to persude him there would be no police proceedings. He was the last one they caught up with. He's scared of losing his job, but he talked. It's a dirty busines, Trace."

Mary Galligan said, "That sort of thing goes on, Johnny."

"No one I know does it," the senator said. "The other accusations Hauser made are fairly standard for these extremists. You listened in on some of the reports. Gately and these Sentinel people are in the Attorney General's computers, but that doesn't mean so very much. We have a congressmen, admirals, generals who belong to Sentinel. Most are retired, like this Colonel Burns. Gately's opinions are hardly more extremist than theirs. But you don't want him here, Trace, tonight or any other time."

"Of course not, Johnny," Tracy said. "How should I go about withdrawing the invitation? Should Mary call?"

The senator shook his head. "I'll do it," he said.

Tracy had been thinking. "He has my check for the house. What do you think is going to happen now?"

"It would seem to me that the house is yours. Gately told you so himself. Talk to your lawyer tomorrow, Trace. Right now this is more important."

"Try to be tactful, Johnny," Tracy said.

"Tact doesn't work with people like that,"

the senator said.

Up before the alarm went off, Leonard Gately was resplendent in party clothes as he went to answer the telephone. Sleep had chased away the blues and he picked up the phone with a cheery, "Hello, this is Leonard Gately speaking. What can I do for you?"

"This is Senator John Callaway," a flat Boston voice stated.

Gately laughed. "That you, Darryl?"

"This is Senator John Callaway and it's no joke."

Gately frowned. It sure sounded like him. What the hell was going on down here? "Sorry, Senator, what can I do for you?"

"What you can do for me is listen, Mr. Gately, The invitation to Mrs. O'Neal's party is withdrawn as of this moment. It was a mistake to have invited you and now I am rectifying that mistake. Do not come to the party, is that clear? Do you want me to go into the reasons?"

Gately didn't know what was going on, but his temper was rising. "Sure," he said harshly. "Why don't you do that, Senator."

"Very well then. A few nights ago you made a sadistic attack on two women, Angela Beal and your ex-wife. You also injured a man named Darryl Bates. Don't try to deny it. It's already been checked out at my request. Thoroughly checked. You could go to prison if any of these people decided to press charges."

Gately's head was spinning. "The whole thing is a lie! My ex-wife is always making up lies about me."

The senator's voice remained flat and unemotional. "The matter has been investigated to my satisfaction. Statements have been taken from the people involved. It's just one more step to the grand jury. Is that what you want? Of course not. Therefore you will not come to Mrs. O'Neal's party and you will not try to contact her again. In the matter of the house, I suggest that you talk to your lawyer."

"You bet your fucking ass I will, Senator!" Gately's face was suffused with blood and his hands shook.

"That's what the courts are for," the senator went on calmly. "I might add that I am a United States senator. I'm not quite sure you know what that means, but you'll find out soon enough if you make the slightest trouble. That's it, Gately. I have nothing more to say."

"Just a fucking minute," Gately roared. "That cunt used me to get that house cheap. Now she thinks she's got it. Like hell she does. What she's going to get is a big fucking ugly motel right in her front yard!"

"I doubt that," the senator said. "Your dealings with regard to the house have been completely unethical, perhaps criminal. The least that can happen to you is the loss of your license. The worst . . . better talk to your lawyer."

Gately ground the telephone against his ear. "You can't threaten me, you son of a bitch politician!"

"I wouldn't do anything so rash," the senator said.

Gately replaced the receiver and went to the kitchen to get a drink. Slopping iced vodka into a highball glass, he drank a quarter of a pint in two gulps. He kicked the refrigerator shut and carried bottle and glass into the Great Hall. With a curse he ripped his tie from his Size 17 collar and threw it away from him. Then he stripped off his jacket and tossed it after the tie. Jesus Christ, but he was mad! The doublecrossing no-good sons of bitches! He'd broken his fucking balls to get her the house and now she'd turned on him like the cunt she was.

How the fuck did she hear about what happened at his party? Had she been checking up on him all the time? Callaway said the cops— no, he didn't exactly say cops—had taken statements from Darryl and the bitches. If not the cops, then who? The fucking FBI? Some other agency he'd never heard of? For an in-

stant there was sudden panic, but he killed it
with another enormous drink. He stared at the
new jacket lying on the dirty floor. The suit
had set him back three hundred bucks, a lot of
money for a summer suit. Fuck the suit! Maybe
Angela the cunt was the one who started the
trouble. Yeah, it figured to be Angela. He tried
to think of his other enemies. Fuck it. It had to
be Angela. Suzie might get mad but she'd
never go through with it. What about Darryl? It
couldn't be Darryl. All right, he knocked the
guy around, but he'd apologized for that. Darryl wouldn't rat on him even for a banged-up
knee. Then what about these statements?
They must have come down heavy on the guy
to get him to make a statement. Aw shit, Darryl could always take it back, that is, if he
made it in the first place. Darryl was always
short of money and a thousand dollars in his
hand would turn him around. Suzie would turn
around too or she'd find herself living in a cold-
water flat on the back side of Beacon Hill.
That left only Angela. How he was going to get
to her he didn't know. Jesus Christ! Why was
she making such a big thing out of a few licks
with a belt? Some women even paid good
money to get whipped. The thing to do was to
call Darryl and get the scoop from him.

Panic came again when he realized that the
line might be tapped. If Callaway could check

him out so fast, tapping a phone would be no big deal. But he'd have to take a chance, just the same. The important thing was to find out how Darryl sounded, how he reacted to the call. The problem was—where was Darryl? Ten to one, he'd be at the broad's place by now. What the fuck was the broad's name? He hadn't a clue. Maybe Darryl had it written down somewhere in his room. The hell with that. There might be a dozen names in there.

Take it easy, mister, he told himself. Don't get your balls in an uproar. The cops were no problem at the moment. Yeah, but could he believe the fucking senator? Could you believe anything those bastards said? They had faked him out on the house, so why wouldn't they try to fake him out on everything else? Mike was right. He should have listened to Mike. He felt like an idiot when he thought of Mike. Keep away from those fuckers, Mike had warned him, but would he listen? Hell no, he was too fucking smart to listen to Mike. Well, maybe it wasn't too late to get back with Mike, that great crusty old guy. He felt a sudden warmth for Mike and all the people who belonged to Sentinel. Even Ira Molson wasn't so bad. Good or bad, Ira was better than the people he'd been sucking up to.

"Call Darryl," he said aloud.

He emptied his glass and dialed Darryl's

number in Boston. It burred twenty times before he gave up. Why the fuck hadn't Darryl called the minute Callaway's goons took off? That meant they had warned him not to call. But that didn't make sense. Callaway had called himself. Shit! He'd better call Suzie and see what she had to say. This was one time when he'd have to be nice to her.

Gately had been grinding his teeth so hard that his jaws ached. He could hear his heart thumping; sweat had soaked through his shirt; he found it hard to think. He dialed Suzie's number but got a digit wrong and the phone was answered by some old woman with an Italian accent. He slammed down the phone and dialed again.

Suzie answered, snuffling through her tears. She sounded drunk. "Whatta you want?" she mumbled.

"This is Leonard," Gately said. "You all right and everything?"

"You must have the wrong number, sir. I don't know any Leonards."

Sweat dripped from Gately's chin; he wanted to kill her. Wanting to do that made his heart beat faster. "Stop kidding around," he said. "It's Leonard."

"What do you want, Leonard! Listen, sir, you could just be pretending to be Leonard. Will the real Leonard please stand up?"

"Knock it off, you bitch."

Suzie laughed drunkenly. "Now *that* sounds like the real Leonard. but it can't be. The real Leonard is in jail for beating women with a belt. I think you must be an impostor, masked man."

Gately took a deep breath. "What did you say to the cops, Suzie?"

"I told them you were a bad boy, Leonard."

"Specifically, Suzie, what did you tell them?"

"You want to know specifically? Specifically I said you were a mean motherfucker. Oh, you want to know *specifically*." Suzie's voice started to go to pieces. "I told them what you did, Lenny, all of it. They weren't sneaky like you, they put the tape recorder right on the table. They said I didn't have to be afraid of you, so I told them."

"Why the fuck did you do that?"

"Because I've had you up to here, that's why. You know what I'm doing. Lenny? I'm feeling the bump in my nose where you broke it. It was a pretty nose before you broke it. Why'd you have to do that, you son of a bitch?"

"Look, your nose can be fixed. I'll pay for it, okay?"

"*You* ought to be fixed. Maybe you are fixed. I'm tired of talking to you, old buddy."

"You'll be sorry for this," Gately shouted.

"When the money runs out, don't come begging to me for more. There won't be any."

"Good. I knew you'd say that, soldier. Old buddy, old hoss, old faggot. That's what Darryl called you that night, only you were too drunk to remember."

"You lying, drunken cunt!"

"It's true, good buddy. Darryl spat in your face and called you a big fat faggot. Your creepy friend was a hero that night. Is your creepy friend with you? Ask him. You've been after his ass but you won't let yourself admit it. You're a big fat faggot, Lenny."

"You're finished with me. You'll fucking starve without me!"

Suzie made a spitting sound. "I'm doing it too, hotshot, spitting in your face. I won't starve, old buddy. I'll wash dishes before I come back groveling to you. Got to go now. Have a good time at the party."

They're all going crazy, Gately thought. The bitch was talking back to him, the craziest thing he'd ever heard in his life. The knob-nosed bitch had to be crazy out of her skull to talk to him like that. What was all that shit about Darryl calling him a faggot? Something stirred in the dim recesses of his mind. Images flickered there like worn-out silent movies. They became clearer in spite of a powerful effort to suppress them. Now there was sound as well as pictures; he heard Darryl's voice. *Dirty faggot. Dirty faggot.*

Gately slopped vodka into his glass and drank it off. The empty glass broke in his hand, cutting him. He dropped it and stared at his bleeding hand. He went to the kitchen to get another glass, then he wrapped his hand in a dish towel and stood breathing through his mouth. Darryl, the two-faced son of a bitch! Darryl, the dirty stinking ass-kissing hack writer! Darryl, the nothing! But would Darryl have the balls to fuck him with Tracy? There was no way to tell, but there was Darryl's long phone call right after the parade broke up . . . no, fuck it, it couldn't be Darryl. It wasn't Darryl and it wasn't Angela. If they did anything, they would go to the cops or they'd sue him for a lot of money. They'd go after the money because they didn't have a pot to piss in. Tracy had rigged the whole thing by herself. She got the house so she said, "Fuck this Gately, this peasant." That was how these people were, ruthless, scheming bastards. Darryl was all washed up with him: no more freebies, no more nothing. It was a good thing he knew what Darryl was really like. A rat. Say no more about it.

Mike Burns was the only straight guy in a nest of rats. Good old Mike. Mike would chew his ass out, but that was all right. He'd go to

Mike and say, "I fucked up, sir, I admit it. I'm ready to take company punishment. I leave that up to you, sir." All that would be a gag, naturally, and he knew Mike would go along with it. Mike looked a little like Henry Morgan, who played the colonel on MASH. Gruff but good-hearted. But first he'd better call the guy.

Mike Burns answered the phone. "This is Burns."

"Leonard Gately calling, sir." Gately grinned stupidly. "You got a minute for me, Colonel?"

"What do you want?" Burns said. "I was just sitting down to dinner."

"I'm calling to apologize, sir," Gately said. "I had too much to drink and I want to say I'm sorry for what I said. It was completely out of order and I'm sorry. Don't be too hard on me, sir."

Gately expected the colonel to bark at him in the old familiar way. Instead, the colonel's voice was very quiet. "It's a bit late for apologies. In my thirty years in the military no one ever talked to me that way. They would have been sorry if they had. But that's neither here nor there."

"I said I was sorry, sir."

"Let's not go into that. I don't know what kind of trouble you're in and I don't want to know. What I do know is I had some government people on the phone this afternoon, asking questions about you and what your connection was with Sentinel. I said you no longer belonged to Sentinel. That's right. You're out and you're going to stay out. How many times have I told you not to do anything that would bring the government down on us? But it seems you've done just that. I don't like to get calls like that. It makes me and the organization look bad. It won't happen again, I can tell you. The monies you have given to Sentinel will be returned by check. Don't call here again."

Gately had another drink and began to laugh. Still laughing, he bumped into a table and knocked it over. Still laughing, he kicked the table to bits. He used the bloody dish towel to wipe the sweat from his face. Everything was going wrong. Every fucking thing that could go wrong had gone wrong. Murphy's law. And all in one day. It was like God woke up with a hangover and said, "I'm going to nail some fucker today." Then God went through his Rollodex and said, "Here's the guy I'm gonna fuck today. Leonard Gately the real estate man. I'm gonna zing it to that cocksucker. First I'm gonna do this, then I'm gonna do that. . . ."

The first quart of vodka was gone; Gately smashed the bottle against the wall. He threw the glass on the floor and it rolled away without breaking. Without knowing why, he took an 18th century Scottish claymore down from the wall and began to hack at the furniture. Raising the two-handed sword above his head, he brought it down, splitting the table in the Great Hall. He picked up a piece of wood and threw it at the bald eagle in the Uncle Sam suit. The stuffed bird fell in a cloud of dust.

After another drink he began to think about guns.

CHAPTER EIGHTEEN

The sounds of Roger deCourcy's orchestra drifted across the darkening waters of Hard Luck Bay. A 1940's foxtrot for the older guests, the "corset crowd," as deCourcy called them. Later there would be other music, especially disco. DuDourcy's musicians could play anything; they didn't play from sheets. Many were old cruise ship hands and they knew how to please.

The governor of the state, on his way to Washington, stayed long enough for a drink and a dance with Tracy, a short chat with the senator. Tracy made him promise to drop in on his way back to Augusta. The governor said he was looking forward to it.

"You shouldn't scare the governor like that, Johnny."

"I'm not out to scare anyone."

"You must have scared Gately. I was there when you called. I'm curious. How did he take it?"

"Not very well, but he took it. Between the two of us, I wish Tracy had met his original price. It would have been simpler. But there's no harm done that I can see. . . . What's so interesting about the parking lot, may I ask? You've seen one parking lot, you've seen them all. Like Reagan and the redwoods. Someone coming that I don't know about?

"You don't miss much, Johnny," Mary Galligan said. "Yes, there is someone, a reporter for a local paper. I met him the other day when I delivered his invitation to the party. He's shy but pretends he isn't. I suppose all reporters think they're supposed to be brash."

"Married?"

"How did you know?"

"He'd be here by now if he wasn't. Why do you think Trace invited him?"

Mary Galligan looked puzzled. "She didn't say and I've been wondering ever since. He wondered himself so I had to say it was because she'd read some stories he'd written about this house."

"It could be that," the senator said. "Take it

slow, Mary. You've been so tense lately. Don't get jammed up."

"I wouldn't mind getting jammed up," Mary Galligan said.

Roger deCourcy and his orchestra were beating out an old disco number made famous by Joanie Summers and all but the bravest of the oldsters got off the floor. "Chicken!" Linwood Duval called to Ormond Bailey as he retreated to a safer position. A fixture at Studio 54 before the IRS moved in and sent the owners to prison, Duval knew all the steps. He was light on his feet, as fat men often are, and now his partner was the rangy publisher of a national feminist magazine who didn't object to dancing with men so long as they were fags. Clad in leather, because leather "breathes" and vinyl does not, she towered over Duval with good natured menace. Duval matched his pudgy body to her wild gyrations.

"Look at that faggot go," Sarah Bannard said to Dee when they came in. "Get me a drink, sweetheart, and we'll show them what a couple of Daughters of Bilitis can do."

"I'm not going to dance with you," Dee said angrily. "This is a mixed party and I'm not going to dance with you. This isn't Antibes."

"Jeepers, I thought it was! Willya look at all the famous rich celebrated celebrities? There's that kid from the supermarket. I want you to run over there and get his autograph. But don't say it's for me because that would be too shy-making. What do you mean, you won't dance with me?"

"That's what I said. There's Cal Cameron. Why don't you dance with him?"

"Dance with the devil? Are you crazy? I'm going to ask Freddy DiSalvo to dance. The little wop just came in. You think that's his Confirmation suit?"

"Jesus, Sarah, you promised to behave. We're not here five minutes and you're getting nasty."

"Grab that waiter," Sarah said. "Take the whole tray. I'm going to play kissy-face with Tracy. You can play kissy-face too if you're a good lesbian."

"How wonderful you look," Tracy exclaimed, taking Sarah's hands in hers, not wanting Sarah to get too close. She allowed Sarah to kiss her. "Wherever did you find that lovely dress?"

"I made it myself," Sarah said modestly. "Whipped it up on the Singer in my spare time."

All Tracy could do was laugh; the woman was out of her mind. "The senator—Johnny Callaway—would like to meet you. He was a very good friend of your father's."

"Dear old dad," Sarah said. "How I miss him.

But off with the old, on with the new, as the fella said. It's a lovely party, Trace, and I'm so glad you invited us. I'll never forget you for this."

"Don't be silly," Tracy said nervously, starting to edge away. "The senator is out on the terrace."

Dee handed Sarah a martini. "Make that last," she said.

"Why? Have they closed the bar?"

"Let's go out on the terrace," Dee pleaded. "I have a headache."

"You're not supposed to say that until you get into bed. 'Not tonight, John dear—I have the most frightful headache.'"

The band played on.

"I wouldn't have thought he was your type," the big feminist said when she caught Duval looking in Freddy's DiSalvo's direction. "That would be doubly queer."

Duval didn't object to the word "queer;" he liked it better than "gay." He always said calling someone gay was like calling a garbageman a sanitation engineer.

"Never get in bed with a Mafioso, not even an old one," Duval said. "There may be a book in him, maybe even a play. Anyway, I want to listen to him talk, to find out where he stands politically. I'm sure he's a reactionary. All mobsters are."

"Remember me?" Duval asked DiSalvo when the feminist turned him loose.

"Oh yeah," DiSalvo said. He couldn't say he hated faggots—what was the percentage?—but he found it impossible to understand them. Why would a guy want to stick his dick up another guy's ass when there was so much sweet pussy around? But live and let live. Reaching into his pants pocket to get his gold lighter his fingers touched the short-barreled .32 Beretta. Earlier that evening, dressing for the party, he thought about leaving the stubby automatic at home. But better safe than sorry; he slipped the pistol in his pocket after checking the clip.

Duval saw that the elderly mobster smoked English Ovals just like Frank Costello, long since gathered to the angels. There seemed to be something terribly honest about DiSalvo, as if he had accepted what he was. "Call me Fred," he said. "I like Fred better than Freddy."

"They call me Linny because my name is Linwood," Duval said. "I'd much rather be called Woody, but no one goes along with it."

DiSalvo nodded. "A lot of things we want we can't have," he said.

Sandor Antonescu came in at the same time as the Delaneys. He was approaching the third stage of his nightly drunkenness; the stage where he moved like the walking dead, steady

357

and straight, slurring his words only slightly. In a little while he would be drunk as a lord, that is, aristocratically intoxicated. He still hadn't decided on a plan of action for Greg Delaney. He just didn't know what he was going to do. Perhaps he would simply offer the aging choirboy a lot of money. His job on the *Star* couldn't pay very much. Jobs like that never did.

Sandor Antonescu was dressed as the Duke of Wellington; let the others dress informally; he wanted to come in style. Now he raised his plumed hat and smiled at the Delaneys.

"My two favorite people," he said. "How have you been?"

"Pretty good, Sandor," Greg said, wanting nothing to do with this guy.

"And how are things in the world of literature?" Antonescu asked Carol.

"Pretty good," Carol answered.

Such brilliant conversation, Antonescu thought as they moved away. The bitch didn't like him; did she suspect something? No, he wouldn't be so crass as to offer money. What he might do was to hint that he was interested in buying the *Star*. If he bought the paper it would be necessary to find a new editor. Hayward, the present editor, was too old, too set in his ways to bring in new readers. Therefore, a new editor would be needed; a young man with a nice ass. Of course he couldn't come right out and talk about nice asses, yet there were ways of saying things without saying them. These young journalists were so ambitious, especially when they had neurotic wives goading them with a sharp stick.

Reviewing his tall, slim figure, Antonescu decided that he looked very much like the Iron Duke in lusty middle age. Wellington's schnoz was a great deal larger, while his own might be described as hawk-like, bold, certainly cruel. He carried his gold plated sword in his left hand; his thigh-high boots glittered when he moved. It was true. He was magnificent.

There was a hard, bright light in Leonard Gately's head; a feeling of total isolation. Sometimes it had been like that in Nam. You were supposed to be part of a team; the truth was that you were alone. The other guys didn't give a fuck about you and you thought of them the same way. Even the guys who like to make friends crawled into their shell after the first, the second, even the third buddy got killed.

Needing other people, Gately thought, was a sign of weakness; a man ought to be self sufficient, never seeking approval for his actions, never explaining what he did or didn't do.

Drunk to the point of madness, Gately knew that he was thinking straight for the first time in his life. All that had gone before had brought the realization that he didn't have any friends and didn't need any. Those who claimed to be his friends had deceived him, but they couldn't have done it if he hadn't been weak. He had given freely; what had he received in return? Nothing but lies. Darryl, Suzie, Mike, Tracy—all hypocrites. But Tracy was the one he hated most; she had made a sucker out of him in front of the whole town. Maybe the whole story wouldn't get out, but the town would know something was wrong. Hell! Who was he trying to kid? Of course the story would get out and then he'd be screwed but good. There would be letters and phone calls; his listings would dwindle; before too long he'd be out of business. After all these years he'd be out on his ass. It wasn't fucking fair.

Maybe he could move to another town and start over again. . . . The hell with that. New England was a small place, after all; the story would follow him. So he couldn't go and he couldn't stay. He wondered if there was any way he could live it down. The answer to that was *no*. They wouldn't give him a chance.

The light in his head burned brighter when he thought of Tracy, the way she said, "Call me

Tracy. All my friends do." He remembered the way she pretended to stumble the day he took her to see the house. That was how she could get up close to him without making it seem obvious. For all her money she was just a whore, using her body to swindle him. She was worse than a whore; at least a whore gave you what you paid for. Then all that shit the day they had lunch. What a lovely lunch it was and how much she enjoyed it, and all the time she was laughing at him. Leonard Gately the idiot. Swigging warm vodka from the bottle, he thought of the jokes she must have made about him to her friends. How the faggots must have giggled. The joke about Gately the dummy would be repeated with embellishments; it would go far beyond Yorkport. The heartless, vicious bastards!

They thought they had the world by the balls. They thought they could walk all over a man's life and get away with it. They hid behind their money and got other people to run interference. Nothing could touch them, nothing could harm them, and when they felt even slightly threatened they ran screaming to their high-powered lawyers. They didn't bribe with money because they didn't have to; just wanting something was enough to get it done. But now they were fucking with the wrong guy and they didn't even know it. It was time to show them how wrong they were.

Gately, carrying the bottle, went to his bedroom and unlocked a closet that contained nothing but a metal trunk. In it was the M-16 automatic rifle that he had smuggled back from Nam so many years before. It was in perfect condition because he cleaned it once a month after he took it to a remote part of the woods and ran off a few bursts just to keep his hand in. He hefted the rifle and aimed at himself in a mirror. He grinned savagely at his sweaty face, thinking of all the little brown brothers he had killed in the jungle.

What he was going to do should have been done a long time before. It didn't matter; he was going to do it now. It was Judgment Day. Everything was so simple if you didn't let the small things get in the way. Was he afraid of the consequences? he asked himself. No. Quite honestly he could say that he was not. That was what made him different, not being afraid, and that, finally, was the measure of a man.

Slapping a loaded clip into the machine rifle, he thought, they're all dancing now, drinking and making smart conversation. The faggots, all the arty sons of bitches, are crowding around her, telling her how lovely she looks and what a lovely party it is, and she's accepting it all as her due, the dollar princess. Or did she think of herself as a queen?

He would burn the house after he killed them; the blaze would light up the sky for miles around. They said the house had cost close to two million; one match was all it would take to burn it to the ground. He wondered what she would say when she saw him behind the M-16, the clip in place, the cocking handle pulled back. Would she come toward him with her arms outstretched, saying it was all some terrible mistake, thinking all the while that her money could save her? They said she had shown great dignity in the days following her husband's assassination. Why shouldn't she? The danger was past and she was richer by ten or fifteen million dollars. By marrying O'Neal she had worked her way up to the billion dollar class. As his finger tightened on the trigger, would she think, "You can't kill me—I'm the richest woman in the world?" One bullet would stop her thinking forever. But he'd give her more than one, a lot more than one. He'd give her a few in the face so that she wouldn't be Wall Street's sweetheart any more. It would be good if she screamed and tried to run. Sure she could run but not faster than a speeding bullet. *Superman.*

Gately drank vodka until he was gasping for breath. The way to do it was to come in through the terrace. There was good cover all the way to the terrace. One or two bursts would take care of the people there. Then he'd be coming through the french windows with a fresh clip in the slot. They would turn, some of them thinking it was fireworks. Then when they saw the M-16 they would be like people frozen in time by a stop-action camera. The rattle of the M-16 would start the pictures moving again.

Gately stripped off the rest of his clothes and dressed in a camouflage suit of jungle green. Then he went to the fireplace in the Great Hall and smeared his face with soot. He slipped a British Army commando knife into the top of his rubber-soled hunting boot. It was long-bladed and rubber-handled, a silent and efficient killer; if the cunt had hired any security men, they would have to die first.

He put two extra clips for the M-16 in his belt, a bottle of vodka in his pocket. His hands no longer trembled; he was calm now, a man with a purpose. What happened after the killing and the burning was of no importance. Would he fire on the police when they came to look for him? He didn't think he would do that. If it came to a trial, he would act as his own attorney. He would explain why he did it, why it had to be done. A man had to stand up for what was right, or he was no man at all.

Walking to his pick-up truck, Leonard Gately blacked out.

Caleb Brown remembered some of the music that drifted out through the open windows. This new stuff, this disco garbage, he didn't know at all. He doubted that these disco numbers even had names. Maybe numbers. That fag bar in the village played nothing but disco. You could hear the thump-thump quarter of a mile away. It was a wonder they didn't lose their hearing with all that noise. There had been complaints, lots of complaints, but he hadn't done much about it because he knew it was a waste of time. Sure he could paper the place with summonses, cite it for disorderly conduct, public nuisance, even go after its liquor license if he felt like it. But he didn't feel like it, wasn't going to do it. Fags were fags, and what was the use of making life harder for them than it was? They called themselves "gay," but it was his experience that most of them were far from gay. Once they got a load on they started fighting and threatening to commit suicide and he could think of a few he'd had to rush to the hospital to have their stomachs pumped. It was like they were always playing a part, like actors. The way they talked, the things they wore. Some of the old summer-people fags—those people never went to the bars—did their best to live normal lives. Talked straight and dressed more or less like everyone else, even smoked pipes, a few of them. One such couple did all their own carpentry, built stone walls, cut their own firewood. Fags like that were no trouble at all. But what was the use of judging people unless they did something really awful? It took all kinds, so live and let live. It was a sensible, charitable way to look at the world, and he wished more people shared his point of view.

The band was playing a Glenn Miller tune. Caleb Brown tried to recall the name, and failed. But it had a nice bounce to it; very catchy. He knew it was Glenn Miller and not Guy Lombardo, or the Dorsey brothers, or Harry James, because it had been one of his favorites. Mellow music, good to dance to, they said.

A disco number started up and Caleb Brown left the beach side of the house and went to take a look at the parking area. All the guests had arrived and no more cars were likely to pull in before the party ended. But, good cop that he was, Caleb Brown checked around before he decided that everything was in order. Then he thought he would take a walk down by the point and get away from that damn disco music. The old Hayes house still stood there; he had known old Lem Hayes, had looked in on him from time to time when he got feeble, had attended his funeral. Now old Lem, a famous drinker of Caldwell's Old Newburyport Rum, was gone like so many oldtimers. Oldtime Maine was just about gone for good, and that was a shame, but there was no help for it.

Of course oldtime Maine wasn't all it was cracked up to be, not when you thought of how they worked you to death, dawn till dusk, and beat you down on the wages every chance they got. The summer people and the tourists might be a pain in the ass, some of them, but they had brought money into the state; they provided jobs. All those motels, lobster shacks, seafood restaurants, camp grounds, summer theaters, gift shops, and what-have-you. The price of land was going up all the time, and farmers who never had a pot to piss in were getting rich selling off parcels of land to builders. So it was dumb to resent the "foreigners," as some natives called them. You had to move with the times or get left behind.

On the point there was a strong night breeze and Caleb Brown stood there listening to the sea. As a young man he had worked on a lobster boat; had pulled traps right off this point. At least there was nothing they could do to change the sea. Not that he was sentimental about the sea—the sea was a cold, deadly killer—but he didn't hate it as most fisherman did. Caleb Brown, in his nearly sixty years, had never swum in the sea; in fact, he didn't know how to swim and never had any desire to learn. For one thing, this sea was too cold even on the hottest day of summer, so he left that sort of foolishness to the summer people and the tourists and the young natives who had learned to appreciate the beach.

Walking around the old fisherman's house, Caleb Brown thought of times past when life in Yorkport was simpler. But was it, or did he just remember it that way? It was hard to decide, looking back over the years. Life was better now, no doubt about that. He had a good job and the pay was all right and there would be a decent pension at the end of it. It wasn't like the old days when the Yorkport police chief *was* the police department, summer as well as winter, and all he got when he stepped down, or was pushed out, was a vote of thanks, a hearty handshake, and maybe a gold watch. No, say what you liked, life was better now in every way. He owned his own house and there was a color TV in the living room, a rotary antenna on the roof; and three years before he had taken Kathy to Florida for a month.

Standing on the point, listening to the dark sea, Caleb Brown realized that he loved Yorkport. Not the whole state of Maine, just his native village. That was it: he was part of it, he belonged here, and that was something to hold onto in a world where everything kept changing. Before too many years had passed Yorkport would disappear into what they called "the urban corridor" that ran right down the coast to Washington, D.C., and he might even live to see it, but what the hell, you couldn't stop progress, if that was the right name for it. Hell, it was happening right now and you were hardly aware of it. Was a time when driving the seventy-five miles to Boston was considered quite a trip because of the roads. Now with the new super highways there were people that commuted to Boston every day of the week and thought nothing of it. And look at the motels they had in the town and along the highway; as slick as anything in California, with their porn movies on pay TV, their heated swimming pools. It was all right to call a place Uncle Ezra's General Store, but on the inside the food was frozen and the cash register was eletronic and "Uncle Ezra" was probably a Syrian from Pawtucket, Rhode Island.

But it wasn't the changes you could see that made the difference; it was the state of mind. Yorkport people, Maine people, just didn't think the same way any more. There was a time when Maine was so different from the rest of America, even from the rest of New England, that it was almost a different country. To be from Maine was special, even if they thought you quaint and old-fashioned and your accent sort of funny. Percy Kilbride of the old *Maw and Paw Kettle* movie series used to get a lot of mileage, a lot of laughs, with his Maine accent. Now even the accent was changing and many of the young people sounded much the same as the young people on the TV. The TV wasn't responsible for all the changes, just most of them. Country people who'd never seen a black man in their life were now tuning in *The Jeffersons* and *Diff'rent Strokes* and getting a big kick out of it. And TV was nothing like the movies he had gone to back in the Thirties and Forties before he stopped going altogether. Back then all the heroes had to have American or at least Irish names. Not so on TV. Today on TV you had heroes that were black, Italian, Jewish, Mexican. Naturally that didn't go down well with loonies like Colonel Mike Burns, but so what—what could he do about it besides rant and rave at those Sentinel meetings?

God Almighty, what a crew they were: Burns, Lizzie Hatcher, Ira Molson, Ollie Masterson, Leonard Gately, to name the most outspoken members of this nut group. There was something wrong with all of them. Why else would they carry on the way they did? Burns had never made general and was bitter about it. Lizzie Hatcher had wanted a husband all her life and never managed to trap one. Ira Molson had a wife he knocked up at sixteen and had to marry or go to jail on a statutory rape charge. Ollie Masterson was just plain crazy. And Gately? What about him? It was hard to say what was wrong with him, but there was a screw loose there.

Think about something pleasant for a change, Caleb Brown told himself. In a few more hours the party would be over, and he could go home, sit in the kitchen in his pajamas and eat a sandwich, drink a glass of milk while he read the Portsmouth *Herald*. He knew he could eat here in Mrs. O'Neal's kitchen, but that sort of thing didn't sit well with him. After all, he wasn't a servant but the chief of police, and he could afford to buy his own meals.

In the morning he would sleep late; he had it coming to him, and the Russians wouldn't take over the town while he was getting his beauty rest. Then he'd get up, eat a big breakfast and maybe watch one of the game shows. They were dumb but relaxing. Caleb Brown yawned.

Gately came in without lights, then switched off the engine and let the truck coast down the road until he decided he was close enough. He didn't use the hand-brake when he stopped the truck and got out. There must be no noise, not a sound. He clicked the door half shut and listened to the sounds of music coming from the house. Disco shit, nigger shit written by Jews for niggers. He looked at his diver's watch: ten minutes before midnight. Too bad it wasn't New Year's Eve. They'd be singing "Auld Lang Syne" when he opened up.

The disco music stopped and the band began to play "Mood Indigo." Good for slow dancing, he thought. Closer now, screened by bushes, he listened to the music, the last music they would ever hear. He savored the moment, sweating with pleasure and anticipation. He could hear them talking on the terrace, no more than fifteen feet away. He heard the senator's voice, that flat Boston accent that was part Irish pol, part Harvard. The senator said he didn't want to be President; now he'd never get a chance to change his mind. One more minute to think.

He raised his head and counted the people on the terrace. Ten. He counted ten. The senator was talking to a fat man with a bald head. Using many gestures, Antonescu was talking to Delaney. Now and then Delaney nodded. Antonescu was dressed as Napoleon, some shit like that. The others on the terrace were people Gately hadn't seen before.

God, how he hated the bastards! It was all he could do to keep from screaming, but he knew better than that. Time enough for screaming when he squeezed the trigger. Then there would be screaming all over the place. But first he had to get in closer so they wouldn't have a chance to run. He had to take them by surprise. Total, absolute, horrifying surprise. Too bad the O'Neal bitch wasn't on the terrace. She was the one he was after, the one who had to die. The whole thing wouldn't count for shit if she managed to go on living. But he'd make her beg a little before he. . . .

This was it, this was close enough. Gately sprang onto the terrace and opened fire.

Four hundred yards away Caleb Brown heard the rattle of the M-16 and started to run. It couldn't be, but it was. He was almost sixty, but he ran as fast as he could.

Gately started his left-to-right swing with the Senator and the fat man. The M-16 bucked in his hands as the first burst cut them to pieces, knocking them back against the low wall of the terrace in a welter of blood and shattered bone. He swung the rifle and killed the others with three short bursts. One woman nearly got over the wall before the last burst stitched bullets across her back. Gately slapped in another clip and walked through the french windows. Their eyes jumped to his as he steadied the rifle against his hip. A woman screamed and Bruce Whipple yelled, "Lenny, what are you doing?"

Gately killed Bruce Whipple, the girl beside him, then the screaming woman, before he turned the rifle on the band and the people who had been dancing. The M-16 rattled until no one was moving. The floor was slick with blood as Gately, screaming with laughter, walked across it. "Tracy!" he yelled. "Where are you, you cunt?" He heard a sound. It was the Galligan bitch running for the stairs. He let her get halfway up before he touched the trigger. The short burst splintered the bannisters; she screamed and tumbled to the bottom. There were other sounds as he moved through the archway toward the stairs. Gately grinned. There was someone hiding behind a couch. Holding the M-16 against his hip, he raked the back of the couch from one end to the other. Then he went behind it and saw Cal Cameron sprawled in death, blood flowing from his chest and neck. Where the hell were the rest of them?

He kicked open the massive doors of the library and cursed when he saw a telephone light winking on a table. God damn it to hell! He'd forgotten to cut the telephone wires on the way in. The bastards were trying to call for help. Enraged by his own stupidity, he blew the telephone off the table in a hail of bullets. Suddenly it was very quiet. Upstairs a door banged, and that was all. Fuck it. Let them call. There was no way the police could get there in time to stop the killing. All he needed was another five minutes.

It looked like there was no one left alive on the ground floor. With a fresh clip in the slot, he started upstairs. He was nearly at the top when he heard a sound and started to turn. He was bringing up the M-16 when Caleb Brown, holding his old Colt .38 with both hands, shot him four times in the chest. He fell and rolled and died.

By three o'clock the last of the bodies had been removed, twenty-five in all. The house swarmed with state troopers and state police detectives and assistant D.A.'s. Caleb Brown was still feeling sick when the district attorney arrived as the last ambulance was pulling out.

A tall man with rimless glasses, the D.A. said, "You displayed great courage, Chief Brown."

"Well, what else could I do?" Caleb Brown said.

But for all the slaughter it was a simple case. Leonard Gately, known to be unstable, had finally gone berserk. It was deplorable that such a thing should happen in a beautiful place like Yorkport, and it was best forgotten as soon as possible. Caleb Brown was the hero of the hour and for a long time to come. Those who had criticized him in the past were silent now; his pension was secure. Only to Katy did he confide how rotten he felt about the killing of Gately. "But, you see, I had to do it," he said more than once. "He'd murdered all those people and I had to stop him from killing more. It was him or me."

A town meeting, in emergency session, was held to discuss the situation. One overseer, an outsider from Massachusetts, tried to introduce the matter of local gun control, but was told that she was out of order.

"People kill people, not guns," was the majority opinion.

The murdered locals were buried according to their station in life. Bruce Whipple and Mary Beth MacVey, both Baptists, were interred in the Yorkport Cemetery. "Amazing Grace," that sweet old hymn, was sung for Mary Beth by her chums at Yorkport High. Leonard Gately's aunt, who was to inherit his modest fortune, flew from England for his funeral, which was attended by no one else. At the brief ceremony, a young Episcopal minister asked God to forgive the madman.

Cal Cameron found his last resting place in his native New Jersey; all the other corpses found their way home in good time. Senator John Morrison Callaway received the biggest send-off; Vice President Bush, House Speaker O'Neill, Senator Kennedy, and many others came to Boston to pay their last respects. Tracy was there, of course wanly beautiful in black. After the funeral Ralph drove her back to Maine.

The Yorkport Massacre, the inevitable name, was front page news all over the world; instant books were rushed into print by the end of the week; writers who specialized in conspiracy theories bent over backward to tie the murders to the CIA, Fidel Castro, the PLO, the IRA, the man who shot the Pope. One writer more fanciful than the rest likened the massacre to *The Laughing Policeman*, the famous Swedish detective novel in which a whole busload of people are machine-gunned to death as cover for a single murder. This theory, when published, sold better than the others; it was, in time, to become a big-buget movie. The producer wanted to make the picture on location, but was forced to abandon that idea in the face of strong opposition from concerned citizens. Instead, the movie was done in Washington State in a resort that had once been a fishing village. It could pass for New England if you weren't quite sure what New England looked like. There was a lot of fog and that helped to sustain the illusion.

Worried about a falling off in the tourist business, the town fathers of Yorkport were pleasantly surprised to learn that all businesses were up by twenty percent. Hotels and motels were booked beyond their capacity; the morbid and the merely curious came from all the fifty states, including Alaska. Mike Wallace came too.

Only to the hippies was Leonard Gately a hero; they boycotted his funeral because they refused to believe that he was dead. One kid said, "Lenny is like Zapata, man. He's in the mountains riding a white horse. That's why they're so afraid of him."

And it was agreed that Lenny, like Emiliano, could never die. His fame spread to the ghettos, the barrios, the crash pad of all the cities across the land. Hell's Angels took up his cause; so did the Klan. He became a hero to the unemployed and the unemployable; to laid-off auto workers and tenant farmers, to the poor and the powerless. His own role as go-getting businessman was forgotten, and he became a selfless revolutionary: a New England Che Guevara. Hippy babies were named "Lenny" instead of "Buffalo" or "America." There were Lenny tee-shirts, even a Lenny anthem set to the music of "The Battle Hymn of the Republic." The first line went: "Let us honor Leonard Gately, let us celebrate his fame."

The editor of one underground paper wrote, "Lenny had no politics. He was the John Wayne of all the people, and not just the privileged few. Alone, he set out to strike a blow for freedom, and he chose to do it on the 4th of July, the most significant day in the history of this so-called democracy, and in doing so he served notice on the rich that no longer would it be business as usual. He wrote his message in blood and bullets; a message crystal clear in its simplicity. Lenny loved the land, the good, simple things of this world: the love of a strong comrade-woman, a cup of cold spring water uncontaminated by toxic wastes. Honor, integrity, friendship—those were the words he lived by. They couldn't stop Lenny, they won't stop us. It is up to us to pick up the fallen banner, to make Lenny's truth a living thing. They may kill us, torture us, lock us up in their secret concentration camps, but there is no way they can stop us. Lenny has shown us the way and we must follow that way. How can we fail?"

Two days after the murders Sarah Bannard sipped a bullshot while she read a special edition of the *Yorkport Star.* "This is going to become a collector's item," she said. "I think my picture came out rather well, don't you think? You look good too, sweetheart."

Dee was drinking iced tea. "There's something ghoulish, the way you keep looking at that."

"Well, it isn't every day I get my picture in the paper. It's going to be fun at the inquest. You'll have to testify too, lover."

"God damn it, I'd like to get away from here. I heard O'Neal is going to sell the house."

"Not through Gately's company, I hope. Old Lenny the Moose, I didn't think he had it in him. In he comes with this tommygun—an extension of his penis, of course—and *tat-a-tat-a-tat* and twenty-six people are dead."

"You weren't so brave the other night," Dee sneered. "You were so shook up you actually said 'please' when you asked me to get you a drink. You should stay scared all the time. You'd have better manners."

"I'm brave now," Sarah said. "I'm very brave now. It's too bad that Tracy is selling the house. I was looking forward to another party before the end of summer. Maybe I should call her and persuade her to change her mind. Goodness gracious, it wasn't her fault all those poor people were killed. That's what I'll do. I'll call her."

Dee's smile was filled with malice. "She's gone and won't be back—ever. Some New York realtor is going to handle the sale. You won't be seeing her again."

Sarah smiled too. "Don't be too sure, angel. McLuhan used to say that the world had become a global village."

"Twenty-six people have been murdered and all you do is think about sex."

Already bright-eyed with alcohol, Sarah finished her bullshot. "You're all wet, dowdy Dee. I mourn their deaths from the heart of my bottom. Gone, all gone. Just think of it. No more will Cal Cameron twitch his devil's mustache. They miss him so much they've closed the theater for the rest of the season. '23 *Skidoo* has gone north to Boothbay. I still say we should try to hire that dizzy little blonde as a maid. But, you know, I think I'm going to miss Gately more than any of them."

"You better be glad he's dead. It could have been our house instead of hers. What do you think set him off?"

"I think he got bored," Sarah said thoughtfully. "You ever get bored, honeychile?"

Dee banged down her empty tea cup. "I get bored with the way you carry on."

Sarah smiled at her life's companion. "I know I get bored. I get bored with everything. Believe you me, I *know* how Lenny the Moose must have felt. I just wish he hadn't killed old man Brown and the kid from the supermarket."

"Too bad he didn't kill O'Neal," Dee said. "She's the one he was after."

"You can't kill a billion dollars," Sarah said. "That would be unAmerican."

Dee said, "Is there no way we can leave this place? Why do we have to stay after all that's happened?"

Sarah went to the kitchen to make another drink; when she came back she was happy and humming. "I wouldn't think of leaving here before Labor Day," she said. "Think of it. We have the whole summer ahead of us. Who knows? There may be a lot more excitement before we fold our tents and steal away. Lots of excitement. Yes sir, that's the ticket."

"Jesus Christ," Dee cried in despair.

"I like fun," Sarah said. "That's what summer is for, to have fun."

And while Dee stared at nothing, Sarah began to sing, "In the summer, in the winter, ain't we got fun."